"No beast so fierce but knows some touch of pity.
But I know none, and therefore am no beast."

William Shakespeare—

THE STREET
ILLUMINATI 2

"Genesis of Monsters"

By David Garcia

(Book 2)

"Genesis of Monsters"

PROLOGUE

"Isha Ra"

CAIRO, EGYPT, PRESENT DAY

Eleven-year-old, Isha Ra, stared at her thin body in the full-length mirror and posed regally, or what she thought regally looked like. After a moment, she took a frustrated breath and determined the posture was unsatisfactory. The imperial robe, like the capes of Wonder Woman and Supergirl, was supposed to signify her importance to those around her. But it had failed. Primarily because her youthful radiance gave her the facade of being far too pretentious.

Isha gripped the lapels, shifted her guise, and tried a look of diplomatic influence.

Now you look like an ordinary tribal teen. She didn't consider herself better than such an individual, only that she had a prophetic destiny to fulfill, and to do so without looking the part would be negligent. Exasperated, she dropped her shoulders, having wasted twenty minutes searching for a look that exemplified royalty.

Veering from the mirror, she nearly leapt from her moccasins. Ahlu, one of her bodyguards, stared at her like a giant African ghost. Across the mammoth sitting room, arms folded, he stood with his back against the ten-foot gold plated doors.

Got me again, Isha thought.

When summoned by Princess Isha Ra, protocol for all palace staff upon arrival was to stand quietly off to the side until she acknowledged their presence. Problem was that the royal guard were assassins trained in stealth-like movement. If Isha forgot she had called one, as with Ahlu, their sudden appearance startled her something fierce.

Isha nodded. "Has Mother returned?"

"No, Your Highness."

"Then you may leave."

Ahlu bowed and quickly exited.

Isha removed the robe and decided to relax on the balcony. Her favorite place in all of Mother's seven global palaces, its position overlooked the Red Sea. It was there, during her daily meditation, that she first discovered her earthly importance.

With the salt air relaxing her mind, she turned her attention to the setting sun. Its fiery glow descended upon the horizon like the eyes of a sleepy child. As she planned her course of action, Isha realized the age of her innocence was gone. She reckoned it was a good thing, though. The best thing. Mankind needed her help, but to help them she had to put away childish things, just as the scripture commanded. How that was to happen—the helping of mankind— was currently being deliberated in the upper echelons of human existence.

Her guardian, Joaquin "Monsta" Marquez, a.k.a. the Dragon, continually stated, usually while drunk, "This ain't no movie. Ain't no superhero gonna fly down and save this shit. Blood and guts reality—that's the fucking world we live in!"

Monsta carried the fierce disposition of a pet tiger. A vicious animal who vowed to never hurt her, and whose rare acts of affection were dispersed in some philosophical gesture. Isha likened it to an actual tiger licking her face as the bloody flesh from a recent kill clung to its razor-sharp teeth.

Whether Monsta's estimation of life was true or not, Isha refused to accept her role as the prophesied savior. A vessel sent to destroy the secret society of global domineers created by French professor Johann Adam Weishaupt. The kingdom known as The Illuminati.

It began fifteen years ago, when the voice of Amen Ra called Monsta to an orphanage in the poorest region of Nigeria. There, he came upon a newborn whose mother had died while giving birth. "This is my daughter, Isha Ra," the voice of Amen Ra told Monsta. "Protect her, for she will judge the hearts of evil men."

Monsta delivered Isha to the most powerful woman on earth, Queen of Suma'at, Sekhmet "Mother" Ra. The series of events constituted partial fulfillment of a prophecy more than five thousand years old.

What followed next was the summation of Isha's life thus far.

Mother took Isha as her own—although she had many children, none were biological—and brought in scholars from around the world. They taught Isha reading, writing, religion, history, mathematics, the six languages she wanted Isha fluent in by age six, including a beautiful song like language called Du'a'ta—known only to Mother and a handful of others—and various disciplines. All of which Isha continued to study at the collegiate level.

Subject wise, Isha loved science and astronomy. To her, both proved the undeniable existence of Almighty God—though Mother used the gods interchangeably, Isha preferred Jah of the Hebrew scriptures—a being whose beautiful creation was a gift without equal. A being who, when opening one astrological door, presented mankind with a room with seven other doors, each promising to reveal something extraordinary about the meaning of life.

The same education had, by age eight, exposed Isha to one infallible truth: she was nothing like the Dragon (Monsta's prophetic name, and the name given to him by the Mexican underworld), a man that rumor said, ended life as easily as he ended conversation.

Belief throughout the Suma'at Illuminati (Mother's name for her secret kingdom) was that Monsta had killed hundreds, even thousands of people. Isha had never seen him kill anyone and believed the rumor a made-up story designed to strike Machiavellian fear in the lower ranks. And it had. On one occasion, she'd witnessed a servant's uncontrolled urination while in his presence.

Meanwhile, Mother had supposedly sanctioned every death, believing each to be a step closer to the prophecy's absolute fulfillment, a thing she seemed to desire more than life itself.

Isha set palms atop the balcony guardrail and considered the few prophetic details to which she was privy.

The prophecy, as best she knew, was born during the Bronze Age, in a time when mankind was most civilized. Early in the reign of Suma'atan Queen, Seriah II, an elderly seer presented her with a gift, a supernatural dialect capable of swaying the heart of any human on earth. History was unclear as to the dialect's original form—whether the elderly seer taught it to Queen Seriah II, or through ancient writings—but the Suma'atan scripture translates:

"And the seer told Queen Seriah II, 'As long as the dialect be used for the good of all people, earthly balance shall remain. But if it ever be used to show favor, one for another, balance shall be lost, and the hearts of men filled with great evil. For such had happened once before when that heavenly creature deceived the first human souls. If likewise, the dialect be misused, the Great One shall send forth a child to judge the hearts of evil men. And by the power of the child's words so shall the kingdoms of the earth be destroyed.'"

Fearful of unleashing such evil, Queen Seriah II used the dialect sparsely, and always for the good of all mankind. And so, it went on for nearly three thousand years.

In the winter of 325 B.C.E., Alexander the Great, Sargon III (King of Suma'at), and ten of the world's most powerful rulers, formed a secret alliance known as the Twelve Universal Crowns. With Alexander as the Supreme Crown (leader), the twelve rulers enacted a constitution and such things as all kingdoms were built upon. However, beneath the foundation of righteous governance lay the invisible *Scrolls of Schemata*, an intricate mind controlling network from which mankind was to be ruled in secret.

At the start, there were five scrolls: *Law, Economic, Science, Religion,* and *Games* (known today as the Entertainment Schemata). The earliest framework was rudimentary, with each schemata containing instruments known as a *Substratum* (plural, *Substrata*). Substrata ensured the Blind—the name given to mankind by the Twelve— followed without question the structure set in place. Thus, it went on for over twenty-two hundred years.

In 1935, for reasons unknown to Isha, the Twelve Universal Crowns split into two kingdoms, with King Sargon X (Mother's father) on one side, and Hermann Faustus's Bavarian Illuminati on the other.

In 1953, the two kingdoms went to silent war.

It was at that time that Mother, a then extraordinary six-year-old clairvoyant, received a vision. In it, the Great One told her the supernatural dialect had been misused. Therefore, earthly balance had been lost, and the child was soon to come. The Great One never explained *who* was responsible, or *how* the supernatural dialect had been misused. Mother kept the vision secret, telling only Monsta— the Great One had foreseen his coming—until such a time as the child arrived and was ready to know the truth.

On Isha's seventh birthday, Mother took her to a secret chamber beneath the Saqqara Pyramids. Speaking in Du'a'ta, she revealed the vision to her: the story of a priestess, a dragon, and the child sent by the Great One to restore balance in the world. In short, Mother explained she was the priestess, Monsta the Dragon, and Isha the child. Together, they were to wage the greatest war mankind has ever known.

Mother finished by telling her Du'a'ta was the supernatural dialect taught to Queen Seriah II and every Suma'atan ruler since. That she too would learn how to use its harmonics to sway the hearts of mankind.

For a prodigy and avid reader like Isha, the prophecy was nothing more than a metaphorical cliché, like those found in movies like *Lord of the Rings*, *Star Wars*, and her favorite, *The Matrix*. The great thinker, Joseph Campbell, called it the *Hero's Journey*.

Nevertheless, over time, Isha learned that for Mother, the prophecy was a literal rendition of things to come, and her kingdom's most cherished prophecy. The pith of which was the child's coming of age, power, and glory in an event called the Baptism of Blood.

The day after revealing the prophecy, Mother added the scrolls of schemata to Isha's daily curriculum, digitized of course, for 21st century consumption. Taught by a man known only as Apollyon, the scrolls were unlike anything she had ever read. When she asked where they came from, Apollyon said Sargon III had created the scrolls at the behest of Alexander.

Throughout her study of the Crowns, the Scrolls of Schemata, Suma'atan scripture, and Du'a'ta—which was powerful indeed—two vital facts kept jumping out at Isha. First, Alexander had chosen Sargon III as his successor; and second, as Apollyon had said, Sargon III created the scrolls at the behest of Alexander.

Isha kept asking herself, *why would Alexander, already the most powerful ruler on earth, share power with eleven other rulers?* It made no sense. And then one spring afternoon, as she walked along the palace courtyard, the answer hit her like a wave of cool air. The idea didn't come from Alexander; it came from Sargon III. He'd obviously used Du'a'ta to sway Alexander in all matters related to the Twelve Universal Crowns. In doing so, Sargon III had violated the seer's warning, thereby starting the prophetic clock. More importantly, Sargon III had somehow implemented Du'a'ta as the driving force behind the Scrolls of Schemata.

Convinced of her findings, Isha decided to tell no one. Instead, while Mother and the Illuminati continued to battle each other for control of mankind, Isha was devising a plan to free mankind in a loving, peaceful way. Her goal, when the time came, was to heal the world through righteous solutions, not deliver it by way of violent acts. But to do that, she'd have to do the one thing she feared most. She'd have to destroy both kingdoms.

As Isha drank in the last of the setting sun, she reckoned the time not yet upon her. *But soon*, she thought. *Very soon.*

PART ONE

"The Street"

Chapter 1

"DJ and Angel"

LAS VEGAS, NEVADA, 2014

Angel Dominguez knew she was in trouble. Seated on the couch between Stephen and Jacob, the once friendly conversation had taken an unexpected turn for the worse. They were no longer discussing campus activities, her MBA, or plans after graduation.

The two men now used explicit language to compliment her beauty. Compliments she had initially fended off with classy retorts; but as the barrage continued, those classy retorts had slowly morphed into slurred speech. Her thoughts now came in... chopped... fragments... of...

You're drunk, she thought. *Really drunk. But how?*

She had followed her one shot, one cup of beer minimum. The buzz was always just enough to relax and stem her social anxiety. Occasionally, she drank wine instead, but even then, it was manageable.

Is it a foreign beer? she wondered hazily. No, when Cindy gave her the cup, she said it was Corona. That it came from a keg of Corona.

But Corona had never made her feel so mentally sloppy, helpless. And she felt mentally helpless, sloppy.

Even now, as she fought to steer the ship, she was telling Jacob about her mother, Gwendolyn. How everyone said she looked like Salma Hayek, and perhaps that was where she obtained her lusciously round ass.

Why am I discussing my ass? Why am I laughing? Why am I acting as if I'm having the time of my life?

Stephen said, "I'm gonna stick my cock in that ass."

"Oh, really?" She didn't mean to say that. She meant to scold him because his reply was lewd.

I'm not being lewd. Where are the other girls that were supposed to be coming? She suddenly wondered.

At last count, it was still only her and Cindy. They had been early. Max, the guy who rented the house, said others would arrive shortly. But no one yet. Except for a bunch of other guys.

Where was Cindy, anyway?

A senior, Cindy had befriended her during one of their weekly finance classes, complimenting her on the outfit she wore, saying how beautiful she was, and the incredible shape of her body.

Angel thought her friendly, thought it refreshing to meet someone not intimidated by her genius. Not to mention, she had found Cindy incredibly attractive, especially her long legs. The two eventually got around to discussing the bisexuality that drew them together.

On Wednesday, Cindy suggested Angel skip her usual Friday night of study—Foreign Exchange and Trade—and go to dinner. Afterward, they could watch a movie at Cindy's place.

Tonight, following dinner at Roy's Hawaiian restaurant, Cindy changed their plans. She first wanted to stop by the party of a movie director friend, which turned out to be Max. An aspiring actress, Cindy said she had lots of friends in the industry.

Upon their arrival, Cindy handed her a cup of beer and said she needed to talk to Max in private. Initially, Angel thought to decline the beer, but she didn't want to seem stuck up, as if the plastic cup were beneath her. That's when Stephen and Jacob stepped in and offered to keep her company. Angel had not seen Cindy since.

She suddenly wondered if her parents were awake. Wondered how disappointed they would be to see her like this.

The song on the stereo changed for what felt like the millionth time. Rock. Not loud, but not low either. Enough that she needed to raise her sultry voice when speaking... slurring.

Stephen was from New Jersey, and midway through a Master's in Sociology. The first to approach, he said he was a member of the hockey team. Tall, blonde, fit, Angel found him extremely attractive.

Jacob was medium height and average looking. A Los Angeles native, he claimed his father was a well-known Hollywood agent who represented Tom Cruise and Jennifer Lawrence. He'd been super nice and respectful, but that all changed in the last ten minutes when he tried to kiss her three times.

"Whoa there," Angel had said, reeling back at his first attempt. "Uh, no thanks."

She thought her response proper, leaving no room for misunderstanding. Jacob apologized; said he had misread the signs. She told him not to worry; it was okay; things happened when people drank.

A few minutes later, he made another attempt. This time, she didn't pull away; instead, she let him enjoy the moment before she subtly turned her head.

After discussing her tension and need to unwind, Stephen proposed a massage. She smiled and playfully warned him against any funny business. As he moved closer, his fingers expertly began kneading her shoulders, sending waves of pleasure through her body.

Inwardly, Angel panicked, but it did not show. She smiled, laughed, and seemed to enjoy herself, eyes closing and throat releasing groans of pleasure as his fingers pressed deeper. Those strong fingers betrayed her, making her crave his touch and sending her mind to a dreamlike realm of want and hunger.

Suddenly, she could hear the voice of her beloved tío, Javy. "Never accept a drink from anyone."

But she had accepted. Now, dream and reality blurred theatrically.

Why are you not resisting?

In a rush of oblivion, her thoughts faded, and she lost the ability to respond.

When Jacob placed a hand on her knee, Angel eyed him and tried to say, "Please, stop." Needed to say it but couldn't. As he moved his hand between her thighs, her mind screamed, "Stop!"

But it was only a dream.

*****

"Which chick is this, homz?" Raul asked, lounging in the Escalade's backseat, sipping Hennessy.

DJ observed that the traffic along Paradise Road was lighter than usual for a Friday night, which explained how quickly he had reached the address. He lowered the stereo's volume.

"The real smart one from class. Remember, we went out a couple of months ago," DJ said.

Jason, Raul's older brother and DJ's best friend, reclined in the front passenger seat, his Raiders cap pulled low. With the window open, he flicked Marlboro ashes into the night as tourists bustled along the Vegas Strip like excited children at Disneyland.

"The one with the Mercedes," Jason said.

"Yeah, that one," DJ said.

Angel Dominguez had texted DJ minutes earlier.

Jack, I feel weird. I think someone spiked my drink. Please come get me. 4367 Tamarus.

In the two classes they shared—and even on the one date they had gone on—she had always presented herself as a sophisticated, young, professional Latina, so the text had her in real trouble.

He continued to weave in and out of traffic, his mind flooded with memories of their shared history.

Angel had captured DJ's attention right from the very first day of class. She was drop-dead gorgeous in her red business suit and skirt, sexy black nylons, and designer heels. While the rest of the students stumbled into class looking as though they'd partied all night, wearing their T-shirts, flip-flops, and sneakers, Angel had an air about her, like she owned the whole place, strutting in as if she were the CEO of some big corporation.

Later, he couldn't help but notice that even Professor Franklin, typically composed, had a wide-eyed, infatuated look on his face whenever she spoke. DJ knew why. She was, hands down, the finest woman he had ever seen, around five-one or so, though it was hard to tell with those heels. She had round, above-average breasts that would make a preacher swear and a curvy ass that could turn heads for days, no matter what she wore.

The word around campus was that she was some kind of business genius who had graduated high school really early, like fifteen or sixteen, and had jumped straight into college. By the time she crossed paths with DJ, she'd already been there a few years.

During weekly critique sessions, where students picked apart each other's work, it became routine to watch her destroy the entrepreneurial dreams of Shark Tank wannabes. Her analyses were so brutal that Professor Franklin nicknamed her Ms. Wonderful. Although DJ barely knew her, he respected Angel.

Two months into their second semester, he presented a long-term proposal for a restaurant along the Vegas Strip. It was the first time DJ had chosen to share with the class.

Several of his classmates praised his plan to the point where DJ believed he had finally gotten the concept. That was until, in one swift economic retort, Angel tore his formula to pieces. Angel's annihilation of his formula was so precise that Professor Franklin, trying to save DJ from embarrassment, repeatedly highlighted its positive qualities.

DJ wasn't mad, though. He could only respect her game.

After class, DJ sat in the cafeteria, dipping mini carrots into a bowl of ranch dressing.

"That wasn't an attack on you," Angel said.

Her voice dripped with honey. He turned to find her standing there, books secured against her chest with both hands. She wore a knee-high plaid skirt, white blouse, and heels. DJ eyed her casually. "Didn't take it like it was," he said. "You were right."

He returned to his ranch dressing. He had seen men of every race attempt to ask her out. Couldn't blame them; her allure was that strong. However, he never heard of her accepting any offers. It didn't matter because relationships required both parties to be willing to play the game of putting their best foot forward. He didn't get down like that, didn't indulge in fantasies played out over the shiniest parts of a person's character. He could be charming, even romantic, but he'd always be the one who brought death to his enemy.

Feeling her eyes on him, he also decided he wasn't going to audition for the lead role in the tired warrior and the princess. She wasn't going to become the cure for his sorrow, the love that healed his battered soul.

She stuck out her manicured hand. "Angel Dominguez."

He turned, wiped his hand on a napkin, and shook her hand. "Jack Johnson. But everybody calls me DJ."

"You mind if I sit down, Jack?"

He nodded toward an empty chair.

She placed her books on the table and folded her arms on top of them. "Why is it you've never attended any of our study groups? I know you've been asked. They're quite informative."

He laughed inwardly. She spoke as if each syllable were made of gold; what niggas on the street would call talking white. He didn't buy it, though. She was as brown and beautiful as any Latina he'd seen in a while.

"Not the sociable type," he said.

She unfolded her arms and interlocked her fingers. "I know. Last year, not once did you eat here."

He surveyed the place. "Didn't even know it was here."

She had the cutest laugh. "Well," she said with a hint of sarcasm, "it's easy to miss out on so much when you rush straight to your Escalade after class."

He instinctively studied her eyes, even though he knew she wasn't a cop. "Real observant."

"Oh, I'm not, uh, stalking you. I mean, we've parked near one another on several occasions. I merely saw how quickly you drove off."

"Didn't say you were. And I know your black Mercedes."

Her eyes narrowed slightly, but he couldn't tell why.

"I'm glad the weekend's here," she said. "Might I ask what you're going to do? I mean, not that I want to know. It's just, you're eating here, so you know…" She sighed, and her voice softened to almost a whisper. "I'm babbling, aren't I?"

He shook his head with a smile. "It's cute." He wiped his hands and pushed the food away. "Why are you taking classes?"

"Well, a year ago my dad had a stroke and..."

"Sorry to hear that."

"Uh, thank you. He's doing much better now."

He glanced at his Rolex, then looked back at her. "You wanna get some dinner?"

She placed a delicate hand over her mouth, clearly surprised. "Pardon?"

"Unless you have other plans?"

She paused and batted her eyes. "Mr. Johnson, are you asking me on a date?"

"A business date," he clarified with a grin. "I figure the least you can do is let me pick your brain after kicking my ass like that."

"Well, I don't have a morning class. Very well, but I get to pick the restaurant."

He stood. "Okay. How about seven?"

They exchanged numbers.

Her simple innocence relaxed him. "I'll text you the restaurant."

He appreciated that she didn't assume he was supposed to pay. "Sounds like a plan."

That night, he stood beside her in the parking lot. "I learned a lot," he said.

"And I had a wonderful time, Jack."

"You have my number. Maybe we can do this again."

"Sure."

He hoped her words were sincere. There was no disputing the fact Angel's intellect and company captivated DJ, and while he avoided dwelling on those sentiments, he couldn't deny his attraction to her.

As the days passed and DJ returned to his usual routine, memories of that evening would occasionally surface unexpectedly.

During those moments, he briefly entertained thoughts about what might have been, then pushed them aside. It didn't matter how he felt, because they hadn't met since, and life moved on as it always did in his world.

Chapter 2

"To The Rescue"

The man swung open the front door, and DJ, Jason, and Raul rushed past him. Their eyes darted around, quickly assessing the vacant living room.

"Where the fuck is she?" DJ demanded, his gaze sweeping the empty space.

"Who are you looking for?" The man asked, bewilderment evident in his voice.

Raul produced a 9mm pistol. "The girl, man," he stated firmly.

"She's in the back bedroom," the man said, gesturing towards a hallway.

Without hesitation, DJ strode to the back bedroom and pushed the door open. He entered and saw two men fucking a white girl woman atop the only bed. Three others stood by, awaiting their turn.

DJ stomped back to the living room. "That ain't her. She's a short Latina named Angel."

"Oh… she's in there," the man insisted, raising his hands in a placating manner.

DJ took a closer look at what he thought was a door to a study or den—just like most frat houses were designed. Rooms originally meant for laundry or storage were transformed into bedrooms so they could charge higher rent prices.

He opened the door and eyed the scene before him. A large bedroom. A dozen men clustered around the bed, obstructing his view.

"Just rip the stocking down the middle and snatch the panties off," a voice said.

DJ stepped between them.

Out cold, Angel lay on the bed in a black skirt, nylons, and heels. One guy, wearing only boxers, had wedged himself between her thighs but appeared unsure of what to do next. The other crouched near her head, his junk inches from her face as he tried to open her mouth.

DJ snatched him by the hair and threw him to the ground. He then spun around and kicked the other guy in the face. Blood gushed from his broken nose as his body stiffened, falling backward off the bed. Unconscious, his calves lay against the edge of the mattress like a stuffed doll.

"What the fuck, man," the guy said whose hair he pulled. He had jumped to his feet and taken a jittery fighting stance.

DJ closed the distance between them and backhanded him to sleep.

Raul and Jason took position between DJ and the rest of the men. Jason pointed the nine-millimeter at them. "Kickback, fools."

DJ scooped Angel into his arms. "Where's her shit!?"

One guy, his left leg shaking, pointed to a black bag on the coffee table. "Uh, she came in the black Mercedes—SUV."

"If any of her shit is missing, I'm gonna come back here and kill all you motherfuckers."

"Call the cops if you want, ese," Jason told the guy who let them in. "But if they come looking for us, mí família gonna come looking for them."

Jason didn't say another word. He didn't have to. Everyone there knew about the Mexican gangs, and how they'd stop at nothing to track you down and end your life.

In the street outside, DJ gently placed Angel in the back of the Escalade while Jason retrieved her car keys from her bag and handed them to Raul.

Twenty minutes later, both vehicles entered DJ's carport. DJ carried Angel into his house and placed her onto his bed. He removed her shoes and covered her with a blanket.

He stepped into the living room and lit a Newport. "Couldn't let them do her like that. Real talk, I feel like going back and smoke'n that bitch."

"Relax, homz," Jason said. "Need to figga out what'chu gonna do with la chicá?"

"Gonna let her sleep it off."

"Hopefully, she don't wake up crazy."

"Hopefully." DJ sat on the couch and took another drag. "Take my truck. We'll hook up in the morning."

Once they left, DJ took off his Jordans and laid on the couch.

*****

Awakened by the sudden squeak of the bedroom door, DJ opened his eyes and sat up. Shirtless, he clicked the table lamp on, glimpsed the clock above the TV. 4:05 a.m.

He eyed the hallway. Even with frayed hair and a crinkled skirt, Angel looked flawless.

She stared at him for a long moment before stepping closer. "Jack? Jack Johnson?"

The sound of her voice sent a wave of electricity shooting through his body. "Yeah," DJ said, standing up.

She took a step back.

He raised hands to calm her. "It's okay, you're safe."

"How did I get here?"

"Do you remember anything?"

"I was with Cindy, and we stopped at a friend's house. It was her friend's house. The friend was a movie producer." Angel stared at the carpeted floor. "She's an actress. I waited for her, and…"

Her eyes spoke a thousand words. Slowly, the memory returned.

"Started talking to some guys…" she continued, looking up at DJ. "Now I'm here."

"She spiked your drink for them. You texted me."

Angel didn't remember texting him. She wrapped her arms around her body, dropped her gaze, expecting the worst.

"Nothing happened," he said. 'I got there right after you blacked out." He motioned to the recliner beside her. "Have a seat."

She did.

He stepped into the kitchen, returned with a glass and a can of Red Bull. He filled the glass and handed it to her.

Angel drank and set the glass on her lap. "I should call the police."

"Was hoping you wouldn't say that."

"Why? They nearly raped me."

"Yeah, but I knocked two of them out." He looked away. "Didn't tell you that night because we were talking business, but I have a reputation for knocking people out."

"I can testify. Tell them what happened."

"Can't stop you, but I don't need the heat."

He also didn't tell her he spent three years in prison for putting another man in a coma. Was currently on parole for the incident. Calling the police constituted *police contact*. The only thing his parole officer would focus on was the guys he put to sleep. In parole terms, it was an act of violence. He could hear the asshole now. *Why didn't you simply call the police? What were you doing there in the first place? Who were you with?* DJ knew he'd be violated.

Angel sipped the glass and huffed. It wasn't an angry huff. More like a '*we need to find a solution to the rapist problem,*' huff.

As she often did during her critiques, she stood and took a contemplative posture. "Well, how do you suppose we keep it from happening to someone else? I couldn't live with myself if they harmed another girl because I did nothing."

"Take three of my friends. See who you need to see. Threaten who you need to threaten."

"And what makes you think they'll heed my warning?"

"Because they will."

She took another drink and eyed him curiously. "I understand. The least I can do is avoid causing you any problems. I'll take your friends to confront the loser whose house it was. Perhaps that will suffice."

DJ grinned inside. This was the Angel he knew: poised, determined, badass.

"My tío told me never to accept a drink from anyone," she said.

"Smart dude."

"The smartest person I've ever known. He passed away."

"Sorry to hear that. Pretty sure he'd want you to pick better friends."

"I agree." Angel straightened her posture and walked up to him. "I can assure you, Jack, it will never happen again."

"My friends call me DJ." DJ towered above her. "That's something else I didn't tell you that night."

"I prefer Jack if that's alright with you."

You can call me whatever you want.

"Jack's cool."

"And about that night, I know we talked about doing it again."

DJ raised a hand. "No need to explain. You don't reach your level of business skill without the discipline to avoid wasting time."

"I wouldn't call hanging out with you wasting time, but thanks for not being mad." Angel stepped in and hugged him tightly. "And thank you so much for saving me."

It was then that she wept.

Chapter 3

"Butterflies"

DJ stood next to his truck, observing Angel as she hurried through the university parking lot. She moved with the grace of a young tigress, her heels creating a soft, rhythmic sound on the asphalt, like the gentle ticking of a clock.

In the eight classes since the incident, she had smiled at him twice, quickly averting her gaze afterward. That was it. No "Hi Jack, thanks for saving me." No mention of meeting up with his brothers to go to the white boys' house as they had planned. Just silence.

After two weeks of almost no communication, DJ was sure Angel had moved past the event, and that meant moving past him too. The same might have happened after their dinner, but the spiked drink had compelled her to seek his help.

DJ wasn't upset. He had watched her in class, and she seemed fine. More than fine. She was stronger, more assertive with her words, and Angel no longer held back.

Like today, during two different critique sessions, Angel lived up to her nickname, Ms. Wonderful. She decisively dismantled Xavier Smith's Java Juice proposal and Cynthia Wilkes' Centered Life Yoga studio idea. In both cases, she cut through their plans with the precision of a Samurai, leaving them exposed in the middle of the classroom, all while wearing the most captivating smile.

"Good afternoon, Jack."

"What's good?"

"Will not be needing your friends after all."

"A'ight."

"Aren't you curious why?"

"I don't do curious." He shrugged. "If you're good, I'm good."

She stepped closer, placed a hand on his arm. "I finally dared to go to Max's last night. That's the loser's name whose home it was. Jacob was there. Remembered him from that night."

"Handled your business?"

"I certainly did. And let me tell you, mister, your impact on them was amazing. Geez Louise, I've never seen two men so afraid. I thought they were going to pass out. At any rate, they assured me their friends were equally afraid, deeply sorry, and wanted nothing more to do with you or your friends. Another guy, Robert, went into his room and returned with five thousand dollars in cash. Strange he would keep so much money on his person."

Not to DJ. Jason had sent some of his relatives to the house to back up the threat he had made.

"Gave it to me for my troubles," she said. "Though I think it was less about my troubles and more about keeping you and your friends at bay."

"Hope you took it."

"Sure did. Then I slapped his face." Her eyes beamed. "Slapped all three of their faces. And they let me. Didn't budge one bit. It was like some sort of hazing ritual. Told them their lives would be in grave danger if I ever heard of an incident involving another girl." She placed a hand on her heart, laughed the sweetest laugh. "Slapped their faces, Jack. Can you believe it?"

"Definitely. You're strong as hell. And you got a nice chunk of cash out of the deal."

"Oh, I don't need the money. Dropped it off at the Ronald McDonald House. Watching them nearly poop their pants was the only satisfaction necessary." She paused, contemplatively. "Hope my threatening them doesn't cause you any problems."

"It won't. And you weren't lying."

"About what?"

"About their lives being in danger."

She smirked. "I was wondering… can I buy you lunch?"

"You don't have to thank me anymore. We're good."

"I beg to differ. I'm forever in your debt. But I'm over what happened. I mean, I was going to give Cindy a piece of my mind when I saw her, but she never returned to class. Rumor is, she has dropped out. Perhaps fearing legal repercussion. Aside from that, I've moved on." Angel folded her arms at the chest. "My request is more about courage. Before that night, I wanted to call you a million times, but I was too much of a scaredy cat."

"Why?"

"I'm not really sure. So how about that lunch?"

*****

Inside the crowded student cafeteria, DJ and Angel settled at a table near the fire exit. Unlike their dinner, which had focused solely on business school, their conversation finally shifted to more personal topics over the past hour. He learned she lived in Henderson and was an only child, much like him.

Her parents, middle-class conservatives, had raised her in a predominantly white environment, and she had attended some of the best private schools available. Despite that backdrop, Angel expressed a deep pride in her Mexican and Colombian heritage, revealing layers of her identity that went beyond her upbringing.

DJ admired the way Angel spoke. Her words carried a sophistication that made her even more captivating, if that were possible. He understood that some might mistakenly associate such eloquence with a desire to be white, a stereotype often imposed on black and brown communities.

DJ knew that was bullshit. An educated manner of speaking wasn't reserved for any race. After all, figures like the Obamas, Dolores Huerta, and Pedro Albizu Campos were all educated and proud of their heritage.

Her upper-class background didn't bother DJ either. His brother, Carlos—not by blood—had a revolutionary mindset and didn't see the world as us (minorities) versus them (all whites). Carlos had taught him about the Young Patriots, white Appalachian revolutionaries who worked alongside the Black Panthers.

"History books don't be talk'n 'bout them," Carlos said, one night after too many shots of Cuervo. "But them niggas was riders. And guess what their logo was?"

"What?"

"A Confederate flag with a white and black hand embracing in the middle."

"Get the fuck outta here."

"Real talk, nigga. It was like this." Carlos reached out and took DJ's hand, holding it up as if the two were about to arm wrestle. "Google that shit. Young Patriots knew the motherfuckas up top with all the money is our real enemies."

Angel confided in DJ that she loved his street swag. He was different from the guys she and her friends had met before, many of whom turned vulgar when their catcalls were ignored. DJ knew the type—guys who couldn't handle rejection. Angel said that even though he had a tough exterior, he was sweet, kind, and confident in himself. He had nothing to prove, which she found incredibly attractive.

DJ and Angel chatted for what seemed like just half an hour, even though two hours had passed, before they started discussing the class dynamics. He teased Angel about her knack for dissecting proposals, joking that her intensity was almost cruel. He mentioned a student, Amos Whitehall, whom Angel had once reduced to tears with her critique.

"You're crazy," Angel said. "Everyone knows how sensitive he is. I took it easy on him."

"Easy on him!? You started walking 'round class in them high heels, talking 'bout..." DJ raised his massive arms, "are you not entertained! Are you not entertained!"

DJ's deep voice echoed through the cafeteria, causing several people to turn and look. He couldn't quite tell if the look in Angel's eyes was one of embarrassment or if she secretly enjoyed the awkwardness their conversation had created.

"Whatever," she said, giving his arm a gentle punch. "Anyway, any investor who lost money because of his proposal wouldn't be concerned about his tears."

"Ouch." He leaned back and feigned injury. He then eyed her beige suit jacket, skirt, nylons, and matching shoes. "You always dress like this?"

"Like what?"

"Like a smoking hot CEO. Goddamn, girl." He raised his hand. "No offense."

"Oh, it would take a great deal for you to offend me. And yes, I love the attire of corporate professionalism."

He bent an agreeable lip. "You're definitely killing it. Anyway, word on the street is you're some kind of genius. Started college at like six or seven."

She laughed. "Sixteen. Studying for my MBA. Plan to open a marketing firm in Vegas. Expand internationally."

"No doubt you'll kill that too."

"What makes you so sure?"

"Cause you're definitely a genius at the business shit. Even Professor Franklin knows that. And because I'm psychic." He looked up, closed his eyes, pretended to see a vision. "Yup. There you are. The sexy, badass, marketing firm-owner-lady."

DJ opened his eyes. Her smile was brighter than ever, the episode at Robbie's place truly behind her.

"Tell you what, if that happens your first campaign is on the house."

"Deal."

"Okay, mister, tell me something about yourself. Something nobody in class knows."

"I like going to the Spring Mountains... by myself."

"Alone? Why not with friends?"

He pouted, playfully. "I don't have any friends."

"Aw, I'll be your friend."

"Cool. But all jokes aside, my niggas ain't on the whole nature vibe."

"Why not? Nature's awesome."

"We'll have to hit the mountains sometime."

"What about now?"

He looked around at the cluster of students. Her gentle nature was messing with his ability to keep the world at arm's length.

She paused, watching his face. His silence spoke volumes. Swallowing hard, she said, "I'm sorry. If you don't..."

"Let's do it."

*****

DJ parked at the far end of the narrow overlook and shut off the engine. He shuffled out of the vehicle, watched as Angel pulled alongside his truck.

A minute later, she still hadn't exited. DJ considered the possibility she might be a little wary since the dense woods were better suited for the disposal of bodies than an afternoon of sightseeing. When she finally stepped out, he saw the reason for the delay. She had exchanged the designer heels for a tiny pair of pink Nikes.

Adorable.

"I like your truck," he said.

"Thanks. Drives awesome, don't you think?"

"My nigga Raul drove it that night. I took you in my truck. What kind is it?"

"Mercedes Brabus AMG. It's super comfortable."

"And super expensive."

"The tío I told you about left me some money."

"My bad. Didn't mean to be all up in your business."

"It's okay."

A short time later, DJ had taken her to his favorite location, an isolated fifteen-foot walkway along the mountain's apex.

Angel took in the view. "God, Jack, it's breathtaking."

"Makes you feel small enough to appreciate life."

"Couldn't have said it better myself."

He examined her Nikes. "Cute."

"My non-CEO attire." She extended a foot. "For my spin class."

"Bike riding? You're turning out to be one sexy little mamí."

"Why thank you, sir," she said, her voice silky. "And you're incredibly hot if I say so myself." She surveyed the entire landscape. "I see why you come here, it's so peaceful."

"My fortress of solitude."

"You're certainly built like Superman." She turned her body to face him. "Enough about me. How long have you lived in Nevada?"

"Why you say that?"

"You have an east coast accent and a different flair than most guys. Especially the ones from... how should I say this... urban backgrounds."

DJ laughed. "I'm originally from New York. Brooklyn. Pops died when I was born. Mom died two years later. Cancer."

Angel placed a hand on her heart. "God, I'm so sorry."

"Got no memory of them. After she died, I had no relatives in New York, so I went to live with Carlos. He's not biological, but I call him my older brother. He and my pops were partners in crime. He's Dominican, like my pops. Moms was from Haiti. We stayed in New York 'til I was twelve."

"I don't mean to pry."

"It's all good, we're kicking it. Enough with the sadness. How did you get so dope with the business?"

"Tío Javy was a shrewd capitalist. I took an interest at a young age—used to ask him all kinds of questions. Once he saw my interest, he nurtured it; taught me everything he knew. I became a sponge and fell in love with making money, which he made super simple to understand."

"Simple to you because you got a gift. But trust me, it ain't simple. If it were, everybody would do it. And the way you be cracking skulls, he must've been a genius too."

"He was. Lived in Miami at the time of his passing. We spent summers abroad, traveling all over the world, which sorta became my classroom."

"Any place cool?"

"Italy. Spain. China. Even Russia."

"He must've been really successful 'cause I'm pretty sure that's hella money." DJ shook his head. "Sorry, I keep getting all up in your business."

"It's okay, Jack. And he was remarkably successful. If a company had an ounce of profitability, he bought it. That's why I'm so thorough. He taught me how to read below the bottom line, which varies from company to company. And yes, now that I'm older, and know the cost of his lifestyle, I realize how wealthy he was."

"Need to keep that to yourself."

"Always do." She walked up and motioned for him to lean over, as if she wanted to whisper something in his ear. When he did, Angel kissed his cheek. "But I'm sharing it with my friend, Jack, who I trust."

DJ fought back a blush. "Growing up, Carlos had a little money. Nigga wasn't rich, but I never wanted for anything. Once we got here, he started making business moves."

"Is he the reason you're taking classes?"

DJ nodded. "Owns two businesses. A small restaurant, and an auto repair shop. Wants me to expand the portfolio. Treats it like some Northside empire I'm gonna inherit." He stepped closer. "I'd go into business with you any day."

"I'll hold you to that." She placed a soft hand on his arm. "I'm sorry, Jack. Don't mean to ask so many questions. I just find you interesting."

"You're good. And I'm having a blast."

"Me too. Never hung out with someone like you."

"Damn girl, *someone like me*?"

"I didn't mean it like that. You're sweet... extremely buff... and god, super-hot. Super, super hot. But the same streets that told you I was a genius, said you were a fighter, and... that you were in prison. I'm not into bad boys, but the fact you're so humble fascinates me."

"Them streets love to talk."

"They sure do."

"Use'ta kickbox. Was undefeated as a pro. Problem was, I fought more in the streets than I did in the ring. One night, I got into it with this one nigga. Before I knew what happened, he was in a coma. Cost me three years." DJ moved to the edge of the overlook. "Prison was good for me. Taught me how to slow down life... reflect... be careful about every step I take."

*****

DJ walked side by side with Angel, stopping next to her truck. He extended a softball sized fist for her to bump. "Okay, my super smart and sexy friend, I'm gonna need you to drive safely. That way we'll get to kick it again someday."

"Soon, I hope." She bumped her tiny fist, leaned against the truck's door. "FYI, I totally enjoyed your company."

"Not as much as I enjoyed yours."

"Don't be so sure." She grabbed his collar, pulled him down to her lips, kissed him.

DJ wrapped hands around her waist. "Shouldn't I have done that?"

"Of course. But I get it. With all that happened, you probably felt awkward."

"Smart..." He kissed her back. "And perceptive."

Angel set hands into his. "Have a confession. Ever since our first day in class, I've had a giant crush on you. Wanted to get to know you better, but I was super intimidated by the fighter, prison stuff."

"Since you're spilling your guts, I would've been holla'd at you, but I heard a few niggas in class had asked you out. That you shot 'em down cold." He shrugged. "Guess you weren't the only one intimidated."

*****

As DJ turned east onto I-19, he struggled with the unnatural feelings running through his mind. Unnatural in the sense he'd never felt them before. He didn't want to even consider the origins, but it was hard not to admit the obvious. There wasn't another woman in Vegas who could touch her. It wasn't even close, not to his taste. A goddess, she was the perfect woman: beautiful, readymade rich, and sweet as honey. And she was feeling him, kept his heartbeat twenty beats above normal, all as he fought the wellspring of hunger rising in his soul.

The phone's beep snapped him back to the present.

A missed text. Picking up the phone, he read: **The butterflies in my tummy are killing me. I already miss the taste of your lips**

Butterflies? That's exactly what this feels like. And they're fucking killing me, too. All he wanted to do was spend every second with her.

DJ texted: **Don't trip, I feel 'em, too. And I could spend the entire night kissing you**

She texted: **Where?**

He texted: **Anyplace you want**

She texted: **Purrrrr**

Goddamn, she's killing me.

Chapter 4

"Tío Javy"

The daily conversations came as natural as the air they breathed, and the trips to the Spring Mountains, a weekly routine. Each time they ended with a progressively longer make-out session. Within a month, the two had become the best of friends, the scent of relational love hovering like a cartoon thought bubble.

A champion at life, Angel was always smiling, always joking, always making DJ feel as if it were okay to want the best that life offered; likewise, to expect it. And not just financial success, but the peace of mind she believed came with it. To Angel, the phrase, 'More money, more problems' was nonsense. More money meant fewer problems.

DJ learned that her father, Luis, was a Mexican American engineer from San Antonio, Texas. He met her Columbian American mother, Gwendolyn, while working on a two-year government project in Miami, Florida. The then nineteen-year-old actress and model had been featured in a dozen local magazines and commercials. She had also had a five-episode stint as a snitch hooker on a popular Columbian novella; her character eventually strangled to death for being, well, a snitch.

The couple married midway through the project and returned to Texas upon its completion. When an opportunity came to work as a Vegas consultant—a job that paid two hundred thousand a year—Luis jumped at the chance. Angel was born the following year.

Estranged from her brother Javier for reasons unknown to Angel, shortly after she turned five, brother and sister reconciled. Tío Javy quickly became Angel's favorite person in the world, and her most influential. A great deal had to do with his charismatic, adventurous nature, and her belief he was the funniest person she had ever known. But mostly, it had to do with the fact he treated her like a princess. The last part was a testament to the guidance he provided, since Angel had not grown up to be a spoiled, stuck-up bitch.

Javy was a childless financier and philanthropist, and based on the scattered details she provided, DJ believed he was a player.

She had spent nine summers, and countless holidays traveling the world with her beloved tío. By age twelve, Angel had become worldly wise, having gone with him on trips to China, Africa, Japan, Italy, France, Germany, Australia, and England.

Javy presented the world through a very provocative lens, transforming his niece into a young woman with expensive tastes. Very expensive tastes. Treated like the child he never had, Javy schooled her on life, the ins and outs of business, all while promising to finance any endeavor she chose, so long as it coincided with the course of *life goals* he'd shown her. Become a drug addict, and she was on her own.

Tragically, Javy died in a small engine plane crash two months after her fourteenth birthday. His death devastated Angel. Not long after, a man showed up at her house and introduced himself as Mr. Clark, executor of Javier Arroyo's estate. He requested to talk with her mother in private.

After a lengthy conversation, Mr. Clark handed her a cashier's check for $500,000, a gift from her deceased brother. He then gave her a debit card in Angel's name. It belonged to a Bank of America account containing $300,000 for living expenses while she finished high school. Mr. Clark told her Angel would receive additional money once she graduated. He briefly set down other details regarding her brother's estate as it pertained to Angel.

Shocked by the $500,000, her mother failed to convey the other details to Angel; specifically, the part where Angel needed to contact Mr. Clark whenever she completed any of the *life goals* discussed with her late tío.

The living expenses, along with the knowledge Mr. Clark was there for her, gave Angel the resilience to continue. She told DJ it was as if her tío was still there, guiding her along the path of life. Filled with the determination to make him proud, she graduated high school with honors at sixteen and was the class valedictorian. After that, things got interesting.

Mr. Clark deposited another $300,000 into the account: her reward for graduating high school. Valedictorian got her another $250,000. Angel thought the money a relief. In the two years since Mr. Clark's arrival, she had spent $212,000 of the original $300,000, on clothes, shoes, jewelry, and other expenses.

Offered more than a million dollars in academic scholarships from UCLA, Stanford, Princeton, and Harvard, Angel wanted to remain close to her parents and chose the University of Nevada Las Vegas. She didn't care about school recognition, believing her tío had given her all the business experience she would ever need.

Days after enrolling, Mr. Clark called and told her he had placed tuition into a separate trust. He explained her tío would have never allowed her to take scholarship money from another deserving kid.

*****

On the afternoon of their ninth week in the Spring Mountains, Angel sat atop DJ's hood, a quilt beneath her skirt. She picked up where she left off during the prior visit, explaining it was shortly after her sixteenth birthday that she finally discovered the other details her mother neglected to tell her about.

It happened the week she'd gotten her driver's license and first vehicle. Angel had walked into a Mercedes dealership and did what her tío taught her to do when she knew what she wanted. She found the nearest sales rep, pointed to the AMG, and said, "I'll take it."

Sticker price: $94,000.

The next day, Mr. Clark asked her to stop by his office. Angel assumed he was going to scold her, as her parents did. That her mother, still angry over the exorbitant purchase, had called and told him.

Angel told DJ she had entered Mr. Clark's office and prepared for the riot act, thinking he'd begin by telling her the vehicle was well outside her financial range. He'd follow it with documentation on how she had already spent a third of her money on personal amenities. Finally, he'd end with a lecture on saving the rest of her money because blah, blah, blah.

She had planned to inform Mr. Clark that she appreciated his concern, but the Mercedes was her dream car, and her tío would have wanted her to have it.

"But when I arrived," Angel said, her arms across DJ's shoulders. "Mr. Clark's like, why didn't you notify me you completed a transportation goal?"

DJ leaned between her open legs, his hands on her waist. "Transportation goal?"

"Right! I was super confused, too. The reason being my mother never told me about the incentive-based inheritance."

"What the fuck is that?"

"Money based on the goals tío and I set for my life. We didn't actually set them, we discussed them. The inheritance coincided with our discussions. Every time I accomplish a goal we talked about, or think I do, I'm to present Mr. Clark with the documentation. He presents it to a board of trustees, whom I've never met, and they check to see if he left me money for accomplishing it." Angel used air quotations on the word *accomplishing*.

"Makes sense."

"Why do you say that?"

"You were like his only child. If I was him, I would've left you everything."

"Funny you should say that, because Mr. Clark suggested I reconsider my purchase. That perhaps I'd like to lease something higher in quality with unlimited miles. That way I could change vehicles every year."

"Cool."

"Cool?" Angel huffed. "It's insane, Jack. Change vehicles like one changes hairstyle? I asked if tío's estate could sustain such amenities."

"What did he say?"

"He laughed. Told me, 'It's a mere drop in the bucket, young lady. A mere drop.'"

Her imitation of Mr. Clark was cute as hell, made him sound a little like Hannibal Lector. Angel had rethought her purchase and returned the next day with documentation for a white Mercedes Brabus G850 G63 AMG.

The fact she presently drove the black version only confirmed Mr. Clark's drop in the bucket theory.

"What's the lease on something like that?" DJ asked.

"I don't know. But fully loaded, which mine is, is around five-hundred-fifty thousand."

"Damn! That's Lambo money."

She dropped her shoulders, embarrassed. "I probably shouldn't drive such an expensive vehicle."

"Hell nah," he said, waving off her comment. "I didn't mean it like that. Your uncle busted his ass so you could have a good life. You gotta live it to the fullest. I would."

She perked up, which made him happy. The last thing he wanted was to make her feel guilty for having money.

"I'm glad you see it that way."

"Why?"

"I'm quite sure if I stay the course, I'll be rich."

"No offense to the inheritance he put down, but even if he hadn't left you any money, nigga schooled you on the game. You'd be rich on your own."

It was exactly what she needed to hear.

"I love you, Jack."

To say he loved her was an understatement. He fucking adored her. But the long-winded conversation about money caused him to pause.

"It's okay," she said, disappointment filling her voice, "you don't have to say it if you don't feel the same way."

"Are you crazy, woman? How could a nigga not love you? You're fine... smart as hell. It's just that..." he struggled to find the words. "I kinda wish you didn't have all that money."

"Why?"

"Then you'd know a nigga loved you, for you."

"You didn't know about the money the night you saved me." She kissed him. "I know who you are, Jack. You have nothing to prove to me."

DJ didn't know why, but he believed her. "I love you."

She kissed him again. "You said no one ever comes up here?"

"They don't. Why?"

"Do you have a condom?"

He drew back, studied her for a moment. "You sure?"

"Oh, I'm sure," she said, pressing her heels against his ass.

*****

Two weeks later, DJ and Angel relaxed inside the Mercedes Sprinter, listening as the rain pummeled the vehicle's roof. The night before, she asked if he wouldn't mind going with her to the dealership in the morning, her parent's anniversary was coming up, and she was thinking of buying them a luxury vehicle. He loved hanging with her and joked that he'd go wherever she wanted.

Angel arrived at DJ's house this morning and handed him the keys to her truck, something she had begun to do during their trips up the mountains, saying she enjoyed holding hands as he drove.

When they pulled into the dealership's lot, Angel pointed to an open space next to a black Sprinter. "That's it."

He'd seen them along the Strip but never paid them much attention, considering the design too boxy for his liking. As she headed inside, DJ waited next to the vehicle. Eyeing the sticker price, he shook his head. $274,783.00. Three months into their relationship, he still struggled with the money at her disposal.

Angel returned, handed DJ a key fob. "We're off."

He examined the fob, which had more buttons on it than most. "You want me to drive?"

"I'd like your opinion. I've already driven it."

"A'ight, but you gotta show me the test-driving route."

She laughed. "What?"

"The streets you use when test driving high dollar shit. I heard every dealership has them."

"Nonsense. We're going up the mountain."

"You're fucking with me?"

"Nope."

He shook his head because only Angel could get a dealer to let her take a quarter-million-dollar vehicle for a joy ride.

Halfway up the mountain, Angel said, "I had initially planned to buy them an RV, but daddy doesn't like super big vehicles. This is way cozier, and has everything they need: kitchen, bathroom, shower, refrigerator, and a bed with a TV. Lexani designed it."

"Drives hella smooth. And this dashboard camera makes it easy as fuck to see behind us."

"They're thinking of going to the Grand Canyon next month."

"Cool. Ain't never been there, but I heard it's dope."

"I'm taking you," she said. "We can stay in one of these."

"They let you rent it?"

"A prolonged test-drive."

At that moment, DJ couldn't help but imagine them as a married couple, out on a weekend trip.

When they arrived, the two broke out a quilt and snuggled beneath her favorite tree. Since making love for the first time—and on each trip since; plus, four off days, where they went to his house—the two had become extremely comfortable with sex.

After a lengthy discussion about marriage and what it took to raise a mentally sound child today, the two kissed. Seconds later, Angel slid her hand beneath his shorts. Before either could say a word, the rain forced them back inside. Seated in the center compartment, she used a remote to start the hushed engine and set the temperature to a comfortable 72 degrees.

She sat across his lap.

DJ surveyed the lavish interior, which was coated with a lacquer that screamed of wealth. To their immediate right was an oak kitchenette with marble countertop, prep area, and stainless-steel sink. Set below the structure were four sizable drawers. To the left of the kitchenette was an oak door, which he guessed led to the bedroom. "Shit's like a mini-suite."

As the heavy rain continued to fall, Angel kicked off her sky-blue Nikes and set her legs across the back seat. She had bought ten pairs, just for their trips to the mountains; to match her outfits, of course. "It's super cozy."

He nodded at the oak door. "Bedroom?"

"Uh hun." She shot up, entered the cabin, and sat on the bed, motioning for him to join her. "Look."

He hunched inside and took a seat next to her. The bed ran parallel to the cab, with a dresser and another door leading to what he figured was the bathroom. A fifty-inch Sony rested on the wall at the foot of the bed.

Angel tapped the keypad beneath the TV, and the screen came to life. Like the dashboard camera, it held an unobstructed view of the area behind them.

"This' some James Bond shit," DJ said.

She eyed the torrential downpour. "It's super dark out there. That was close."

"We're good. This area never floods."

She used the keypad to dim the cabin lights, then turned and studied DJ. He'd worn a black tank-top and matching athletic shorts. "Do you have any idea how hot you are?"

"No," he said, in a deep murmur, "but you can tell me."

"Oh, I'll tell you." She pushed him back onto the bed and mounted his knees, her skirt climbing an inch above the stocking's edge. She ran fingers along his groins noticeable imprint. "I can't get over the size of this thing."

"It's not that big."

"Nonsense," Angel whispered, her breath warm and inviting as she slowly unzipped his shorts. With gentle fingers, she eased the fabric down his legs, her touch sending shivers up his spine. His arousal, firm and insistent, pressed against the confines of his boxers, begging for release. With a subtle flick of her wrists, she pulled the boxers down, baring him to her eager gaze.

Her hand enveloped him, her touch sending sparks through his entire being. "My fingers don't even touch."

He felt the warmth and softness of her palm as she stroked and caressed. Her movements were slow and deliberate, her eyes never leaving his as she savored the power she held in that moment.

"That's because you have small hands."

"Or you have the biggest, thickest penis I've ever seen." She bent the sweetest brow. "I'm sure you'd like to know how many I've seen?"

"Everybody has a past."

"Glad you're not holding me to a different standard than you'd hold yourself." She stroked his flesh. "You like that, baby?"

He groaned. "Love it."

"Started taking birth control."

"Yeah?"

"Uh hun." She raised the skirt to her waist, adjusted her hips above his flesh. "Should warn you," she said with a smile. "I've been holding back."

"What'chu mean?"

"I like to talk dirty." She batted her eyes. "And I want you to do the same."

"My sexy little freak," he said with a chuckle.

She punched his arm gently. "I'm not a freak. I just find it a turn on."

"Don't trip. With you, I'm willing to get as freaky as you want."

Her eyes widened, a spark of intrigue igniting within them. The corner of her mouth curled upward, matching her raised eyebrow. "Well, well," she purred, leaning in slightly. "Now that's interesting." Her words hung in the air, ripe with potential.

"No doubt." He took hold of his flesh, eased her body downward. "So get to talking."

*****

Forty minutes later, DJ exited the bathroom, naked. He held the toothbrush over the garbage can. It had been part of a display, along with toothpaste, floss, and mouthwash. "Here?"

"Yes. We'll replace everything on the way back."

He lay on the bed, gathered her beneath his arm. "You're definitely a talker."

"That's because you know what you're doing. Geez, I've never orgasmed so hard. I nearly passed out."

He kissed the top of her head. "A nigga can't get enough of you."

After a long pause, she said, "I want to start going out."

"Going out?"

"It's something I've been thinking about."

"And when you say out, you mean—"

"As a couple." She lowered her eyes. "If that's alright with you."

"Could get complicated."

"How so?"

"Your parents? Friends? We don't exactly come from the same hood."

"They'd see any guy as a threat. But I love you, and don't care what anyone thinks. Fact of the matter is, I've never met a man strong enough to be with me. Most were too fragile. Mentally and physically."

"That's a bold statement."

"A truthful one, nevertheless. The few men I've dated were insecure or held energy that let me know they were the controlling type. I could never be with someone who tried to control me."

"Insecure and controlling? You got that all on a first date?"

"I'm excellent at reading energy. And once I do, there is no second date."

"What about the guys who had positive energy?"

"I'm extremely selective, and sorta high maintenance. No need to pretend. And just so you know, excluding you, I've been with three men. Two were only one time."

"Why only one time?"

She grabbed his penis, which had recovered nicely, and stroked it. "Because they lasted less than five minutes."

"You kicked them to the curb for that?"

"Couples need to be sexually compatible. A man who does not make his woman's climax a priority is a selfish man."

DJ glimpsed his watch. "We did about thirty, and you came. Guess I should feel lucky."

"I'm the lucky one. We talk about genuine issues. You're playful, gentle…" she slowly kissed down his chest with each statement, "considerate, and God, we're definitely sexually compatible."

"I think we make a good couple."

"I agree," she said, taking him into her mouth.

Chapter 5

"Love and Gangsters"

That Friday, DJ and Angel celebrated their official relationship with dinner at her favorite restaurant, L'Atelier de Joël Robuchon, inside The MGM Grand. The most expensive restaurant DJ had ever been to, the maître-d' greeted Angel as *Ms. Dominguez.*

Tightly wrapped in a thigh-high dress, Angel's voluptuous figure snapped the neck of every guy. The best part, seated among a sea of white faces, it wasn't as if they were a Hispanic couple masquerading as socialites. Angel reeked of money, carried herself with a level of class equal to any person in the room. She ordered dishes in various languages, selected wine like a connoisseur, and looked and sounded like brown royalty—the daughter of a Saudi King.

When the bill arrived, DJ insisted on paying, but Angel refused. "Allow me, baby. Remember, I asked you out."

Although slightly offended, he did an excellent job of masking it. But that slight offense turned to shock once he glimpsed the $1,700 bill. Angel handed the server a Platinum American Express card. It was then DJ understood why she insisted on paying. People with actual money, wealthy people, never paid cash. Cash was beneath them, the equivalent of a crackhead trying to buy a $50 rock with a jar of pennies.

Afterward, they walked hand in hand to the suite, their first night together. In a bizarre twist, DJ had the odd feeling Angel was on something. Even before the wine at dinner, her eyes held a red gloss. As he smoked a blunt inside the suite, he asked if she ever got high.

"Well, I hope you don't think less of me…" she said, staring at the floor, "but I love taking ecstasy."

"Ain't you full of surprises." He shook a playful finger. "You're on the shit right now."

"Are you mad?"

"First off, you can do no wrong in my eyes 'cause I fucking love you. And second, where's daddy's tab?"

She giggled like a schoolgirl and wasted no time digging into her purse. As he washed down the tab with a gulp of wine, DJ knew he loved her—mind, body, and soul. She was all he needed.

The sex had been long and unusually rough. Along the way, he realized their union was perfect; perfect in the sense that they knew how to let go and enjoy sex free from judgment. More animalistic than sensual, they didn't make love; they fucked. Fucked as if hunting for the most pleasure filled orgasm they could find. And whether it was the ecstasy or a natural fire within her, DJ finally experienced the full brunt of her sexuality. An explicit lust that commanded him at will.

No wonder two out of the three guys she had been with couldn't last five minutes. She had a fiery energy that could overwhelm most men's minds. By day, she was the picture of elegance, and by night, she turned into an adventurous lover, eager to please her partner. He felt the same way. Her scent, smooth skin, and her essence—she had climaxed on his lips—tasted sweet like honey. That's why he didn't hesitate to kiss her nylon-covered toes—which she said drove her wild—and trace his tongue along her backside. After DJ climaxed in her mouth for the first time, he was eager to marry her.

In the morning, they drank mimosas and dropped two more tabs. Whoever the supplier, the ecstasy was as potent as he had ever taken. Once it kicked in, they entered the giant shower where he bathed her and finally tapped that luscious ass. She had handled a good amount of him, talking dirty the entire time.

After breakfast, Angel told him to invite Jason and Raul to dinner at Sage; a personal thank you for also helping to save her that night. DJ was a bit surprised, but the gesture solidified the fact she was all in on his life. He had to admit, the idea of proposing to her had gained mental traction.

That night, the four of them ate, drank, laughed, and had the time of their lives. Outside the restaurant, Angel gave Jason and Raul a hug and presented them with a bottle of wine.

"What's this for, Nena?" Jason asked.

"You said your mom loves red wine. Since her birthday's a week before Jack's, you can surprise her."

"Oralé." Jason grinned ear to ear. "Why don't you come through with mí hermano."

"I'd be honored."

On the surface, the invitation appeared casual, a gesture of friendship. What Angel didn't know was the Abregons rarely allowed outsiders into their world. A family of sicarios—led by patriarch Renulfo Abregon, a legendary sicario from Sinaloa, Mexico—they were more feared than the Bonucci crime family. That's because Abregon relatives from Mexico would not hesitate to cross the border illegally, enter a target's home, and kill everyone inside. And like the patriarch, that included women and children.

At the birthday party, Angel shined like a star. She came across as humble and truly honored to have been invited. She listened, spoke when appropriate, and silenced any idea she might think herself better; even helping Mama Cecilia—the Abregon matriarch—clean up afterward. Later, Mama Cecilia told DJ she loved Angel, and that he had better marry her before someone else did. DJ laughed and said he'd work on it.

"Bullshit." She waved a crooked finger at him. "Close the fucking deal."

"Yes ma'am," DJ said as he and Jason respectfully held back a chuckle. As deadly as her husband, Mama Cecilia didn't fuck around. She wanted Angel in her family, end of story. But that was Angel's allure; a person couldn't help but fall in love with her.

Days later, it was Angel's turn to invite her closest friend to lunch, a gorgeous white model named Cat. Tall and beautiful, she had accepted DJ without question, even calling him a chocolate hunk. And like Jason and Raul, they had a blast. The difference was DJ sensed a connection between the two women. He couldn't tell for sure if it were the ecstasy—she and DJ had taken a tab, and he was pretty sure Cat did too—but they had flirted a lot. A whole lot.

Other women he knew played with each other like that but weren't fucking. Still, Angel said nothing when Cat suggested an extremely graphic threesome. In the end, he blamed it on the ecstasy, wine, and the type of friendship they had, one with lots of joking and sexual innuendo.

If Angel was bisexual, DJ loved her enough to accept her for who she was. Truth be told, he didn't have a problem with two fine chicks getting it on; but two guys were gross as fuck. The world called people like him homophobic. He didn't give a shit. Morbidly obese men and women were also gross as fuck, and yet the same world that said being morbidly obese was okay—and judged anyone who said otherwise—never voted them *People's Magazine's* sexiest man or woman alive. Neither did they hire them to serve drinks at Hooters, or walk the runway as a Victoria's Secret model, or whatever the fuck.

After Cat left, the couple stopped at Tiffany & Co. There, DJ bought Angel a $5000 diamond necklace. Placing it on her neck, he couldn't help but notice how small it was compared to her other jewelry.

The afternoon ended inside another suite. After fucking for more than an hour, Angel mentioned she'd like to hang out on the Northside. To finally meet Carlos and a friend other than Jason and Raul, though she loved hanging out with them.

DJ said he would set it up.

However, be it the fear of losing her, or the shame of knowing she was too good for him, he worried about exposing her to the darkest parts of his life.

In all the time spent in the mountains talking about their past, laying out the childhoods which made them who they were, not once did he mention the fact Carlos never wanted children, let alone a little brother. And for good reason, Carlos was a New York O.G. who loved to hustle, stack money, and fuck beautiful women. A player through and through, he fucked his *lady friends*, as he liked to call them, anytime, anywhere. As a kid, DJ often awoke to the sounds of Carlos's headboard smashing against the bedroom wall of their Brooklyn apartment.

When they moved to North Vegas, the nightly escapades increased. Mainly because Vegas women loved a New York nigga skilled at seeing the angles. Eventually, it became normal for the women who stayed the night to interact with DJ as he readied for school. They cooked him breakfast, answered questions about class subjects—girls really were smarter than boys—and taught him about the way their minds and bodies worked. Specifically, foreplay and the clitoris. And when he was old enough to explore further, Carlos had no problem with *his* lady friends becoming *DJ's* lady friends.

At fourteen, DJ lost his virginity to Peaches, a gorgeous white girl—Carlos loved his fine-ass white girls—with giant breasts and long legs. Though he lasted minutes, she used her mouth to give him a second chance. She then guided him through a slower, lengthier love-making type session. Once done, she told him his massive penis would go a long way toward pleasing the ladies. And she was right. When word got out, his own list of lady friends grew.

Before long, as Carlos slept off a night of heavy drinking, DJ became the proverbial fat kid in the candy store. Society called it child endangerment, or worse. DJ called it the greatest childhood in the history of mankind. A childhood Angel didn't need to know about. A childhood that taught him the differences in a woman's body.

Although most women were tight to him, Angel was overly tight. The kind of constriction that came from inaction. She hadn't been fucked regularly before getting with him. All the same, DJ knew she'd been with more than three guys. Not a lot more, but men who were older, more experienced. She was two hands-on with his dick. Too familiar with each position, and way too explicit in her verbal expressions. Didn't matter, though. Like he told her, everyone had a past.

Despite Carlos's lack of fatherly experience, he had taught DJ valuable lessons, like to own his choices, even the bad ones, and to always love and respect his roots. "Your bloodline is black and brown," he said from time to time, "wear that ship with pride."

Carlos also taught DJ not so valuable lessons, like drug dealing, violent retribution, and murder.

Spanish speaking, DJ's east coast accent—though Vegas's dialect had since taken to him—gave him a swag alien to the Northside. Over the years, he had come to mix the New York slang of *nigga* and *son* with the Chicano's *homz* and *ese*.

As a teenager, his expanding physicality, and years as an up-and-coming kickboxer in New York and Vegas, caused gangsters from all races to gravitate toward him. But a lightning quick temper and propensity towards violence—fighting solved everything—cost him three years of his life.

DJ had hated prison. Hated being told when to eat, shit, and sleep. Above all, he hated being at the mercy of white prison staff; many of them took joy in telling a young nigga what to do. The majority were cowards. On the street, they wouldn't dare talk shit to him, but given the power of lock and key, they suddenly became the toughest motherfucker walking the planet.

Another reason DJ struggled to expose Angel to his life had to do with him and Jason's other family, Vegas's fastest growing inner-city gang: the Las Vegas Kings. DJ, Jason, Raul, and Cornelius "Gun" Dawson made up the King's leadership. Of the four, DJ was the most intimidating, though he was not the most feared. That honor easily belonged to Jason, who, at twenty-three, already had eleven murders under his belt. Ten were contract killings; four of which DJ helped to execute.

There were key factors related to the King's rapid growth. First was its racial diversity, a byproduct of DJ's upbringing. Though most members were black and brown, there were Native Americans, Asians, and even whites. Second, its members refused to acknowledge there was a gang at all. Their rumored existence was just that, a rumored existence. Last, its members came from and were still part of existing gangs. Gun's family descended from Chicago's Gangster Disciples.

Presently, other non-affiliated gangs were trying to figure out how to best deal with the King's rise to power. Rumor had it their leaders believed the Kings had gotten too big, too fast. What that meant exactly remained to be seen.

Law of the streets told DJ the figuring out process might end with a move against them, and that was the primary reason he hesitated when considering whether he should expose Angel to his life. All it would take was an enemy to see them together. To know what she meant to him. After a little research, it was about opportunity, which Angel made easy. She stayed on the move, was a socialite with friends all around town.

In the land of monsters, there was no telling what an enemy might do. *Rape? Torture? Murder?* He had watched Jason—extracting information for an Abregon associate—cut the fingers and toes off a sixty-year-old man.

DJ knew he could never live with himself if something like that ever happened to Angel.

Chapter 6

"Dream Killers"

Mexican rap thumped from the stereo as young men and women ate and drank around the inground swimming pool, a rarity for that part of town. At the picnic table, Abregon relatives up from Mexicali played a game of cutthroat spades. One of them, a heavyset man, barked something in Spanish as he slammed a card onto the table.

Across the yard, DJ and Jason relaxed on folding chairs. "I'm pretty sure he left her a couple mill," DJ said.

Jason gulped the bottle of beer. "Way more than that, homz."

"How you figga?"

"She said the vato worked around the world. And you can tell she ain't stress'n 'bout no fería. Her truck... the restaurant she took us to..."

"She had a blast. Wants us to do it again, asap."

"Oralé. Shit was fun as hell. All of them gringos when we walked in—nervous an' shit."

"I think she loved watching them trip as much as we did."

Jason nodded. "Mí familía loves her. Even before moms found out about the wine."

"Wine?"

"From the restaurant. Moms never heard of it… checked the internet. Twelve hundred a bottle." He motioned to the platinum chain around DJ's neck—Angel's birthday gift. The diamond encrusted medallion glistened like a flattened chunk of crushed ice. "Twenty-five."

"You think?"

"At least." Jason gulped what remained of the beer. He motioned for a male teen to get him another. The youngster opened a nearby cooler, rushed it over, and returned to his position. "Your girl's a boss, homz. La Chicá Napoleona."

DJ's face sank. "Her parents gonna think I'm some bum ass nigga try'na hit a lick."

"Fuck 'em. Angel loves you. And you ain't never been wit' no chicá six months."

"No doubt. But real talk, she's too good for me."

"She's too good for any vato, like mí Marcella." Marcella was Jason's five-year-old daughter. He had two boys. "But if she the one, she the one." Jason paused as if to acknowledge the love DJ felt; the kind that scraped against a man's bones like heroin withdrawal. "We make'n serious fería. Finish the school shit, get the degree, open a couple more businesses. After that, her parent's gonna be good."

DJ reached into his front pocket, pulled out a black box.

"Get the fuck outta here!" Jason grinned. "You bought that shit."

"And it's the one you picked out."

Jason examined the ring. "I picked it out 'cause I didn't think you was serious."

"She got us a suite at the Cosmopolitan. Whole weekend." He checked his watch. "Gonna be there in a few. Might ask her tonight. Maybe tomorrow."

"If you don't, Nana gonna smoke us both."

"Yeah, she ain't fucking around." At peace, DJ returned the box to his pocket. "You think her parents gonna be cool once I put down a few moves?"

"Fuck no."

The two laughed.

"Ain't about the money with us, you know, it's about—"

"We all know what it is, fool."

DJ stood up, dapped him. "You good with meeting the nigga, Chrome?"

"He's just another vato look'n for a connect."

"Maybe. But watch him. My gut tells me he's a snake."

"You think every vato not with us is a snake."

"Need to let me knock him out."

"Gotta fine ass honey wait'n to kick it, and you talk'n 'bout sock'n some fool up. Get the fuck outta here."

"Love you too, nigga."

*****

DJ stepped onto the terrace, took a deep breath. He moved to the balustrade and gazed upon the radiant metropolis. The Strip looked different from there... the throne of wealth... a future as bright as the North Star. It looked like a Christmas tree. No, a Christmas city.

"When you get here?" he asked.

Angel eased up from behind, wrapped arms around his waist. "A few hours ago. Wanted to take a hot shower, make sure everything was perfect."

"When we check out?"

"Monday morning."

"First the chain... now this." He turned, eyed her from head to toe. Dressed in a pink silk robe, matching stockings, and Giuseppe heels, the outline of her hard nipples told him she was naked underneath. He pulled her body into his, inhaled the sweet perfume. "You didn't have to go all out."

She kissed him. "I'd give you the world if I could. The Chelsea Penthouse will have to do for now."

Give me the world? The pain of unworthiness pressed against his mind like the barrel of a gun. "Got something a thousand times better than the world." He kissed her. "I got you."

Angel grabbed his hand and walked him through the 3,700 square foot suite. Earlier, he had researched the cost of a Chelsea Penthouse, then spent all day wondering what $5,500 a night bought. The result was insane. Floor-to-ceiling windows, terrace, wet bar, crystal-encrusted wall textures, marble that ran forever.

"Been in Vegas a long time..." He shook his head as they stood in the bedroom. "Ain't never seen one of these from the inside."

"Glad you like it." She retrieved a black silk robe from atop the bed, handed it to him. "Bought it this morning. I'll pour us something to drink."

DJ moved into the bathroom, put on the robe, and reentered to find her extending a glass. "What's this?"

"Scotch whiskey, Bowmore single malt." She interlocked arms. "A toast to the day you were born."

He stared at the mirror, admired the way the chain looked against his bare chest. He swigged the scotch, held the glass eye level. "Damn, shit's hella smooth."

"Like my baby." She unlocked her arm, set her glass atop the lampstand. She crawled onto the bed, lay backward, and patted the space beside her. "Feel how soft it is."

DJ glanced at the silver tray on the other lampstand: half an ounce of Kush, eight hits of ecstasy. He lifted the tray. "You hustlin on the side?"

"Cat knows a guy."

"How many you take?"

"Two. Plan to fly away this weekend."

"Let's fly baby girl." He popped two and washed them down with a gulp of scotch.

Usually, he'd wonder if she had an ecstasy problem, but those glossy red eyes only showed up on nights like this. The rest of the time she was clear-eyed and as focused as a sniper. He set the glass next to the tray and joined her on the bed. Nestled beneath his arm, the two stared at the mirrored ceiling like love-struck teens

"Is this soft or what?" she asked.

"As feathers." He kissed her forehead. "Been thinking about what you said. I want a business career. Just never pictured it until I met you."

"You don't know how happy that makes me." Angel retrieved her glass, mounted his midsection, and fed him a drink.

"Try'na get me drunk?" He removed a pack of magnums from the robe's pocket.

"Of course. That way I can seduce you." She took the pack from him, having failed to get her monthly birth control. "Sorry, baby, my physician's on vacation."

DJ moved his hands along her calves. "It's all good."

"I love you."

"I love you. Never thought I'd say that to any woman."

"Never?"

"Always considered love a weak emotion."

"Why is it different with me?"

"'Cause you make a nigga feel strong."

"You are strong, baby." She sipped, set the glass down. Returning to his side, she lay her right leg across his thighs. "We're going to do remarkable things together. Things that will help you... and your family."

"Appreciate that, but Carlos is good."

"I mean Jason... and the others."

"Others?"

"I hear you on the phone, Jack. Not to mention, you've spent over twenty thousand since we started dating. Last time I checked, no one left you an incentive-based inheritance."

"What'chu try'na say?"

"They're gangsters... like you. Twenty thousand means you're involved in some kind of illegal activity. Most likely drugs. The only question is, how much money do you have?"

He eased her leg off him, sat up. "Where you going with this?"

Unfazed, she smirked. "I'll tell you once you tell me."

Up to that point, their relationship, their love, had been unconventional. But she was ready to prove she was his ride-or-die chick. Not the one willing to hide the murder weapon, or drive ten kilos across state lines, but the one willing to use her business intellect to help him succeed. Problem was, to do that he'd have to do something he'd never done with any woman. He'd have to trust her with his life.

DJ nodded. "About forty-five thousand."

"Is that you, or everyone combined?"

She's really going there.

"Together, we could get eighty. Maybe ninety. Niggas got bills… lifestyles."

"I only ask because I know how much you want our relationship to reflect financial equality."

"If by equality, you mean I ain't try'na live off your money."

"Correct. Therefore, I propose a joint business venture. That way, once it makes millions, it'll be all of *our* millions. Your brothers included."

"Wasn't expecting that."

"Tío taught me how the Italians used ill-gotten gain to establish legitimate businesses. As did the Irish and Germans. Why can't black and brown people?"

"'Cause the rules are different for us."

"Different when you have no legal capital. But in your case, you have other options."

"Name one."

"Your brother has two businesses. He can cosign a loan."

DJ shook his head. "Sorry to rain on your parade, but that nigga ain't risking his businesses for nobody."

"No risk. You give him the principal in cash, plus fifteen percent interest as compensation. He'll put the principal in a safe deposit box and pay back the loan incrementally. Meanwhile, you and I will take it from there."

"Never thought of that angle. But how do we *take it from there*?"

"We open a corporation, become venture capitalists."

"And if it fails? Niggas done a lot of dirt to get that money."

"I'll ensure the money, Jack. But we won't fail."

"No one's perfect, mamí."

"Have faith in me."

DJ felt an overwhelming rush of love for her. He took a long moment to consider the offer. "I'll do it... on one condition."

She sat up on her knees. "Name it."

DJ shuffled off the bed and headed into the living room.

"Where are you going?"

"Need to get something."

When he returned, she noticed the black box and covered her mouth.

"You're my heart for real," he said, dropping to one knee at the edge of the bed. "I want more than a corporation with you. I want a life... kids... a house... the white picket fence." He opened the box. "Angel Dominguez—"

"Yes, yes, yes, yes." She jumped into his arms and smothered him with tear-soaked hugs and kisses.

*****

With the celebratory excitement died down, they had returned to the star-gazing position atop the bed. Angel extended her hand toward the ceiling, admired the ring. "Angel Johnson. Mrs. Angelica Athena Johnson, wife of business tycoon, Jack Johnson."

"Don't know about tycoon, but we'll be okay."

"We'll be better than okay—we'll be great."

"Whatta you, Tony the Tiger?"

Angel giggled. "Grrreat!"

DJ pulled her close. "So what'chu need from us?"

"A hundred twenty-five thousand. I'll match it. That'll give us a significant line of credit. But we'll still have a lot of work to do—those involved, percentages, taxes. That's for later. This weekend is about my baby's birthday."

"And our engagement."

"Our engagement—woohoo."

He reached down, ran his hand along her lower thigh. "You love you some stockings."

She extended a leg in the air. "They look super sexy. Don't you think?"

"Yours are already sexy, and you got the cutest feet in the world. But I ain't gonna lie, they get a nigga going."

"These—" she opened the robe, exposing the stockings edge and her shaven middle, "are from Victoria's Secret."

DJ turned toward her and slid a leg between her thighs. "I fucking adore you, woman."

She ran fingers down his chain, scooped the medallion into her palm. "You like it?"

"Best birthday present ever."

"I have another present." Angel scurried off the bed, disrobed, and went to step out a heel. "Off or on?"

"On." He tossed her a weighty grin. "I'm about to blow your back out."

The talking had begun, this time with him as the initiator. Most times she started with, *"Fuck me like I'm a married woman and we're having an affair"*, or *"your bitch"*, or *"a prude you forced yourself on."* Crazy shit that, once he smoked the weed, swallowed the tab, fucked with a nigga's head on some aggressive shit.

She purred like a tigress, crawled back onto the bed. "I don't think you can."

DJ got up and discarded the robe. He lay back down and set hands behind his head, taking in the full breadth of her soul.

Angel mounted his knees, leaned forward, and kissed his chest down to his flaccid penis. She took hold with both hands, looked up at him, her long black hair glistening like filaments of onyx. Splayed, it covered her face, giving her a look of fiery tease.

"Happy birthday, baby." She took him into her mouth.

DJ placed a gentle hand on the back of her head, groaned as she struggled to consume the upper part of his shaft. She cupped his lower region, stroking his penis with each upward motion, doing so until he was hard. DJ thought it intoxicating to see her red-painted lips around his flesh; a woman so beautiful she could have any nigga in Vegas. Yet here she was, sucking him, loving him as if her life depended on it.

A few moments later, DJ found the sight of her bobbing head and the audible, wet sounds of her stretched lips unbearable. He scrunched up his face, struggling to hold back his climax. In an effort to delay, he carefully pulled her upward and rolled them both over, positioning himself between her legs. He then buried his face in the space between her thighs, inhaling her intoxicating scent.

As his tongue delved into her aching folds, Angel let out a stifled exclamation, "Fuck!" She arched her hips, seemingly presenting herself to him like a platter of lust. With a firm grip on his hair, she sank her ass into the mattress, grabbed her knees, and spread her legs wider.

DJ drank from her middle as though it were the source of everlasting life. Within no time, she let out another muffled scream. Only when she caught her breath did he come up for air, her nectar dripping from his lips. "I love the taste of you."

"God, you're amazing," she panted.

He loved the fact she always treated sex like the pleasure-filled event it was. Expected him to do the same. He was sure that in marriage, she'd keep her body and wardrobe tight, her fire as abundant as an active volcano. They'd always fuck—at least he believed they would—like a man and woman who lived for the taste of each other.

DJ ripped open a condom and sheathed his flesh. He knelt between her thighs and grabbed both ankles, extending them outward. He scooted forward and set her left ankle on his right shoulder. Gripping his shaft, he rubbed the tip against her saturated opening.

"God!" Her entire body trembled.

"God can't help you." He slid into her tight, wet fold.

She pushed against his midsection. "You're too big."

The statement was part of her hunger. He knew she wanted him to feel as if he was tearing her apart. Wanted him to fuck her without mercy.

A thousand breaths passed; her labored moans transformed into a cosmic song of profane gibberish.

DJ set both ankles atop his shoulders and plunged into her with everything he had as she screamed through gritted teeth. Pounding nonstop for twenty-plus minutes, DJ was in awe at her ability to endure. All as she talked and commanded him the entire way. It soon became a battle of wills, though she held a distinct advantage, her pussy an unending reservoir of juice. Angel screamed… shuttered… came… screamed… shuttered… came. Niggas didn't have that luxury. There was always recovery time, a pause in the action.

Somewhere around her third or fourth orgasm, her viselike fold tried to wrestle the seed from his body. He turned her around, set her on all fours.

She raised her ass, arched her back.

DJ entered, and, catching the pace of her rapid breath, found a rhythm. A violent rhythm. Rougher, more animalistic. He stared at the side of her bliss-covered face as it lay against the pillow and picked up the pace. Eyes shut, her head jammed front and back as her cries grew louder and louder with each forceful thrust.

Another fifteen minutes passed before a distorted sense of pride appeared. A pride that convinced him it was their best sex yet; and as good as anyone had ever fucked her.

An hour after they began, the sound of wet slapping flesh engulfed the room. Draped in sweat, the veins bulged from his entire body as he continued to tear into her plump backside.

Without warning, her body stiffened, and she screamed into the pillow. At once, he felt her warm juice spilling onto his scrotum, the ensuing rush of euphoria unstoppable as he let out a series of throat-filled grunts and exploded.

The two collapsed in a flurry of heavy breathing.

*****

Angel held a fresh glass of scotch as they cuddled in front of the fireplace. "Could do this all night."

"Me too." DJ's cellphone went off, but he silenced it. "The way you carry yourself, make a nigga wanna fuck you until he can't walk."

"Good, because I bought five outfits. Was hoping to do a little roleplay—if you're game."

"What kind of roleplay?"

The phone rang again. He bent a brow, silenced it.

"French maid and the gangster. Nurse and the gangster. Schoolteacher and—"

"The gangster."

"No silly, the student."

When the phone rang a third time, she knew something was wrong. "That's not good, is it?"

"Something's up. Niggas know not to bother me this weekend."

Her face held a glint of disappointment. "Hope it's nothing serious."

DJ grabbed the phone and read the number. Dialing, he waited.

Chapter 7

"Honor Your Brother"

DJ weaved in and out of traffic. He had no memory of looking back at Angel, of getting dressed or saying goodbye. Hearing the news, his mind had simply cracked into two distinct realities. The first, a blurred vision of heaven on earth. Angel, his angel, had said yes to marriage. All that remained was the *happily ever after.* A perfect reality, filled with young love, weekend suites inside luxury hotels, and the type of sex that fulfilled every man's fantasy. A reality that promised business ventures, riches, and growing old with the woman he loved.

The second reality started with a simple phone call, like the sudden shift in circumstance that accompanied most murders. The phone's chime begged him to step away from the first reality for just a moment. To meet the stranger in a back alley. A setup. But DJ knew better. A moment was all it took for an enemy to get the drop and put your lights out. Determined there would be no drop tonight, he ignored the phone's chime, treated it like a third-world child begging for loose change.

But the child continued to beg. And he continued to ignore.

The third time, the child didn't just beg; it clung to his sleeve, pulled down on his wrist, and forced DJ to look into its eyes.

When he finally answered the phone, it took a second for Gun's words to register. At first, DJ expected him to express stupidity for having bothered him. "My bad, bro," he was supposed to said. "I forgot you were with your girl."

But Gun hadn't said that. Instead, caught between choked tears and garbled rage, he said, "Chrome jus' smoked Jay in the park. Cops are everywhere."

A million miles from heaven, DJ struggled to breathe, the ecstasy wringing his stomach like a filthy rag. With the euphoria long gone, the poisonous discharge now threatened to drown his existence in a hundred-foot wave of grief.

Smoked? he thought, as the cars whizzed by on each side. Not *hit*, or *shot*, words that more often than not included sentences of hope, like, "He's on the way to the hospital," or "He's in critical condition." If that were the case, the call would have made absolute sense; DJ needed to get to the hospital to sweat it out with the rest of his niggas. The doctor, periodically stepping inside the emergency room to give an update, would eventually ease their pain by walking Jason back from the edge of oblivion. And once he was safe and sound back on earth, DJ and the Kings could get to hunting his hell bound replacement.

But *smoked* was different. *Smoked* held one meaning, and one meaning only: Jason was dead.

*****

The crowd gathered on the street in front of the park, a length of yellow caution tape separating them from the crime scene. News reporters stood with film crews at one end of the tape as a hoard of police shuffled along the yellow barrier, ordering people to stay back.

DJ turned onto the only accessible street and parked behind a Cadillac. He bolted from the truck and headed toward the crowd, at once noticing the group of Kings standing off to the side. Some cried, some held blank stares, as though sleepwalking. Many, like Gun and Milz, held grimaces so contorted they appeared demonic.

Gun approached, pointed at a teenage Mexican nearby. A sleepwalker. "Youngsta said a car pulled up and the back window rolled down. It was the nigga Chrome. He waved for Jay to come over. Brah walked up to the window, and they got to talking. Next thing he know—"

"Where's Raul?"

"Was at his girls," Milz said. "Some of the Abregon's were here, but they left. Went looking for Chrome."

Leaving the body in the middle of the street was the Abregon way. DJ had been with the family long enough to witness the death of loved ones: uncles, cousins. Each time, Jason had shown no emotion. Like the Aztecs, they were a clan of warriors. You honored a warrior, did ceremony to return their souls to the source of life, but you never mourned their departure from this world. To mourn for the inevitable was an act of lunacy. Even when they were murdered—died in battle was the Abregon term—you didn't get emotional, you simply put on the war-paint of vengeance and handled your business.

DJ tried to focus on each detail of Gun's statement but couldn't. His eyes locked onto the one-of-a-kind black Jordan's protruding from beneath the coroner's sheet. He and Jason had stopped by

Premium Outlets four days ago. A lifelong Laker fan, DJ had never seen him in anything but traditional Cholo Nikes.

"Kobe gonna disown you, nigga," DJ had told Jason as he held the Jordan's and considered the purchase.

Jason had examined the $700 price tag and grinned. "Bean'll forgive me. These is clean as fuck."

DJ inspected the coroner's sheet, wondered why another sheet lie around the body.

"Blew his fucking head off," the male voice said, coming just off to the side.

The words, their emotional disconnect, twisted the knife into DJ's soul like a corkscrew. As far as he was concerned, vengeance could begin without delay.

DJ snapped his head around, saw the uniform cop, arms folded. Crowd control, his leisured stance and fat pink face held a nonchalant grin. The death of his best friend, his brother, meant nothing more than overtime.

He's probably thinking, 'just another dead spic.'

The name on his uniform said *Langford*. DJ made a mental note. Maybe he'd double back in a couple of weeks, have him followed. Smoke that ass in his driveway, coming out of church, wherever.

*****

The zipper's echoing slice cut through DJ's heart like a surgeon's scalpel. As three men situated the body bag into the coroner van, the second reality took control of his mind. He would never see Jason again. Never. And for that, Chrome needed to die.

*****

On the street outside Jason's home, DJ stood before the Abregon patriarch, Renulfo. "I should've been there," DJ said in Spanish, tears flowing from his eyes. "He was my brother."

With a granite-like stare, Renulfo puffed a cigar and examined the surrounding scene. A group of Abregons stood on the porch, that frigid glare painted across every face. All were ready for war. Inside the house, silence. DJ knew Jason's mother, Violeta, was in there, gritting her warrior teeth like a vice, waiting for news that the person responsible was dead. It was the only comfort she wanted… needed.

"This is the life we chose," Renulfo said in Spanish, his voice deep and powerful; his words calmer than the moment required. "Death is friend to no man. I have buried many of my family." He chuckled. He actually chuckled. "But I have buried many more enemies."

"I'm gonna kill him." DJ clenched his fist. "I promise. I'm gonna find this mutha fucka and kill him."

"You have become a grandson to me." Renulfo pointed the cigar at DJ. "You are Abregon here—" he tapped his own heart. "You honor your brother—this is good. But killing one man… is not honor."

DJ understood.

*****

Night came, and DJ gathered to discuss the next move. Chrome was leader of the Ruthless North, a dimwitted crew of wannabe gangsters. Never had they exhibited the type of ambition killing an Abregon represented. An act as suicidal as it was brazen. Abregons didn't lose wars. Ever. They sent as many relatives as it took to end your life, even if it meant treating the lives of your women and children like steps on a ladder.

In the middle of the meeting, Angel texted: **I'm here for you, baby. Please call when you can.**

She must know, though he didn't remember telling her.

The devil on his right shoulder said, "Your brother's dead, and all this bitch wants to do is talk about some fairytale shit."

"Look, nigga," the angel on his left interjected. "In all fairness, she doesn't know your level of pain. Street love is different from regular love. Remember, this is not a fairytale. It's hope. A future. The start of something special."

"Hope!?" the devil rebutted. "This ain't about no fucking hope. It's about avenging your brother. It's about doing what Jason would've done had it been you. About killing as many motherfuckers as it takes to ease your pain."

In dark times, the devil always got the last word.

DJ didn't respond to her text. He had never done that before.

*****

"As soon as he moves, nigga!" Gun hung up the phone and turned to DJ, Raul, and Jason's fifteen-year-old brother, Malo. The two Abregons held an unyielding determination to avenge, not their older brother, but the clan from which the slain warrior came. "Flip said the nigga just sat down. Gonna call when he's about to leave."

Flip was the owner of *Easy Times*, a small bar in the blackest part of the hood. DJ knew the place well, having served coke to Flip for the better part of two years. A weekday night, there might be a dozen people drinking and shooting the shit before heading home.

"Who you know around there?" DJ asked.

"Smoker named Mook," Gun said. "Lives with his moms, like two blocks away."

"See if he's home. If he is, tell 'im you're coming through. Need to use his driveway if he got one. Otherwise, the spot out front. That you'll hook 'im up with a nice piece." DJ checked his watch. "Then call Flip back. Tell 'im to leave the back door unlocked."

*****

Three hours later, the stolen Lincoln sat in Mook's driveway as Gun listened to the phone. He hung up and started the engine. "Nigga's bounce'n."

Two blocks away, Gun pulled up to the alley as the faint whisper of a police scanner spouted code. DJ, Raul, and Malo jumped out. Each wore a mask, gloves... carried a weapon: Malo an AR-15, Raul a Glock 17, DJ an AK-47.

As Gun drove off, the three entered the darkness. Midway through, they stopped next to a dumpster. DJ pointed two businesses down: Easy Times rear door.

The Abregon's took position. Raul turned the doorknob until it clicked open, then nodded.

DJ continued down the alley. Two thirty-round clips, taped together at opposite ends, lay in the AKs belly. Another double clip set in the waistband at the small of his back. As he trotted along, the words of the Abregon patriarch played in his head like a doomsday clock. "Killing one man is not honor."

The mental declaration was followed by Carlos's words, spoken on the night DJ successfully committed his first murder: Timothy Watson. DJ was fifteen then, like Malo. Watson had been arrested for fondling the daughter of Carlos's closest friend and released on $25,000 bail. Five months later, Carlos got word the prosecution didn't want to put the six-year-old on the stand and offered Watson a two-year plea. Furious, Carlos told DJ it was time to put in work.

Days later, DJ caught Watson exiting his vehicle in a rundown Northside apartment complex and shot him in the head five times.

Later that night, Carlos downed his sixth or seventh celebratory shot of Patron. "I'm so fucking proud of you. You move just like your pops. He was a stone-cold killer. Use'ta say, 'Motherfuckers stay sleep. Be think'n death never gonna come. But I'm come'n motherfuckers.'"

Carlos followed the statement with a weighty hug. DJ likened it to the pride a white father felt—those from states where hunting was as popular as high school football—whose son had killed his first deer.

At the end of the alley, DJ dropped to one knee, took a deep breath. Gun's job was to pull caddy corner to Easy Times front door, forty yards in the opposite direction. Seeing Chrome, he'd blow the horn.

DJ glimpsed around the corner. The low lighting was perfect, his line of sight guarded by the graffiti-stained post of an old telephone booth. Chrome and Little Ant, a Ruthless North lieutenant, talked with a group of young girls. Chrome's back was to DJ as the girls leaned against an emerald-colored Chevy Tahoe. DJ couldn't tell if there were three or four girls. The closest was a Latina. Tall and thick, she said something to Chrome about the truck's shimmering rims.

Suddenly, the adjacent corner lit up like a prison yard.

Another deep breath.

Honk.

Chrome and Ant turned, snatched guns from their waist.

Honor.

The Latina asked Chrome what was going on when his head exploded into her mouth, the same bullet removing a chunk of skull from her shiny forehead. Both slumped to the ground as automatic gunfire serenaded the once silent night. Little Ant froze. The two remaining girls froze.

DJ swept the AK across their bodies, dropping them to the ground beside Chrome and the Latina. All but one was dead.

A girl.

Black.

She gurgled a high-pitched moan, clawed at the concrete, her salon-painted nails snapping off like tiny icicles.

He placed the barrel behind her head, splattered her face onto the concrete.

Honor.

DJ sprayed Chromes face until there was nothing left. He then sprayed the other bodies until the weapon locked. Turning the empty clip over, he slammed it into place and ushered in another round.

Gun pulled curbside. "Call went out, we gotta go."

DJ moved into the bar.

Breathe.

Raul and Malo had everyone on the ground, faces to the floor, including Flip and Pinky, a Mexican waitress. In the open space in front of them, a female customer coughed and spit up blood, the result of a bullet hole in her back. DJ looked at Raul, who nodded at Malo, acknowledging him as the triggerman.

DJ set the barrel to her head, pulled the trigger. He scanned the room, counted eight more customers, all whimpering in some form of muddled prayer. Only Death had the power to transform a bar into a church.

He eyed Flip, who lay on the floor at Raul's feet. A coat of sweat painted his thin black face. Pinky lay next to him, a white apron around her waist.

"Who else?" DJ asked.

Before Flip could answer, a man to DJ's right climbed to his knees, hands raised in the air. "I ain't had—"

DJ shot him in the chest. The man bent forward, gasped, as the others continued with their godly negotiations. DJ walked over and put another bullet in his head. He turned, nodded at Raul and Malo. The two executed Flip and Pinky.

"Help the cops," DJ told the rest, "And your children die."

*****

Night vision goggles allowed DJ and Malo to drudge a quarter mile down the isolated hillside. The Spring Mountain location sat in an area that forbid people from entering. A decade earlier, following heavy rain, three hikers stepped onto a wide section of loose dirt, the unexpected mudslide carrying them off the hundred-twenty-foot cliff. As a result, signs prohibited visitors from entering the location or be subjected to a $1500 fine.

With the evidence soaked in bleach, Malo dropped the last shovel of dirt onto the four-foot grave. An Abregon burial ground, there were countless graves scattered along a seventeen-acre radius. DJ had lied to Angel. He hadn't discovered the beauty of the mountain through a love of nature, but a process of death. He didn't know how many graves there were. Some held weapons, others held human heads taken from victims to make an Abregon point, but most held bodies. Men… and women.

One woman was Angel's drink spiking friend, Cindy. Two days after she set up Angel, an Abregon female confronted her outside her apartment, told her she needed to drop out the classes she shared with Angel, or she'd regret it. Terrified, she agreed. He waited a week before using another Abregon female to befriend her during an audition for a local movie. She enticed Cindy to a location under the guise of an audition few knew about—an urban flick that had a streetwise white-girl character.

Once there, DJ knocked her unconscious. He then set the plastic, dragged her into the middle, and drove a ten-inch knife into the base of her skull. When he was done wrapping the body, the Abregon female transported it up the mountain, where the open grave he'd dug the night before awaited. Ironically, she was buried less than a hundred yards from the place DJ and Angel first had sex.

Back inside Malo's Impala, DJ glimpsed the text: **Done.**

Sent minutes earlier, Gun and Raul were on their way back from a barren section of California desert, ten miles outside of Primm, having left the Lincoln engulfed in flames.

DJ eyed the phone, broodingly, then wrote his last text to Angel: **Never forget how much I love you. To protect you, I gotta let you go. You'll understand in the morning. Please forgive me. Don't contact me ever again.**

Cold, it hurt like no pain he'd ever felt, but it was the best he could do. It was what he *had* to do. Teary-eyed, DJ hit send and removed the SIM card.

Five miles down the road, Malo pulled over. DJ got out of the car. On a single dreaded night, he lost the two people he loved most in the world. One violently taken from him, the other he had to let go. He placed the phone on the ground, crushed it beneath his boot, and tossed the shattered ruins into the darkness. Heat and rain would do their part in disposing of the past.

Another five miles down the road, DJ flicked the bent SIM card out the window like a smashed cigarette.

Chapter 8

"Noss"

LAS VEGAS, NEVADA, 2020

"He said as soon as you can," Alissa said.

"A'ight, love, I'll head out in a few," DJ said.

"See you then."

Alissa hung up the phone, walked to the rear office, knocked twice, and opened the door. Nathaniel "Noss" Robles sat at his computer. "Mr. Johnson said he'll be heading out shortly," she said.

"Send him right in when he gets here."

"Okay." Alissa shut the door.

Noss took a bite of the pastrami sandwich. As a teen growing up in Dallas, Texas, he had the extraordinary ability to hack computer systems anywhere in the world. Systems agency minds believed impenetrable. It was an ability so rare, the NSA—after watching him frustrate Russian intelligence for more than a year (what else is a thirteen-year-old computer genius to do?)—had him spying on foreign governments a week into his high school freshman year. Not long after, they gave him the codename: Nostradamus. Noss for short. The name wasn't a byproduct of his hacking skills, but an even rarer ability to piece together information in such a way as to predict future events.

During the next thirty years, Noss became a cryptographic god in the realm of cyber-warfare. That career ended in 2010, when he retired abruptly. Earlier that year, agency heads had refused to help rescue his younger sister, Carol, from her violent drug-dealing boyfriend, Rodger. Director Jim Davidson had told Noss, "I'm sorry, but the agency cannot get involved in personal matters. She'll have to file a restraining order like everyone else."

Left with no other recourse, Noss convinced Carol to follow Jim's advice. A week after being served the order, Rodger kicked in Carol's door and broke her nose for the second time. The short police chase ended at a busy intersection, his Harley slamming into the side of a Nissan Pathfinder.

Police inventory of the impounded motorcycle uncovered a kilo of meth inside the leather satchel. Noss thought it a blessing in disguise, especially after Rodger was sentenced to three years for drug possession. However, the day after his sentencing, a dark-colored motorcycle pulled next to Carol's Mustang at a red light. The helmeted rider fired three shots into the driver-side window. Fortunately, her split-second recoil placed his best attempt into her left shoulder. It was then that Noss discovered Rodger's brother was a top member of the Marauders motorcycle gang.

Haunted by guilt, he retired, moved Carol and his family to Arden, Nevada, and took a job as a high-paid security consultant. The following year, he opened Genesis Technologies (Gen-Tech for short), a home, office, and cybersecurity firm. To his surprise, those extraordinary skills translated well in the civilian world. At present, Gen-Tech ranked third in the state.

Success was not without cost. Upon release from prison in 2013, Rodger showed up to the office accompanied by two members of the Aryan Brotherhood—prison had expanded his criminal associations—and demanded to know Carol's whereabouts. Noss told him he didn't know where she was, nor would he tell him if he did. Without making a scene, Rodger slid a cellphone number across the counter and whispered to Noss, "You got two days to give me an address or one of your daughters gonna get a visit. Same shit'll happen if you call the fucking police."

All three of his daughters attended college out of state.

That night, Noss tracked the number to a motel on the outskirts of Vegas. He then reached out to gym owner, Alejandro Abregon. A year earlier, Alejandro had hired Gen-Tech to do background checks on all gym employees. The two had developed a solid friendship, Noss quickly becoming well acquainted with the family's infamous reputation. He had even done *favors* for Alejandro; favors that included looking into whether members of the Abregon family were under criminal investigation.

Noss explained the situation to Alejandro who suggested he meet with his grandfather, Renulfo. Over a glass of Jim Beam, and a thorough frisking, Noss reiterated his predicament. "And Mr. Abregon…"

"Renulfo."

"Renulfo. I gave the agency thirty years of my life, and they did nothing. Even after she was shot." Noss paused, got to the point. "I think my skillset has been extremely valuable to you."

A calm, cigar puffing, Renulfo asked, "What exactly do you want from me?"

"I want him gone."

"I have no power to make him leave Vegas."

Noss understood the cautious wordplay. "Then I'll be forced to leave Vegas."

A long silence followed.

"Safety of one's family is most important," Renulfo said. "If we were family, I would do everything in my power to protect you... to protect *your* family. Because *your* family would be *my* family." Renulfo nodded. "Do you wish to become part of my family?"

"Yes."

"Understand, Mr. Robles, years down the road, one cannot simply walk away because one no longer wishes to be family."

"As you can see, I don't walk away from family."

"Very well. I'll look into the matter."

The next day, Jason Abregon stopped by Gen-Tech and told Noss to take his wife out to dinner. He did. While they dined at Nunzio's Pizzeria inside the Stratosphere Tower, Rodger and his cohorts were executed in the motel parking lot.

After a week—with no one showing up to question him—Noss hacked Vegas P.D. He learned police had found six ounces of cocaine inside the motel room, along with $12,000 in cash. The lead detective had determined the murders drug related. Most importantly, Noss was not a person of interest.

A year later, when a rival gang down gunned Jason Abregon, Noss protected the family's retaliation; an event still known today as the *Easy Times Massacre*. Monitoring the investigation from afar, Noss discovered the moment police located a key witness. The report said the bartender's nephew had arrived with his girlfriend a half hour before the murders. The nephew was told to leave because *Mexicans were on their way to smoke a nigga.*

The report further stated the girlfriend's sister had later contacted police to collect the $50,000 reward. Picked up and questioned for over three hours, she told them everything her sister had told her, except the names of the Mexicans, which she didn't know. Based on the information, police suspected it was the bartender who called the shooters and was killed by the same individuals to cover their tracks.

Homicide detectives tried to question the girlfriend but couldn't find her. Moving on to the bartender's nephew, they found him on his living room floor, bound and gagged, his throat cut to the spinal cord. They discovered the girlfriend in the bedroom, having suffered a similar fate. Only her tongue had been cut out, which they could not locate.

The coroner determined they were executed within nine hours of their bodies being discovered. She had also found the tongue... inside the dead woman's vagina. The sister's headless body was discovered in a Northside dumpster seventeen days later.

Since then, Noss had become the King's most valuable asset, and the sole reason law enforcement gained no traction in the last seven years. His specialized program—hidden in the office computer of a Berlin, Germany, toy-maker—scanned targeted law enforcement databases once a week for anything related to the Kings and its five leaders.

Noss provided the Kings with burner phones, the newest bug technology for sweeping persons and locations, and met with DJ twice a month to discuss moves the Kings and Abregon's were looking to make. The two groups moved independently of one another.

The reason for the present phone call had to do with Carlos's potential business partner, Ronan Carter. DJ had again asked Noss to investigate his background, something Noss had already done. Though Ronan had come back clean—no law enforcement ties—DJ now wanted Noss to focus on his business associates.

*****

Seated at the edge of the bed, Angel retrieved her bag from the nightstand, removed a phone, and began texting. She returned the phone to her bag, bent forward, and adjusted the ankle strap on her shoe. "Have to go."

Joshua Delaney emerged from the adjacent office, a glass of WhistlePig whiskey in his left hand, a legal envelope in his right. "You just got here."

"And yet, we're done."

"Sorry, it was a long day. Stay the night—I'll do that thing you like."

"Have a ton of meetings tomorrow," she said, uninterested. "Besides, my car will be here in five minutes."

Joshua struggled to hide the disappointment. He had again underperformed in the sex department, and she let him know it. "Report on the Sloan project," he said, handing her the envelope. "You were right, Crown Point sold sixty acres west of the interstate."

Angel placed the envelope into her bag, stood. "Subdivision?"

"Galindo is planning to build two hundred plus homes, starting in the mid four-hundreds. That gives you plenty of options."

"I'm not concerned with them; they're building another Southern Highlands. But I'll need more research."

"What for?"

"I have several businesses I'd like to position."

"Minority owned?"

Her brow creased. "Why do you ask?"

"Father wanted me to... he would like to be part of Serenity's entrepreneur program."

"Two months to go and suddenly he's worried about Quincy Taylor?"

"Always to the point."

"Because any other direction leads you astray." She checked the time on her Patek Philippe. "Your father should have no problem. Quincy's agenda is way too progressive, even for Nevada."

"Sounds like you know him?"

"I know a lot of corporate lawyers. Is that a problem?"

"Of course not. Anyway, since he's African American, data shows dad is vulnerable with the Hispanic vote." He shrugged. "Republicans and the minority vote… like oil and water."

"Doesn't have to be." Angel placed a hand on his forearm. She understood the difficulty Joshua faced walking in his father's immense shadow. "I want *you* to write up a bill your father will support; a tax credit for minority-owned businesses. We can negotiate the details."

"You'll do it then?"

"If you truly want a political career, you'll have to create your own legislative identity."

Joshua followed Angel into the living room, held her jacket as she slid into it. "How do you suppose I do that?"

"By becoming the one Republican who treats minorities as something more than a vote. To substantiate that narrative, you'll need a track record of bipartisanship."

"With you by my side, I could be president." He bent his clean-shaven face into a broad smile, walked her to the door.

She kissed his cheek. "Take care."

"Mom keeps asking me when we're going to set the date."

"Sounds like you need to talk with her."

"She's just dying to call you her daughter."

"Please, don't remind me."

"When will I see you again?"

"We'll do something when I get back from London."

"I love you."

She opened the door, patted his chest. "Don't forget the tax credit."

*****

"Hey, beautiful," DJ said.

He handed Alissa a sly grin. A month ago, Noss had let it slip that he thought the young Brazilian had a crush on him. Although married, DJ had a feeling she'd go if given the chance. He'd been laying the foundation ever since.

"Hey handsome," she said in Spanish, her plump lips pursed in a mischievous smile. "Follow me."

Of the four currently in the office, DJ knew she was the only one who spoke Spanish, so he tested the waters. "I'll follow you wherever you want to take me."

"Good to know." She strutted to the back office, her thick ass jiggling like a jelly-filled medicine ball. When they reached the door, she placed a hand on his arm. "He's waiting."

"Thanks, love."

"Anytime."

"You have my number."

She glimpsed the surroundings and, seeing no one, whispered, "I do."

DJ walked through the office door, bottled water in hand. "Noss the boss, tell me something good."

"Three years ago," Noss said, getting down to business, "you had me research a friend of yours." He motioned to the computer screen, tapped open a file, clicked the Jpeg.

DJ studied the photo. It was a group of twenty Asian men and women, a ribbon-cutting ceremony for a restaurant. Ronan was

91

inches from being cropped out. Easy to notice, he was the only black person in the photo. At the center, an Asian woman held a giant pair of scissors around a gold ribbon.

The photo wasn't the issue. The issue was the person standing next to the woman.

"It's a stupid question, but how the fuck did you find this?"

"Facial recognition software. Lady with the scissors… it's from her restaurant's website." He eyed DJ with half a grin. "In Tokyo."

"Should've fucking known."

"Who is she? You never told me exactly."

DJ leaned against the desk, eyeing the photo like a mirage. "Proposed to her the night Jason was killed. After we did what we did, I had to cut her loose. Ain't seen or heard from her since. She's an investor?"

"Took a while to untangle the paper trail but there are no investors. It's just her." Noss spun the chair to face him. "She paid a million two for the plaza. And get this, she bought it two months after Carlos purchased the laundry-mat."

"You're kidding?"

"Afraid not."

"She's been following us?"

"Seems that way. Question is, why?"

DJ paced. "She's like a genius on the business shit. Had a rich uncle who taught her the game. Left her a boat load of money when he died."

"Well, based on everything I've seen, the genius part is an understatement."

"What'chu mean?"

"Owns a multinational conglomerate. Serenity Corporation. Six thousand employees worldwide. It's the most versatile portfolio I've ever seen. Agriculture, real estate, stocks, entertainment."

His words brought a smile to DJ's face. "Believe it or not, I was supposed to be part of that. Was gonna give her a hundred grand in dope money to wash, pool it with hers. After the wedding, we'd open the corporation together." DJ looked up at Noss. "Makes sense now. She'd know our influence on the neighborhood."

"What are you going to do?"

"Don't know."

"Tell you what, I'll grab the GPS on her phone and car just in case you want to meet up."

"A'ight." DJ stopped at the door. "Gotta ask—what's her company worth?"

"One point three."

Chapter 9

"Joshua Delaney"

Joshua sat in the Fendi Casa leather chair, a Christmas gift from his mother two years ago. Sipping the whiskey, he stared at the crumbled bedsheets and suffered in silence. Joshua had had his share of beautiful women, but Angel was the most beautiful woman he'd ever seen, let alone made love to. Handsome, albeit slightly overweight, he was a well-respected criminal defense attorney, and son of Republican Senator, James Delaney.

Angel was different for too many reasons to list. Hispanic genes and an incredible sense of style gave her the appearance of a 21st-century goddess. When added to the intellectual strength of a Michelle Obama, and the business savvy of a Jeff Bezos, she was a woman capable of capturing the heart of any man. She had surely captured his; held it in her tiny hands like an ordinary piece of gum, Joshua powerless to do anything about it.

The relationship began seven months ago, at the mansion party of Priscilla Hewlett. Called to Washington last minute, Joshua's father had asked him to fill in on behalf of the family. A former Ms. Nevada, Priscilla was the wife of billionaire Raymond Hewlett, his father's biggest campaign contributor. She had celebrated the opening of *Priscilla's Cafe and Dessert* inside the MGM Grand, her young franchise's third such opening in as many years.

An hour into the event, Joshua entered the spacious living room and gave it another forty minutes before he left. He watched from the opposite side of the piano as Priscilla stood near the foyer, her long statuesque body draped in a magenta Oscar de la Renta dress and Gianvito Rossi shoes.

"My god, Pree, the new place is fa-bu-lous," an older woman raved.

Priscilla tossed back her auburn hair. "Eleven thousand square feet. We have two marble staircases... an elevator...."

Joshua walked away. He despised everything about Priscilla and her circle of trophy wives. She had married Raymond three years earlier, when he was fifty-two. He had four children from his earlier marriage, the youngest of which was three years older than his new wife.

Renown attorney, Angus Cooper, had overseen the couple's prenuptial agreement. A longtime family friend, Angus told Joshua the lengthy document, sealed through court order, ensured Priscilla never sought children, engaged in intercourse at least once a week (Raymond's preference), and kept her weight under 135 pounds.

Also, she had to attend social functions (with or without Raymond), establish her own business, and meet with the benefactors of his multiple charities twice a month. Beyond that, she was free to shop and hold elaborate dinner parties for friends and associates. Should they divorce for any reason, except for an extramarital affair, Priscilla kept sole ownership of her business and received ten million a year for life.

However, if she had an affair, her business went to his children, and she received nothing. Not even the clothes on her back. An insane prenup by human standards, save those of Vegas's elite.

Joshua stepped through the mansion's rear French doors and into the immense backyard. He lifted a flute of Andre Clouet champagne from the tray of a passing servant and examined the crowd beneath the colossal pavilion. Moving onto the freshly cut Bermuda grass, he nodded at fellow lawyer, Tyler Watts and his stunning fiancé, Nina, a half African, half Native American Barbie doll.

Joshua entered the pavilion and eyed the delicious assortment of cocktail food. He considered a plate of Matsutake mushrooms but, glancing up, was at once smitten. Angel stood across the room, between the tuxedoed jazz band and a pink bougainvillea. She chatted with Eric Lampley, son of real estate giant, Ronald Lampley.

A well-known playboy, Eric was medium height, attractive, and ripped. Last month, they had featured him in a Vegas Lifestyles magazine article. The accompanying photo spread had a picture of him doing shirtless bicep curls at a private gym.

Joshua scanned the immediate area. Many of the best-looking debutantes were nowhere to be found. Usually, a man of Eric's social stature had a dozen following his every move. Joshua understood the reason behind the desertion. Angel possessed the type of beauty they refused to stand next to, especially when a wealthy bachelor like Eric was nearby. The visible discrepancies were so stark as to be embarrassing.

Joshua made his way over, examining Angel from head to toe with each measured step. Up close, she was downright mind-blowing. Her blue, skintight Michael Kors dress ended mid-thigh. Prada shoes and matching hosiery presented shapely calves that caused some men to steal salivating glances. A smidgeon of makeup revealed a natural allure that many women in attendance paid thousands to reproduce. All had failed in comparison.

When Lampley stepped away to answer a call, Joshua wasted no time approaching from the side. "For a moment, I thought you were Kim Kardashian."

Angel gave him the once-over. "Sorry to disappoint you."

"I'm not disappointed at all. Are you here with Eric?"

"Who is Eric?"

"Eric Lampley. The gentleman you were just talking to."

"Oh, him. He started talking to me. We never got around to introductions."

"Well then, please allow me not to make the same mistake." He extended a hand. "Joshua Delaney."

"I've seen you on TV." She shook. "Angel Dominguez."

"My law firm indulges the media from time to time. Anyway, you look like an angel. So, who dragged you to this enormous display of opulence?"

"Priscilla. And we do not drag friends to successful milestones. We look forward to celebrating them."

"Been to lots of Hewlett parties—how is it we've never met?"

"I'm not a social butterfly. In fact, I was about to leave."

Joshua checked his Rolex. "Plan to give it another half-hour before excusing myself to *meet with a client.*"

"An appropriate excuse."

"If not all too common."

"And how do you know the Hewlett's?" she asked.

"Raymond attended mine and my father's Alma Mata. And since he's in Washington—"

"You're filling in like the dutiful son."

"I am."

"Since I have you—"

"And you do have me. From the moment I laid eyes on you."

She winked. "Of course, I do. I'm curious, though, is the Senator also a member of the infamous Skull and Bones fraternity?"

"As am I." He wasn't sure if she was flirting or being sarcastic. And though she held the upper hand—someone that beautiful always did—she had known who he was, and his Alma Mata Yale. It meant she also knew the Delaney name carried a sense of awe for most women in Vegas. At the very least, her question allowed him the chance to level the playing field. "Priscilla loves talking about the fraternity more than Raymond's net worth. Why do you think that is?"

"Perhaps some women find that kind of power more attractive than wealth."

"I thought the two went hand in hand?"

"They do not. You can be wealthy and not possess the kind of power I'm referring to."

"And what kind is that?"

"They allege your fraternity to have placed several men in positions of significant power. The Bush's. John Kerry. Men capable of altering a person's life in an instant. Raymond has ties to the Koch family, known for their super-PACs. And if the rumors are true, your father's political future knows no limits."

"Well informed, I see." Joshua raised the empty flute in offer.

"No, thank you."

He set the flute onto a table and motioned to a nearby server. The man extended the tray while a different server retrieved the empty flute. Joshua grabbed the drink, tilted it in her direction. "You sure?"

"Always."

"The question is, do *you* believe that kind of power more attractive than wealth?"

"If used for good, it's more attractive than physical appearance." She touched his arm, gestured toward the partygoers. "But that's not the kind of power on display here."

Joshua grinned. The already stimulating conversation had produced an unusual topic. "Please elaborate, Ms. Dominguez."

"Angel."

"Angel."

"Some of these men offer the power in their wealth. That's because they know some women, if given the opportunity to live a lavish lifestyle, will sleep with an unattractive man. And some of these women offer the power behind their beauty because they know, if given the opportunity, *all* men will sleep with a beautiful woman, the most beautiful woman possible. In this situation, either party can thwart the power exchange, making it contrary to the power I speak of."

"Thwart?"

"Yes. If you don't find me attractive enough to sleep with, you can withhold your offer of an extravagant lifestyle. And if I'm not at all swayed by an extravagant lifestyle, I will not entertain such an offer. Thus, neither can forcibly alter a person's life."

"Are you saying you don't care about money or sex?"

She dropped her gaze, as if expecting more from him. "Who doesn't enjoy money and great sex? I'm saying I can do without your power, money, and cuteness."

He tapped a finger against his chin. "So, what holds power over you?"

"Nothing." She glimpsed the time on her Omega. "It's been a pleasure."

"Have dinner with me."

"And why would I do that?"

"Like you said, nothing has power over you. Therefore, it'll be a simple dinner with friendly conversation."

"Right." She eyed him with a glint of humor. "As entertaining as that might be I'm going to pass."

"I'm serious. I believe you when you say you're not at all impressed by this…" he nodded at the crowd. "Not only is that different from what I'm used to, but it's also refreshing. And though I find you insanely attractive—like Charles Manson insane—I'd like the chance to enjoy dinner like a normal person."

"As opposed to what, every woman's fantasy? I get it. You have the name, money, and good looks, but I'm a self-made woman. And I can assure you, Mr. Delaney, I'd require a great deal more than superficial enticement."

"Brutal." He clutched his chest as if shot. "All I'm saying is you presented a unique perspective. I'd like to hear your take on other issues. But if you're the person whose point of view is the only one that matters, I understand."

"Oh, did we also minor in psychology?"

"That and beer pong."

Angel smiled. "What exactly do you have in mind?"

"Yui Edomae Sushi."

"I have several errands to run. Let's do seven?"

"Seven it is."

*****

Joshua dried the glass with a hand towel and placed it in the overhead cupboard. He returned to the bedroom and the Fendi Casa and checked the wall clock: 10:23 p.m. Angel was home, should be home. He couldn't be sure. She wasn't a person who called to say she arrived safely, and to wish you a good night. He thought to text her but decided against it.

Instead, he revisited the dinner at Yui Edomae Sushi. Joshua had arrived dressed in a black Bottega Veneta suit, Angel in a rose Versace skirt, and matching shoes. Her outfit road curves so pronounced men had tossed him envious glares like hand grenades. Having grown up around wealthy fashionistas—his mother and sisters' wardrobes held every high dollar name in the industry—Joshua recognized stylish women with expensive tastes.

Based on their earlier conversation, he had surmised she didn't do casual banter, and he was right. Throughout dinner, Angel discussed the world with a fervor he had never seen or heard from any person, man, or woman. The more she spoke, the more attractive she became.

Spellbound throughout the evening, Joshua believed her confident disposition removed any pressure or social advantage associated with being part of Vegas's most esteemed family. And her elegant yet entertaining persona fit well with his robust and straightforward demeanor. A demeanor that had always intimidated women, no matter how beautiful.

Several people had stopped at their table to tell him that his father could rely on their vote next election. Each time, with hands folded in her lap, Angel grinned, amused at the level of reverence.

By the time the check arrived, Joshua was convinced he'd done well in impressing her. That was until they reached the outside curb. She stopped next to a black Rolls-Royce Phantom, a square-jawed driver's hand on the open door. Angel smirked. Like the half million-dollar vehicle, her look mocked him for being too confident.

Old money? New money? he wondered.

Delaney was old money. Joshua's great-great-grandfather, Lawrence, had arrived in America from Europe in the mid-1800s. Within two years, he started the lucrative mining company—still in existence—that became the cornerstone of the family fortune. Delaney's owned several multi-million-dollar businesses, including Delaney Automotive, the largest dealership in Nevada.

If the money were hers, its inclusion ensured his chief weapon—the offer of an extravagant lifestyle she correctly surmised—would have zero effect in swaying her heart.

"Nice car," he said.

"It gets me around."

He asked to see her again. Angel agreed to dinner the following Saturday, at Twist by Pierre Gagnaire.

Overwhelmed by her lingering presence, every woman he met throughout the week was unattractive, insecure, shallow, or intellectually deficient in comparison.

Saturday arrived, and she did not disappoint. When they entered the restaurant, Angel turned the head of every man... and a handful of women. Like a scented rose, Chanel perfume swathed a red Valentino dress that ended four inches above her knees.

She completed the look with Miu Miu heels and black leopard print nylons. The image ignited every fetish known to man: breast... ass... legs... feet.

Laughter marinated a conversation that traveled everywhere. Besides her social and political views, Joshua discovered the origins of her wealth. Founder and CEO of The Serenity Corporation, her company had been the talk of town for the last three years. It held other revered enterprises of the same name, including Serenity

Marketing, the number four firm in Vegas. Her fast-growing real estate company, Serenity Premier, had outbid Delaney's London Finance for a ten-acre parcel just outside Boulder City.

Joshua's oldest brother, Aaron, had planned to build an office complex there.

For all her amazing qualities, Joshua had encountered one potential issue. When asked direct questions about personal information—friends, family, and private interests—Angel responded in vague terms, much the way his father did when asked a policy question he had no intention of answering.

Joshua gave her the benefit of the doubt, deciding she was a woman who shared morsels of personal life based upon a friend's emotional progress. A nice touch since most women he dated surrendered every detail of their lives, along with their bodies, in a single night.

On the way home, Joshua texted: **Had a great time. Must do it again... soon.**

Her text arrived minutes later: **Any suggestions?**

He had plenty.

The texts journeyed into the next day. Each time her jingled response sent a jolt of electricity shooting through his body. In the beginning, he answered almost immediately, but her delayed reply, sometimes as long as two hours, was a message: take it slow.

Caught in the rush of newness, and her continual deflection when asked personal questions, Joshua did what most men and women do when considering the possibility of a meaningful relationship—he investigated her. His efforts turned up little, save her company's net worth ($1.3 billion), her title as Serenity's CEO, and her board position on several minority-run organizations. No Facebook... Twitter... Instagram... Snapchat... nothing.

While everyone else was busy with social media and self-promotion, her life was so private it was almost like a secret. So, even though he knew a lot about Angel, he really had no idea who she truly was.

Although they continued to stay connected, the ensuing months saw little to no emotional movement in the friendship. She was regularly out of the country, sometimes for as long as three weeks. During those periods, she seldom, if ever, answered his texts. And when she did, they were brief and accompanied by a declaration of, "Super busy, will call when I get back." No date for *getting back* was ever attached.

One night, Angel returned from Italy and called to see if Joshua was up for lunch the following day. He told her yes but asked if she could first stop by his downtown office. He wanted her to meet a friend of the family. Angel said she hated surprises but agreed.

Once there, Joshua introduced her to Michael Blakeman, COO of Sam's Club, who was in town visiting Senator Delaney. Blakeman explained to Angel that several of his retailers were looking for a marketing firm in Vegas and asked if she'd be interested. The potential contracts were sure to be seven figures.

Angel said she'd love to meet with them, provided Blakeman her contact information, and ended with small talk regarding her interest in one day purchasing a vineyard. Earlier in the conversation Blakeman had mentioned he owned a Napa Valley vineyard. He offered to show her around if she were ever in town.

Two things resulted from the meeting. Blakeman, who was handsome, married, and in his forties, was drawn to Angel. Normally, this wouldn't have bothered Joshua, but Angel seemed to reciprocate. The energy between them was like the early conversations in many extramarital affairs. Joshua, experiencing this intense jealousy for the first time—it made him feel sick—promised himself he would never allow such a situation to happen again.

Later, as the two sat alone in his office, Angel told him she loved the gesture but didn't want his help in obtaining clients.

"Just trying to network," he said, relieved.

"And I appreciate the gesture. But I don't want some obscure form of quid pro quo entering our friendship."

"Is that how you see me... as a friend?" He realized the desperation in his voice. Not to mention, she had recently hinted at the fact she was not looking for a relationship. "Wait, I mean…"

"I know what you mean. And yes, I consider you a friend. Someone I enjoy spending time with. We laugh, have fun, but the last thing I want is contracts obtained through associates of yours."

"I would never hold something like that over your head."

"I would never allow you to."

"God, you're so strong." He raised hands. "Please don't kill me, but I researched you."

She shrugged, unaffected. "The times we live in."

"Couldn't help it. I like you."

"And I like you. But I'm a private person. If you want to know something about me, ask. If I don't wish to share, I have no problem saying so. Anything else is an unwanted intrusion."

"You're such an independent woman."

"I am. And just so you know, you'll never be able to control me. I was Angel Dominguez before I met you, and I'll be Angel Domínguez should we ever part ways." She took his hand in hers. "If you can accept that, I'd love to continue seeing you."

"I can accept that."

She guided him to the office couch, sat him down, and gave him a summary of her life; details which included the relationship with her beloved uncle Javy.

The next night, having dined at Estiatorio Milos, Joshua and Angel stood in the parking garage of the Cosmopolitan hotel. As her driver lingered in the distance, he said, "Once again, love, I had an amazing night."

"Is it over already?"

"Uh, what did you have in mind?"

"A nightcap—your place."

A woman of strong conviction, Joshua believed Angel when she hinted at not wanting a relationship. However, to her, a relationship and intimacy were two separate things. She told her driver she'd call him if he was needed and got in Joshua's Ferrari FF.

When they arrived at his condominium, Angel shut the door and kissed him. Locked in a passionate embrace, the two stumbled into the bedroom, undressed, and slid into bed. It was over in less than ten minutes.

Although she claimed to understand, her initial, "You're done?" coupled with an utter look of disappointment, had left him feeling embarrassed and emasculated. He tried again a short time later, faring better. What *he* thought was better.

"It's okay," she said as the two lay in bed. "Some people are not compatible."

"Take it you failed to orgasm?"

"Not in fifteen minutes. Besides, for that I need uninhibited oral stimulation."

Joshua believed he knew what she meant and jumped at the chance to redeem himself. He spent the next hour with his face between her thighs, licking, sucking, and bringing her to multiple high-pitched screams.

As he walked her to the door, he said, "I take it we're compatible."

"Not if you consider that uninhibited oral stimulation." She kissed his cheek. "Still, I had a lot of fun."

The next day, he called his brother, Mark, and told him what happened. Mark suggested he try the pill he used when fucking women other than his wife, Anne. He called them his magic pills. Joshua picked up a dozen.

It took a week before he got Angel to give him another shot. That night, they made love... twice. And thanks to the pill, he'd lasted over twenty-five minutes each time.

Since then, they had made love twice a week—when she was in town—and always at his condominium. He had once suggested they go to her place. "I like it this way," she'd replied, her tone definitive: her place was off-limits.

After one session, she said, "Mind if I take a shower?"

"Not at all." He handed her a puppy-like grin. "Can I join?"

She winked. "Only if you're going to follow my every command."

Unsure of what she meant, he said, "Okay."

They stepped through the glass walls of his custom shower. Angel adjusted the desired water temperature and poured scented body wash into a blue loofah. As the warm beads cascaded their flesh, she faced him, presented the loofah. "Bathe me."

He again felt as if Angel were getting him to do something she planned to evaluate. A test. Like when she set her nylon-covered toes against his chin and told him to "Suck." And he sucked and lick, from her toes to her knees, bringing her to multiple orgasms.

Joshua took hold of the loofah and started with her full, pert breast. Angel closed her eyes and moaned as if his touch were stirring her insides. He worked his way down to her flat stomach. Before he could continue downward, she took hold of his wrists and moved his hands to the crack of her ass. He slid his fingers from both hands between the taut flesh. She bit her lower lip, let out a soft purr.

"Here, let me help you." She turned around in his arms and again guided his wrists to her ass.

He pressed the loofah between the plump crack and washed her. As he did, Angel rocked her hips in an up and down motion, riding the loofah and letting out another soft purr. She grabbed the railing, spread her legs, and arched forward. Though she said nothing, he knew what she wanted from him.

Joshua knelt.

After an especially vocal orgasm that caused her entire body to shutter, he removed his tongue. It was his third time pleasing a woman that way.

Angel caught her breath. "That was amazing."

"I've never done that before."

"Neither have I." She giggled. "And I never will, so don't ask."

"Well, what do I get out of the deal?"

"The satisfaction of knowing you can make your woman cum."

"My woman?" he asked, trying to hide the excitement.

A week later, Joshua invited Angel to his parents' home for dinner. He'd already filled them in on the woman he'd been dating for months, her impeccable character and incredible success as a businesswoman. By night's end, they too were head over heels in love with her; especially his mother, Helen, who called her the most beautiful creature she'd ever laid eyes on. She even told Angel, "You and my son would make me the most beautiful grandchildren."

Angel didn't miss a beat. "You're far too young and beautiful to be anyone's grandmother."

The next night, after a half-hour of sex, and another thirty minutes of orally pleasing her, Joshua reached beneath the bed and presented the open black box.

"Marry me," he said.

She looked at him with a mixture of surprise and slight amusement. "You don't want to marry me."

"Uh, seeing as I'm holding a half-million-dollar ring, I'm going to disagree."

"Half a million?"

"Yes."

"Very observant, but I don't think you thought this through."

"Help me understand."

"Being a Delaney means social functions, mingling, having your name on everyone's lips. All the things a private person like me despises."

"Then stay a mystery for all I care. Love you better that way."

"And what of my trips? What would be your expectations?"

He paused, knowing what she meant. If he dared to change her life in any way, she was lost forever. "Being my fiancé. That's it. Nothing changes. And we'll keep it a secret until you're ready for it *not* to be a secret."

"And your parents?" She eyed the almond-shaped diamond. "I cannot keep this thing a secret."

"I hadn't thought of that."

"We'll tell them together."

He looked up, excited. "Whatever you want."

"I keep my condominium. No cohabitation until we're married. And I'm not setting a date for at least a year."

"Anything else?"

"I'm serious, Joshua."

"Is that a yes?"

"One last thing. I will not get pregnant."

"You don't want children!?"

"I want children. I'm just not destroying my body to have them. We'll use a surrogate."

*****

As Joshua continued to ponder their future, he still couldn't believe she'd said yes. All the same, the sex earlier was terrible. Five or six minutes terrible. Afterward, he tried orally pleasing her, but she pushed him away and dressed.

He realized he would need to always have a steady supply of magic pills. He wasn't sure, but he suspected that if he ever consistently underperformed, neither marriage nor uninhibited oral stimulation could keep her faithful.

Joshua didn't know why he struggled without the pills, since he'd bedded other beautiful women for as long as he wanted. Maybe not as long as he wanted, but longer than ten minutes. He believed it had to do with Angel's size and fiery persona. Demure, she had a way of making him feel as though he were annihilating her. Her firm body, sultry cries, and outright vulgarity stirred his loins like nothing else.

He realized he'd become like the countless addicts he saw around the courthouse. The struggle they faced with their drug of choice. The constant pining for even the smallest taste, to bring a glint of normalcy back into their lives.

Normalcy? he thought. *My life won't be normal until she's my wife.*

Chapter 10

"Young Tigress"

Angel clenched the bank statement. "Seventy-seven thousand? When?"

"Last Wednesday," Gwendolyn said. "During the meeting with John. I added Arclinea tables, Trussardi Casa sofas, and Zeville crystal decanters. They're all trending."

"This is an antique shop, mother, not home decor for the affluent."

"I've been thinking about that. Perhaps we should reconsider our brand."

Brand? Angel wanted to say, 'You don't have a brand.' Unless one considers overspending for unnecessary inventory, a brand. But it was pointless to tell her mother anything. She was not business savvy, she was bourgeois. The love of antiques belonged to her father, Luis.

Two years ago, Angel had encouraged him to buy and sell antiques online as a hobby. Knowing him to be a longtime collector of fine craftsmanship, she believed, if given the chance to engage potential customers, her father's warm personality would be well received. And she'd been right. A relationships person, Luis walked potential customers through a myriad of selections, filled them in on histories and valuations, and granted them the respect spending enormous sums of money on a single item warranted. His first year online had surpassed her wildest expectation.

Following a lengthy conversation about the sacrifice needed to run an actual shop, Angel helped him to open *Royal Antiquity*. It was an overnight success. Luis carried an air of social refinement, developed through years of interaction with corporate bigwigs. That refinement meshed perfectly with Angel's entrepreneurial genius, and his customers noticed. Some even credited him with her meteoric rise in the business world.

On the other hand, her mother was nothing more than a social media aficionado. Market research for her meant watching tons of reality TV, scrolling social media, and mimicking the counterfeit lifestyles of America's most popular caricatures. If a so-called influencer said this or that product was to die for, she simply bought it.

Like the four Zeville whiskey decanters she paid $6,000 apiece for. Featured at the start of a recent *Housewives* episode, one of the aged divas threw the decanter across the room at her nemesis. She then spent the rest of the episode complained to anyone who'd listen, "That was a Zeville whiskey decanter. You know how expensive they are."

Sadly, Luis's stroke a year ago had deprived the business of its most important asset… him; and so, there wasn't much Angel could do about her mother's lack of business know-how. With Serenity Corporation in need of her undivided attention, Angel had hired a manager for *Royal Antiquity*, who reported to her daily. That way, she didn't have to micromanage the shop or stop in every time she was in town. Still, she wanted her mother to feel a part of something special, and so she entrusted her with minor tasks, like the ordering and restocking of inventory. A big mistake. One that forced Angel to stop by the shop today.

"I specifically asked you not to have the meeting without Laura," Angel said, finally responding to her mother's unauthorized purchases. She held up a stack of bills, aimed them at the clutter of furniture: chairs, lamps, tables, nightstands, and clocks. "We have a surplus. And you've created a look of eccentricity on the showroom floor."

"What was I supposed to do? You're always off, flying around like a movie star. I'm trying to keep your father's business afloat."

"And you're doing a wonderful job." She wasn't. Neither was his business in dire need of rescue. "But there's a process, mother. That's why I hired Laura. Trust me, Mr. Reynolds doesn't care if you sell the merchandise or not."

"I disagree. John was quite insightful. He wants me to succeed."

Angel eyed her warily. "That's the second time you've referred to him as John. Is there an issue?"

"Don't be silly, that's his name. Anyway, I don't get it, you rich people buy this stuff all the time."

"*Us* rich people don't all have the same tastes. Daddy's shop has a certain clientele. One that does not keep up with the Kardashians, or the Real Housewives of wherever." Angel stood, gathered the bills into a small stack. "You've given me an idea."

Gwendolyn's face brightened. "What idea?"

"By necessity, we now must make a distinction. Laura's going to create space for your modern purchases. That way the eccentricity will seem deliberate. As though *we're* presenting trends. Perhaps we can tap into a younger customer base. Come on, I'll show you."

The two entered the large showroom floor and took a position next to an oak desk. Angel motioned to the right of the entryway, at a section in the far corner. "We'll start small. Ten or twelve items, with a sign depicting modern influences. But you'll have to work the section, mother. Put your twist on things. If it works, I'll find another location—for *you*."

"Right, míja," she said, excitedly. "I knew you'd figure it out."

"Only time will tell. I just need you to hold off on any more purchases."

"No more, I promise"

"I'll be setting up an eighty-inch flat screen on the inner wall, just out of view. I researched some of the brands you've chosen. A handful had glamorous presentation videos."

"That's why you're so rich. You can make lemonade out of oranges."

"If it works, you'll have done that, mother."

A classy older woman walked up to them. "Good morning, Angel. I'm surprised to see you here."

"Good morning, Mrs. Wolfe. Checking on my mother. I see your chandelier arrived."

"Laura called me first thing."

"She's a godsend."

"That she is." Mrs. Wolfe leaned forward and whispers to Gwendolyn, "Your daughter is so beautiful."

"Thank you."

Mother and daughter watched as Mrs. Wolfe headed toward the front door.

"Bitch," Gwendolyn said in Spanish. "You're engaged to a Delaney and suddenly I'm worth speaking to."

Angel walked to the register and retrieved her Chanel bag from beneath the counter. "It's the reason I should call the damn thing off."

"I love Joshua."

"So do I, but I hate the artificial esteem associated with that family."

"Well, she's right about one thing…" Gwendolyn assessed her daughter's outfit. "You could be Ms. Universe."

"I'm five-one, mother."

"So what. You're stunning, like me."

Angel laughed. "I have meetings the rest of the day. I'll call you tonight."

*****

Inside the Gothic-styled loft, artist Enrique Ceron, stood barefoot in front of the five-foot canvas. Dressed only in a pair of black sweatpants, he dabbed red paint into the iris of a young, brown-skinned woman. The color choice gave her the desired effect, a hint of demoniac as she peered from the castle's top chamber window. The contrast worked well with the surrounding landscape, painted in a grayish fog, the captured misery unmistakable.

He enjoyed working on the painting while Angel was there, especially after handling her body the way she loved. The castle woman symbolized a powerful soul fraught with internal conflict—his interpretation of her own.

"His mother's pressing," Angel said, buttoning her blouse.

"They're like the fucking Royal family. Can't wait to plan the wedding of the year."

"I doubt they'd place me on the same pedestal as Kate Middleton."

"Fuck that milky bitch. She's not even in your league."

"Sweet of you to say."

"I still can't believe you're marrying him. You know it's a step down for you."

"It can't be that bad."

He applied more red. "Says the woman of a thousand secrets. You hate having anyone in your business."

"I'm well equipped to keep the looky-loos at bay. Case in point, you and I manage."

"That's because we've been doing this for two years." He turned to her. "Tell me again why *we're* not married?"

Angel retrieved her bag from the empty chair, removed her phone, texted. "You're too high maintenance."

"And your fiancé is not?"

She eased up behind him, placed a soft hand on his eight-pack, kissed his right shoulder. "Behave. And his vanity pertains to social status. Yours is purely psychological."

"Meaning?"

"You get off on fucking a woman's mind."

"This is true, my love." He chugged a bottle of Merlot, applied more red. "Never forget, the mind is the soul's aphrodisiac."

"I need no such enchantments." She backed away, eyed the incoming text. "Only your penis's ability to endure pressure situations."

"Is that what we're calling your tight little kitty these days." He stepped sideways, examined his work. From that angle, the woman's stare was ominous, as if threatening anyone who dared to look her way. "Still too much for him?"

"Stamina-wise, he's improving."

"Gotta be taking something."

"You think so?" she asked, a brow raised.

"One does not go from premature ejaculator to cocksmith overnight."

She giggled. "Who said anything about cocksmith?"

"Right. What is he, five inches erect?"

"Not everyone is as you, my dear."

Enrique was an intellectual with antisocial tendencies. Having attended one of his shows years ago, Angel was instantly drawn to his work, arcane and dark. Apart from his gift as an artist, he had three unique qualities: a thick, above-average-sized penis, the ability to control his climax, and an uninhibited desire to pleasure her without reciprocation. In return, she compensated him financially.

They fucked weekly (when she was in town), and for no less than an hour. Longer, if she desired. Although completely in control, she willfully submitted to him, and he knew why. Angel dominated men and women on every level; occasionally, she needed to be freed from the reigns of her power, to be dominated herself, if only for an afternoon.

A trusted friend with benefits, Enrique helped her to experience, free from judgment, the dark seductive realms that lay deep within. He also knew she'd grown tired of relational wantonness, thus her acceptance into the Delaney clan.

Certain that Joshua could never satisfy her appetites, he doubted it would last. Eventually, she'd grow bored and find the simplest excuse to part ways.

"Who could blame him if he took something," Enrique said with a shrug. "Women who look like you, who carry that kind of fire, it's difficult for any man to hold back. Even me." He gulped the Merlot and applied a bit more red. "You get to moaning, screaming that *fuck me* shit—takes everything I have not to explode."

"Or lick my tush, which he did recently."

"Let me picture that a moment; the one and only Delaney prince."

"Gave him enough hints."

"Any good?"

"Always room for improvement. But no one licks mamí like you."

"That's because you present yourself as a savory dish no man can resist. Your ass is as mouth-watering as your kitty." He pushed up behind her. "I can understand his need to satisfy, though."

"Excuse me?"

"Your sex drive... how should I say this... is a tad bit aggressive."

"Most men would consider that a good thing."

"And I am most men. But you expect to have an orgasm every time. Get pissed when you don't. A lot of men would find that intimidating."

"Who cares? Men *always* climax. A woman should expect the same." She examined the painting. "How'd the exhibit go?"

"Sold the abstract and print."

"Which print?"

"Number four: Leviathan."

"Beast Descends from Heaven. I loved that one."

"Then you should've purchased it? I would've given you a sweeter deal."

"You said you didn't want my help. If I remember correctly, you called it pity."

"Charity, my love. I called it charity." He caressed her cheek. "I'm already a slave to your body. The last thing I want is to become one of your money."

"Then why am I the one paying for great sex?"

"Because you're the one who brought money into this. And you don't pay for great sex, you pay to have me abscond from your life afterward."

"This is true. What did they sell for?"

"Twelve hundred, and two thousand, respectively."

"I'd given three for the print."

"Which serves my point."

"And what point is that? That I want you to be happy."

"I am happy," he said. "Like you, I'm doing what I love most."

"Fine." She removed a white envelope from her bag, placed it on the table. "I've included this month's rent."

"Why? It's your building."

"Discretion."

"I see." He put down the brush. "You spoil me."

"I pay for performance. Nothing more."

He stared cautiously. Angel had many faces. Some were gentle and endearing. Others belonged to a merciless creature few people knew. One capable of exiling a person from her life without so much as a text, giving less than a shit about the repercussions, in their case if he told Joshua everything. "And where are you going?"

"Home. I need a shower and a new outfit."

"The boyfriend."

"God no. A business dinner."

"Be safe," he said, returned to the canvas.

Angel headed to the front door. "Friday after next. I'd like a little role-play this time. Number six."

"You sure? Things got intense last time."

"Number six."

"Your wish is my command."

"I should hope so."

"Why are you so mean to me?"

"It builds anger. A hunger for vengeance."

She was right. There were times he hated her for the power she held over him. Hated her so much he tried to punish her. "And that's a good thing?"

"The best thing we have."

He didn't reply.

"I'd like to purchase the painting when it's done." She removed keys from her bag. "I find her delightfully unsettling. I think she'll hang in my new office."

Enrique put down the brush and met her at the door. Interlocking fingers behind his back, he said, "Nine thousand."

"Seven."

"Eighty-five hundred."

"Seven."

"Okay. Eight."

"Seven."

"Seventy-five hundred, and that's my last offer."

"Oh." She reached down, slid a hand inside his sweatpants. "Six."

Chapter 11

"Jack move"

Noss stared at the monitor as the black dot inched along East Fremont. Angel Dominguez was on the move again.

Yesterday, following the conversation with DJ, Noss hacked into her Verizon account, copied her GPS records from the last six weeks—she had three cellphones, always carried them on her person—and did the same to the OnStar account of her Bentley Continental GT, Aston Martin, and Rolls Royce Phantom. He also acquired the flight journals from her company jet, a Bombardier Global 6000. The same six-week review had shown her to be incredibly busy: Dubai, Japan, London, and New York. However, when in Vegas, although still highly active, she was a creature of habit.

Noss had written a special program that allowed him to gather specific information within colored balloons. He could view times, dates, and addresses—pinned to within five feet—visited more than once during the six-week window; as well as the average time spent, and a summary of who or what resided there.

The most noteworthy occurrence so far had taken place last night, when she left the residence of Joshua Delaney at approximately 7:32 p.m. Son of Republican Senator, James Delaney, Noss had yet to confirm if the two were a couple, but several shared texts indicated they were.

At 8:12 a.m. this morning, she stopped by Royal Antiquity. Records showed the business belonged to her father, Luis Dominguez. A hundred and twenty-six minutes later, she drove to one of her properties, a three-story building in south Vegas. Records had four apartments on each of the first two floors. The entire third floor was a loft, currently rented to, Enrique Ivan Ceron. A brief review of his social media revealed he was a sought-after artist.

A hundred and two minutes later, she was home.

Noss thought it strange that she visited the building once a week, within the same pocket of time. He wasn't sure what to make of the rigid pattern but knew it had something to do with Ceron—her dot moved throughout the building—whom Noss thought extremely handsome. Business? Friends? Lovers? Whatever the case, she clearly wasn't the same person DJ knew seven years ago.

Based on the dot's current position, she had arrived at one of the two Vegas restaurants she owned. Noss picked up the phone.

*****

Encased in the sweet scent of Joy Baccarat, Angel entered the restaurant in a white Donna Karan blouse, black mid-thigh skirt, off-white hosiery, and black pumps. "You're looking quite dapper this evening," she said.

"Glad you made it home safe." Seventy-year-old Roberto Ochoa examined her from top to bottom, hugged her warmly. "Young lady, you're going to give me another heart attack."

Angel smiled, turned to her assistant, Michael Flanders, who she'd met in the lobby seconds earlier. Michael presented Roberto with a black box: a bottle of Orphan Barrel Whiskey. "Mr. Ochoa."

Roberto cradled the box like a newborn. "Thank you, Angel. Keep telling my Lola, if I were twenty years younger, I'd run off with you."

"And if it weren't for your lovely wife, I'd take you up on the offer."

He extended an arm toward the dining area. "Mr. Hall is waiting."

The restaurant was her favorite place to conduct business while in Vegas. One of her first clients, Roberto had hired her firm to audit his books and inventory, and to evaluate the business for any needed improvements.

Operating in the red for more than a year, her team discovered intricately woven bleeding spots; particularly, employee skimmed food and drinks. When added to fresh competition from nearby restaurants, mediocre service—staff was not as engaging as they needed to be—and the neighborhood's unsavory appearance, the ambiance of the once-thriving establishment had diminished.

In her seven-page analysis, Angel suggested a staff overhaul and a sizable revitalization campaign. Roberto had studied her throughout the month-long process and came to respect Angel's military approach to doing business. Beauty aside, she commanded any group that stood in front of her like a field general. "We need a guardian of fresh blood," he told her after reviewing the last report. "Someone like my Rebecca."

His oldest daughter, she had died from leukemia eighteen months before Serenity's audit. Angel believed her death had played a critical role in the restaurant's rapid decline.

"I agree," Angel said. "If you're suggesting monthly audits, we can certainly accommodate you."

"I'm suggesting partnership."

As luck would have it, Angel had the unusual habit of appraising any business she entered. Be it fast food, or a comic books store, an internal valuation began the moment she entered: type of business, number and average age of patrons, location, building size, potential profitability—the list went on and on. The fact it was Hispanic owned forced her into sincere consideration. "I'd want complete control in decision-making," she said.

"As did my Rebecca."

"How much are you looking to sell?"

"Twenty percent—for one hundred thousand."

A fair offer, Angel thought, if one knew how to turn it around. And she did.

From his end, the offer was nothing more than a plea for help. Even with her suggestions, he needed a fluid, innovative mindset. Without it, the place wouldn't survive another year.

"Thirty for one-forty," she countered. She was foremost a shrewd businesswoman.

Roberto feigned contemplation, then happily agreed. After the contract was signed, Angel hired two new managers and relegated Roberto to host duty. Like the Roman Empire, she conquered, established a new order of doing things, and then left the captured to self-govern. The restaurant had since returned to its glory days.

Amid a feverish work schedule, the restaurant's serene atmosphere functioned as a psychological massage.

In the previous four months alone, she had kept a watchful eye on her father's antique shop; interacted daily with the management of her various global enterprises; worked with designers on the look and feel of her new office; successfully launched Ad campaigns for Monark Premium Appliances, Kraus, Lago, and Roman Times; and saw the completion of Serenity Estates, an ninety acre Good Springs complex.

Summer homes for business juggernauts, Serenity Estates were her first attempt at a massive real estate endeavor. Built for wealthy foreign nationals—who, much like herself, spent a great deal of time abroad—the complex rested sixty miles south of Las Vegas.

Each five-acre parcel held a ranch-style mansion (built to the owners' specification), multi-car garage, in-ground pool, and every amenity known to man. Down the road, the remaining ten acres held a private airstrip and hangers for the personal jets of its residents.

All sixteen lots were sold before the breaking of ground.

*****

"It's been a pleasure," Gabriel Hall said.

"The pleasure was all mine." Angel stood. "Michael will call you in a few days with my initial draft."

Gabriel lumbered to his feet and extended a hand. "Look forward to collaborating with you, Ms. Dominguez."

"As do I." She shook his bony hand. "And please, call me Angel."

"Good night, Angel." He nodded and walked away.

Angel removed sanitizer from her bag, squirted a few drops, cleansed her hands. "That went rather well." She checked her Cartier. "And in record time."

"Yes ma'am," Michael said. He knew not to add anything else.

Angel's goal had been to keep Mirage CEO, Gabriel Hall, off-balance from the moment he laid eyes on her. And she had. Three feet from him, she pulled her chair out far enough from the table to grant a full view of her body and took a seat. Fair-skinned and semi-balding, Gabriel stayed a total professional as he tried not to ogle her legs. Much to her amusement, he appeared genuinely relieved when it was over.

Business meetings were an act of seduction for Angel. Long before the opening of her company, she understood the clothes and attitude that made her insanely desirable to men... and women. Even as a teenager, when her womanly parts formed, men had hit on her, wanted to fuck her. They hadn't cared about her age, relationship status, sexual preference, or whether they attracted her; they simply desired to have her... possess her... but none could.

Still, by the time she was seventeen, the wealthy bachelors—the ones yearning for a beautiful wife—had approached the idea like a business proposal: a life of luxury and pomp for being their trophy. The majority were average-looking and terribly out of shape. To date, the women she knew who accepted such an offer controlled their husbands with incredible ease.

Next were the playboys, whom she loathed with a passion. Incredibly arrogant, if they found a woman worthy, she might receive jewelry and clothes; uninhibited enough, a pricey condominium and car note.

Married men were shameless, offering enormous financial compensation for the occasional romp. Like the playboy, uninhibited sex could call for a sumptuous, albeit secretly kept lifestyle.

Finally, there were the connivers. Those who tried to seduce women under the guise of mentorship. Fatherly types—like her college professor, Mr. Franklin—who tossed advice, money, and business opportunity at her feet like rose pedals. Somewhere along the way, they let it be known exactly what they wanted.

As an ambitious thirteen-year-old prodigy, tío Javy had discussed the potential obstacles. "Listen, míja," he said one night while they dined in Monaco. "All men are full of shit. Especially wealthy businessmen. Trust me, they won't hesitate to sleep with you."

"Gross," she said.

"For some women. For others, it's a means to an end. Either way, your beauty places you in a unique position. It can be a hindrance or a powerful asset. Honed, it will become your greatest weapon in controlling the mind of any man you meet. For all our social dexterity, we are mere lapdogs with a woman we want to fuck. Even if we cannot have her."

His words were often brutal because, as he continually stated, the world of business was unmerciful. That night he'd given her three books by *Robert Greene. 48 laws of Power, 33 Strategies of War, and the Art of Seduction.*

By year's end, she had read all three, cover to cover, thrice over; at which time, he suggested Niccolò Machiavelli, Sun Tzu, and Carl von Clausewitz.

Although the dogmatic overtures seemed excessive, she'd gotten tío's point. There was a process by which powerful men ruled, and if she wanted to rule them—to be a successful businesswoman, she would have to—she needed to out-think them at every turn. To do that, she had to first understand *how* they thought.

Therefore, like the modern divas, Angel created a mind-melting persona whose undeniable power was clear to any person who engaged her. Coupled with extraordinary business acumen, she was irresistible. A touch of the arm as she suggested a costly expenditure, a crossed leg at the right angle, and she quickly had them eating out of her diamond-laced hand.

Fourteen minutes into the meeting with Monark owner, Adam Clement, he'd wired the $250,000 deposit into her business account, suggesting they have dinner *one of these nights*. With the sweetest smile, she graciously declined, citing her rule of never dating clients. He took it in stride and moved on. But Angel understood. In his mind, the $250,000 was an open door toward later opportunity. Little did he know, unless an emergency occurred, he'd never get another chance.

*****

Angel finished reviewing the notes she'd taken, handed them to Michael. "Email me a copy by night's end."

"Yes, ma'am."

"Have Daniel secure the Parsons delivery first thing in the morning."

Michael jotted the information onto his tablet. "Shall I store them at the office?"

"The warehouse for now. And make sure he doesn't leave them lying around. They are expensive clubs."

"I'll have them locked in the storage room."

"That'll suffice." She looked up from her phone. "How's Andrew?"

"Nervous. They have stalled our adoption papers."

"Any specific reason?"

"None that we were given. He thinks the agency's out to get him."

"Him, or you both?"

"No, Andrew," he said, giggled. "He's the most victimized gay man on the planet."

Angel smiled dryly. "Anything I can do?"

"Short of calling the director, I don't believe so."

"Forward me the information."

"Thank you so much, Ms. Dominguez."

"Angel," the voice called from outside her periphery.

She paused, her weighty breath instinctual. Angel had envisioned the reunion many times, and always with a sense of calm. She placed hands on her lap and turned. "Jack," she said, her voice soft.

"Small world," DJ said.

Calm, but needing time to regain her composure, she told Michael, "Mr. Johnson and I attended the same business class in college."

Michael stood, extended a hand. "It's a pleasure to meet you."

DJ shook. "Didn't mean to interrupt the couple's night out?"

"Heavens no," Michael said. "I'm Ms. Dominguez's assistant, Michael."

Angel stood and opened her arms. "God, I forgot how big you were."

"And you're still the finest woman on the planet." DJ swallowed her up in an embrace.

"You're much too kind. So, what brings you here?"

"Ronan Carter." He let the statement hover while his eyes did the rest.

Angel nodded at Michael. "Please excuse us."

She used the phrase sparingly, the meaning always the same: it was time for him to leave. The abruptness caused Michael to eye her with a glimmer of concern. Her responding glare told him such concern was outside the scope of his significance.

"Yes, of course." Michael quickly gathered his things. "I'll secure the Parsons delivery first thing in the morning."

"See that you do. And do not forget my notes."

"Yes ma'am."

When he was gone, Angel took a seat and crossed her legs. "I don't know what I'm more shocked about, the fact you found me, or my connection to Ronan."

"Private investigator located a photo of you two."

"Bullshit."

He furrowed a brow, stunned at her choice of words. "Japanese restaurant deal."

"I know the photo. It's the only one in existence—a mistake on my part. However, I didn't much care because it's on a Japanese website, which made it a needle in a haystack."

"My guy specializes in finding needles."

"Obviously by circumventing the law. And how did you know I'd be here?"

"That's irrelevant. Remember, your guy approached my brother. Don't get mad 'cause I got people too."

"What do you want?

"Look, I know you got a ton of crackers kissing your ass, but don't get it fucked up—that's the question *you* need to be answering."

Touché. She had certainly painted herself in a corner. "Fair enough. I miscalculated your brother's reaction."

"You didn't. A room full of pussy… the nigga's ready to run with it. You just underestimated my part in his decision." He surveyed the restaurant. "Were you ever gonna tell me?"

A bolt of nerves shot through her body. "Tell you what?"

"That *you* took over the club."

"I hadn't planned on it."

"Then we got a problem."

"I can assure you, Jack, there's no problem. If he doesn't want to do it, I'll take the loss."

"On the whole plaza?"

Damn investigator! He or she was good. "It wouldn't be the first loss."

"Maybe, but I can't let you do that."

"Oh, and why not?"

"Because for what it's worth, I fucked everything up between us."

"That you did," she said, feeling the knot in her stomach loosening. She pondered a moment, wondered if the next move was the right one. "Have you eaten?"

He eyed the seat vacated by Michael. "No."

*****

Angel nibbled on a salad. "I bought into it some years back," she said, covering her mouth as she referred to the restaurant. "It had been operating at a loss for quite some time. Made changes, did a sizable marketing campaign."

"Food's definitely on point." DJ washed down a piece of chicken teriyaki with a healthy swig of wine. "This some good stuff."

"Corton-Charlemagne, Grand Cru white Burgundy."

"Sounds expensive."

"So how many businesses does your brother own now?"

"Four."

"Purchased two more since I last saw you."

"Small shit. A corner store, and the laundry-mat inside the plaza." DJ placed forearms on the table. "Not like the deal you got going."

She was genuinely surprised. "You've kept tabs?"

"Tried to find you a year after everything went down, but you fell off the map. Checked again three years ago—same nigga who found the picture. By then you were doing your thing."

"But not since?"

"No."

"May I ask why?"

"Don't know."

"I left the country after Jason's funeral. Initially, to take a break from school and try to understand what happened. But Mr. Clark suggested I finish my studies. That my life would change drastically once I did." She dabbed the corners of her mouth with a napkin. "I spent the next few years restructuring my priorities, got my degree, received a financial windfall, and went from there."

"Been killing it ever since."

"Not exactly. The first two ventures failed. Lost nearly two million." She cocked her neck. "I was not aware of some people's level of corruption… though I should have been. My tío warned me constantly."

"Scammers?"

"Businesspeople adroit at masking their skullduggery. I made the adjustments, and it all came together."

"Like I knew it would." He emptied the glass.

"What about you? You appear unharmed."

DJ bent a lip, knowing exactly what she meant. "I'm good."

"Do you suppose I'll ever know what truly happened?"

He eyed her warily. "News told you what happened. All you had to do was fill in the blanks."

"The blanks do not explain why you left me. Why you asked me to never contact you again."

His instinct told him to let it be and not bring up the nine murders that were part of the past. However, since he was the one who insisted on meeting, he realized he needed closure just as much as she did. "Maybe one of these days we can meet someplace private. I'll tell you everything I can."

She finished her glass, set it down. "What about now? Is my penthouse private enough?"

He leaned back. "Really wanna do this?"

"There's no way I'm keeping the plaza if we don't."

Chapter 12

"A thousand secrets"

Angel drummed red fingernails against the armrest as the driver eased through the evening traffic. Enrique's words continued to roll through her mind like a news ticker. *Says the woman of a thousand secrets. You hate having anyone in your business.*

He couldn't know the depth of that statement. Those secrets. No one did. Secrets were her life's blood, the foundation of everything that mattered to her. The first thing tío taught her was, *'To become rich, you'll need to have secrets. To stay rich, you'll need to protect them.'*

Either DJ had lied regarding the way he found her, or the so-called private investigator had access to enormously powerful and very illegal computer capabilities.

She was familiar with facial recognition, knew it wasn't a civilian tool. The U.S. government limited the technology's use—Clearview the leading developer—which could eventually allow the instant location of every photo on earth with a person's face. One only needed to consider the ramifications. A serial killer walks into the local mall, sees someone he likes, sneaks a picture, and within minutes has their entire history stored away for later consumption. There were privacy cases in the federal courts fighting against such intrusion.

And how did he know I'd be at my restaurant? Has someone been watching me? Following me? Hacked my GPS?

At the very least, she'd get to the bottom of it. Make sure it went no further than his desire to understand her motives.

Angel calmed down enough to focus on the immediate issue. His investigator had uncovered her plaza purchase. DJ now wanted to know why? She had avoided the query, but that would change soon enough. The answer was convoluted. So much so, she was no longer sure of it herself. To make money. To help DJ and the Kings enter a life of legitimacy. At worse, her simplest excuse had been set in place years earlier: I did it for Jason.

She'd still have to provide convincing motivation. Like the fact that while Jason's family and friends focused on vengeance, Angel's heart broke for his daughter, Marcella. She was supposed to be her adopted niece. A little girl whose eyes lit up every time she saw her favorite tía, the one who spoiled her rotten. Thin, it would have to do.

The most obvious answer to why she bought the plaza was simple: because she could. Rich and powerful, Angel had kept a watchful eye on DJ's life for seven years—studied it for the better part of three; all, as she waited for the chance to quietly step back inside. That moment arrived when Carlos bought a small laundry-mat in the rundown plaza.

After his purchase, and following three exhaustive weeks of research, Angel met Ronan at her New York high-rise. One of the many professionals at her disposal—tío Javy left her a Rolodex (provided by Mr. Clark) of men and women who specialized in corporate espionage—Ronan's expertise was intelligence gathering.

Dressed Cleanly in a three-piece Kiton suit, the fifty-two-year-old Harvard graduate had sipped fruit juice and explained his findings. "Plaza has ten businesses, including a strip club," he said. "It's owned by Margaret Johansson. She's eighty, and lives in Texas. Fifteen years ago, her now-deceased husband paid eight million for the property. There were several developmental projects on the table. He planned to join the plaza to those projects—like what you did in Albuquerque. But the projects fell through. When he died five years ago, she put the property on the market for the price he paid."

"Liquidation?" Angel asked.

Ronan nodded. "He had a sizable portfolio. In the plaza's case, there were no takers. Price has dropped steadily ever since. Currently sits at two-point-four. You could get her down to two, maybe as low as one point eight."

"Why the significant decline?"

"Last nine years, forty-one businesses have failed. There have been three-hundred-twelve reported break-ins; three-hundred-seventy-eight car thefts; two-hundred-sixty-four robberies on, or within a mile of the plaza. A month ago, a man was killed outside the club. Murdered. Police reports say it was gang related."

"Husband failed to monitor the changing environment. Crime has slowly diminished the property's true value. Tío called it trapped money."

"I remember the term." Ronan placed the glass onto a coaster. "Insurance alone is reason enough to balk. I'd pass if I were you."

"You're right, it's a potential money pit. But what about crimes against Carlos's businesses?"

"None at the laundry-mat so far. The restaurant had one break-in. Twenty-fifteen. A drug addict." Ronan nodded, conceding the point she was preparing to make. "Shot in the head six days later."

"As Jack used to say, the streets talk. And the Kings are always listening with an unforgiving ear. Criminals are scared to death of them." She stood, moved to the window overlooking Central Park. The sky was blue, not a single cloud. "Have Theresa take the plaza. Offer seven hundred thousand, cash."

"And the cap?"

"The one point eight you suggested. Plaza's a mile from Carlos's restaurant. Twenty minutes from the strip. If I'm right, I should be able to free up a substantial amount of the trapped money." She spun on her heel, motioned to the bank deposit bag on the table. "There's fifty thousand. I want you to seize the club. The murder should make it easy enough. Bring Carlos in as a partner."

"Very well."

While Theresa went to work on Margaret Johansson, Angel and Ronan spent the next two days fine-tuning her plan; at which time he flew to Vegas in the company jet. To avert suspicion, he began eating at Carlos's restaurant prior to obtaining the club. Soon after, a rumor surfaced that a civil attorney—representing the family of the murdered man—was putting together a class-action lawsuit against the club's owner, Tyrone Matthews. Another rumor had law enforcement and policymakers preparing to shut down the club because of the same incident.

Ronan approached Matthews, posing as a local investor, who, having heard the same rumors, was looking to take over the remaining sixteen months of his lease. Matthews waffled but caved the instant Ronan offered thirty thousand under the table.

Margaret Johansson, eager to rid herself of the property, agreed to one point two million. The day after Theresa closed on the plaza,

Ronan made contact. Dressed in jeans and a sport coat, he saw Carlos seated in the back of the restaurant, talking with a man he knew to be the manager. When the man entered the kitchen, Ronan walked over, introduced himself, and praised Carlos for the excellent food.

"You the one who got rid of that piece of shit?" Carlos asked.

Angel told Ronan Carlos would be leery of unfamiliar faces, and so, once he started eating there, he'd certainly ask around.

Ronan handed Carlos a feigned look of confusion. "Piece of shit?"

"Freaky T's."

"Oh, that. I kept it open."

"Wasn't talk'n 'bout the club."

"I see. Well, I didn't know the guy personally. Just thought he might be looking to get from under the lease. You know, 'cause of the homicide. Figured I'd reopen under a new name, give it a shot."

"I heard. Club X."

"Yeah. Should've done the research, though. The place is a crime magnet. Motherfuckers tried to steal my Corvette."

"Too bad you didn't eat here sooner. Could'a saved you the headache."

Ronan scanned the flood of customers moving about the restaurant. "Doesn't look like you need any aspirin."

Carlos eyed him cautiously. "Food keeps 'em honest."

"Which again is excellent. Especially the enchiladas. Anyway, I'll give it a couple months. Shit don't change, I'll dump it. Dirt cheap if you're interested."

"I'll stick to the enchiladas."

"Lucky for me." Ronan went to leave. "Nice meeting you."

"You gotta get the neighborhood's respect," Carlos said, taking the bait.

Ronan stopped, presented a genuine look of interest. "And how do I get the neighborhood's respect?"

"I'll stop by tonight. We'll talk."

"You don't have to. I mean, the last thing I want is some asshole fucking with your car."

"I'll be there at nine."

Following a night of free drinks and half a dozen lap dances, Carlos offered Ronan a handful of tips on getting that neighborhood respect. To his surprise, however, Ronan offered him a ten percent stake in the club.

"Why would you do that?" Carlos asked.

"I'm no dummy. I've been watching you all night. Everybody here respects you. Even the ones who've been genuine pieces of shit to me. I get it, you're a neighborhood fixture—an O.G. I figure, with you as a partner, maybe that respect will extend to the club."

"What's ten percent gonna cost me?"

"Nothing out of pocket. Show up, let me introduce you as my partner. I'll set aside ten percent each night until I reach fifteen thousand. That'll be your buy-in. Should take a couple weeks. If the bullshit ceases, we'll make it official."

"Let me talk to my little brother. He's the guy with the business degree."

*****

Obviously, he did a lot more than talk to Jack, Angel thought as her housekeeper, Ysabel, met her at the front door.

The older woman took her jacket. "Would you like a cocktail, Ms. Dominguez?"

"Not right now. I'm having company."

"Yes ma'am."

"You and Mateo will remain upfront and make yourselves available."

"Yes ma'am."

Angel went into the bedroom, removed her heels, and fell backward onto the bed.

*****

"Still, it was a very shitty thing to do," Angel said, standing on one of her four balconies.

DJ leaned against the rail, Bellagio's fountain behind him. Eerily reminiscent of their last night together, she felt a sudden twinge of sorrow. Her onslaught of guilt ladened questions seemed trivial when Jason was added to the equation. Since that night, she had only focused on her feelings, her loss, never once considering things from his perspective. From that of a man who'd lost his brother. "It's not like we were dating—we were engaged. And Jason was my friend, too."

"I know," he said. "And the nigga loved you. Everybody loved you. Believed we would make it as a couple. But you were right about us being in the game. What you didn't know about was the enemies."

"I went to the funeral. I mean, the cemetery."

"Black Rolls—tinted windows. Thought that was you."

"I was trying to help you guys walk away from that life."

"And we would've. But it wasn't gonna be easy. What'chu offered, the whole corporation deal, it would've been me, Jay, and you know, the immediate family."

"The Kings?"

He paused. They had picked up right where they left off. The inquiring mind. "Got niggas who rely on me. They got families. Couldn't just leave them hanging."

"What were you going to do?"

"Stay in the game until you and me put down our move. After that, I'd hand over the drug shit to my lieutenants. Finance any moves they wanted to make. That way they could still eat. We'd be out the loop, though."

Her posture wilted. "You broke my heart, Jack."

"I'm sorry. But don't get it twisted, I was crazy in love with you."

"Not enough to choose me over—," she paused, struggling to control her emotions. "How could you just leave me?"

"It was a closed casket." DJ gripped the rail with both hands, tears in his eyes. "I couldn't take a chance on you being next."

A long silence.

"The things I saw on TV the next morning—"

He glared at her. It was a onetime deal. He'd never speak on it again. "Everyone but the bartender and waitress."

Angel turned away, his statement's impact twisting in the wind. He just admitted to murdering seven people. And based on the countless articles she'd read, six were innocent bystanders; five young women with bright futures, and families that loved them very much. Most disconcerting to her was the sudden lack of empathy she felt for them. "I don't know what to say."

"Ain't nothing to say. I made a choice that night."

"Why not call? We could have met somewhere. Talked."

"If we had, I would've tried to make it work. But I kept thinking about your parents... your tío... the life he made for you. I wasn't gonna fuck that up. Not even for love."

Angel thought of the day inside the Sprinter. She pictured Jason's killers standing outside, riddling the vehicle with bullets, she and DJ caught in the throes of passion. She thought of her parents, her tío if he were still alive, the shame they would've felt knowing she died in such a precarious position. DJ was right. It would have utterly devastated them.

Suddenly, the decision to leave her seven years ago wasn't selfish, it was near heroic. If he loved her as much as she loved him, his walking away was the greatest act of love possible. Angel straightened her posture. "And yet, here we are."

He seemed genuinely surprised by her response. *As he should be,* she thought. *What woman in her right mind would want any part of such a man? A killer of the innocent.*

DJ took hold of her hand, eyed the giant engagement ring. "But here ain't there."

The tears finally arrived. "You have no idea how much I missed you."

"I've never stopped missing you. Which is why this feels like a dream." DJ wrapped arms around her. "When's the big day?"

Irony hovered like a storm cloud. "We've yet to schedule a date."

"For whatever it's worth, I'm happy you found somebody."

"What happened afterward? It doesn't sound like there's any more danger."

"I never sleep on the possibility of danger, but we got bigger, made sure niggas understood the cost of trying us. Eventually, the streets surrendered. Things been chill ever since."

"I'm glad. It's crazy… thought I'd always stay mad at you."

"What? You ain't mad no more?"

"You did what you did to protect me. Because you loved me."

"I'll always love you, má."

"I feel the same way. So no, I'm not mad. I'm ecstatic you found out about the plaza. Though I'd like assurance, your investigator will cease all further inquiries."

"I'm already knowing. Nigga ain't got no other reason to be in your business. You got my word on that. But full disclosure, I'm still about that life."

"Maybe we can change that." She let the statement linger a moment. "At least they stopped blaming you guys for the incident."

"Had a lotta help from the nigga who found the picture."

Angel hugged him, placed her head on his chest. "And you truly believe there was no way you and I could have made it work?"

"Truth?"

"Always."

"Niggas went at the people you loved. See what went down after Jason. Had my enemies known what you meant to me; they would've tried something."

"Like what?"

"Kidnap. Rape. Murder. Anything to hurt me." He stroked her back. "But real talk, once everything died down, I thought about going to get you."

"What happened?"

"I don't know. By then you were doing your thing. Plus, my hands had too much blood on them. It would've been a major step back for you."

"I disagree. You were my heart."

"Yeah, but... at that point, I would've been living off your success like some bum ass nigga."

"It was never about money between us. It was about having each other's back. We were a team."

"Never thought of it that way but we were a team."

Chapter 13

"Soul-searching"

DJ sat up in bed, squinted into the darkness, the purple Kush blurring his mind like a layer of thick fog. He centered his thoughts and searched for the iPhone, the source of his abrupt awakening. The phone rested atop the nightstand, right where he set it before closing his eyes for the night.

Kristal shifted her nakedness, placed a soft hand on his chest. "Want me to leave?"

"You're good."

She kissed his arm and rolled over.

DJ shook loose the cobwebs, picked up the phone, tapped open the text.

UP? Sent: 1:37 a.m. He eyed the clock in the upper right-hand corner. 2:10 a.m.

What the fuck?

He considered the unfamiliar area code and prefix. Only a handful of people had the number, and none of them would bother him this late at night. Not on no casual shit. Grabbing the lighter next to the charger, he pinched the half blunt from the ashtray, slid off the bed, and moved into the living room. He lay on the sectional, brought the flame to life, and inhaled the sweet smoke. He typed, **Wrong number** and hit send.

Drained mentally, he lay the phone onto the coffee table. Noss had researched her condominium on Dean Martin Drive; said she paid $18 million for it. DJ thought the number beyond comprehension. But seeing the shit from the inside—servants, gold and black furnishings, ivory pillars, paintings, marble everywhere— had rocked him like a brick to the face. Her lifestyle was remarkably different from the life he and the Kings led, a life of drug dealing, violence, and street governance.

Damn, she looked good. Finer than the first day he laid eyes on her. She had greeted him in a white silk robe, white hosiery, and white fluffy slippers. They moved to the balcony, where the cool air turned those succulent nipples hard as a pacifier.

Once the explaining ceased and he left for the night, DJ needed to fuck something sweet and sexy. He called Krystal on the ride home. A Filipino showroom model, he'd met her at a car show a month ago. The crazy part was, as the two went at it, all he could think about was how many times he'd driven by Angel's restaurant.

Bought into it some years back, she had said. Right under his nose. Visited it... right under his nose. Fine ass Monopoly girl, buying shit up like the old cracker in the top hat. He still couldn't wrap his head around her company's worth: one point three... billion. Oprah money. And how long had she been watching his life from the shadows? *Why buy the plaza three months after Carlos bought the laundry-mat? Why had she asked the number of businesses he owned?* She was too thorough not to know the answer.

Thanks to Noss, DJ caught her two or three moves into whatever she was planning. The fact he did seemed to upset her. But Ronan Carter had drawn red flags. The rules set in stone long ago—always pay attention to unfamiliar faces. Therefore, Carlos right away noticed the polished nigga in the charcoal grey Corvette Z06 ($80,000), though he initially thought nothing of it—random people ate at the restaurant all the time. But the same rules said multiple visits required further investigation.

And so, by the time Ronan introduced himself, Carlos already knew his name, and the fact he'd purchased Freaky T's from Tyrone, renaming it Club X.

After his conversation with Ronan, Carlos called DJ, filled him in on what he and Ronan talked about. Said he was going to the club that night to check Ronan out.

"Think he's a cop?" DJ asked.

"Don't know. He talks street, but the nigga don't sound street."

"What'chu mean?"

"His flow got education. Said shit like *crime magnet*."

"Probably a Stringer Bell wannabe," DJ said. "Or the feds. Want us to come through?"

"Nah, I'm good. Gonna let it play out for now."

The next morning, Carlos told him about the ten percent offer. DJ asked him to email the restaurant video from the previous day. Carlos did. DJ sent it to Noss, who isolated the portions with Ronan, and took less than a day to find the picture with Angel.

His Angel.

Seven years ago, she had stolen his heart, a feat no woman had done prior to, or since. That's because killers loved few things in life. Loved them in a way that incited pain. And love for Angel had incited pain. A pain that lasted years and took sex with more women than he could remember before DJ felt she was out of his system

But seeing her again, he realized she'd no more left his system than the memory of a fractured life. He had simply learned to cope with the pain of letting her go. And *he* had let her go. Done so to protect her.

The relationship might have survived had Chrome been the only one to die that night. But love for Jason had required more. The Abregon patriarch had required more. Honor had required more. Yet more went against the basic rules of murder; specifically, *never bring unnecessary heat to ordinary death*. Chrome was ordinary death. Innocent bystanders were not.

DJ puffed the blunt and shifted his thoughts to the morning following the murders. As expected, the *Easy Times Massacre* was the lead story on every channel. He recalled how strange the number sounded back then. *Nine*. As in nine people dead. A baseball team. Massacred. The concept differed vastly from his version of events. Back then, the blacked-out rage only allowed him to hear one word: *vengeance*. Its soothing whisper eased his conscience every time he dreamt of the *nine* bodies scattered about the scene like fallen leaves. Technically, the number was *eleven*.

With no one knowing, the Abregon patriarch sent family members to Mook's house early the next morning. They handed him an envelope; said it held thirty thousand in cash, compensation for use of the driveway. He opened the envelope to look inside. Never saw the silencer tipped nine-millimeter. Neither did his mother, asleep in her bedroom.

By day two, the media had turned the nine into actual people, labeling each a *victim*, and putting names to faces. They even interviewed family members. One victim in front of the bar had been the youngest daughter of a prominent reverend. His tear-soaked news conference days later came complete with pictures of his little girl as a child at home, school, and church. He talked lovingly of his daughter and asked the community for help in bringing her killers to justice. Midway through, his wife lost it, ripping microphones from the podium, and screaming, "Help me, Jesus."

The heartbreaking visual was all the excuse police needed to swarm the Northside like a wave of locust, strong arming every two-bit hustler, dope fiend and snitch on file. Within hours, Jerome "Chrome" Braxton, was allegedly gunned down in retaliation for the murder of Jason Abregon.

Luckily for DJ and the Kings, Chrome had a colored rap sheet that included attempted murder, aggravated assault, and drug trafficking. Though it raised more questions than answers for law enforcement, it didn't stop the media from reporting on the gang epidemic, the immigration epidemic, and any crime not committed by a white person epidemic. As a result, public fear rose like a malaria laced fever; a fever that disappeared the instant video surfaced of the reverend's daughter taking more dick than a gas station urinal. It featured none other than Chrome himself, exploding across her smiling face.

Video or not, police took countless people into custody, including the Abregon patriarch, and the King leadership. With solid alibis, Jonathan Wright and his team of high-powered attorneys secured their prompt release. Weeks later, the investigation and its faceless suspects crossed the border into Mexico—the land of dead ends, and even deader snitches. Meanwhile, DJ and the Kings received word the remaining Ruthless North members wanted a truce. And DJ knew why. Like the infamous Valentine's Day Massacre, the murders were quickly becoming the thing of legends, revered by black and brown youngsters alike.

DJ sent word. "No truce."

Within hours of his declaration, the same black and brown youth began gunning down Ruthless North members like targets at a carnival; all, as members inside the Nevada prison system, were treated like human pincushions.

Not long after, police arrested three Mexican nationals for the murders, even though murky surveillance video outside Mandalay Bay appeared to show one of the men smoking a cigarette and talking to friends at the time of the murders. Like Chrome, the three had extensive rap sheets, and were eventually coerced into signing plea deals. *Life in prison.* DJ thought it fucked up. But what was the alternative? *Confession?* The best he could do was secretly drop money to the families from time to time.

With no real enemies in sight, and the police backing off—because of Noss—DJ spent the next few years in mental transition. His mantra: *Trust no one not a King.*

Not wanting Angel's name on anyone's lips, his first attempt to find her had been nothing more than a Google search. But she had disappeared, fallen off the face of the earth like one of those milk carton kids. He tried again on the massacre's fourth anniversary, this time with Noss.

"The woman you had me look into," Noss said, calling DJ at home. "Angelica Athena Dominguez?"

"Matches the parents?"

"Luis and Gwendolyn Dominguez."

"What'chu got?"

"Lives in Dubai. Owns a multinational conglomerate: Serenity Corporation. She's been incredibly busy the last few years."

DJ didn't want to ask, but curiosity got the better of him. "What's she worth?"

"Four hundred fifteen million."

Fuck! La Chicá Napoleona.

"A'ight, thanks."

The news had been bittersweet for DJ back then. Angel had made it. Did exactly what she said she would do.

Prior to leaving her condominium tonight, Angel finally told DJ her fiancé's name: Joshua Delaney. Of all the people in Vegas, it was yet another bizarre twist in an already insane plotline. Not only was Joshua Delaney the son of Senator James Delaney—arguably the most powerful man in Vegas; and a man many believed had his sights set on the White House—he was a high-dollar criminal defense attorney used by Malo and several others within the Vegas underworld.

DJ hadn't shared the last part with Angel.

Financially, Joshua held no advantage over him. Angel had her own money and was the type of woman no man could control. But in lifestyle, he completely outmatched DJ. Vegas royalty, the Delaney's rubbed elbows with foreign diplomats, movie and pop stars, and anyone who mattered. Marrying into that family was the perfect accessory for the woman who had everything.

"We met at a friend's party," Angel had said as she and DJ sat on her living room couch.

"Heard he's a badass lawyer."

"He is." When she crossed her legs, the tip of her left slipper grazed his shin, the robe's hem riding her nylon-covered thighs. After all these years, her tactics hadn't changed. "And he works hard for his clients."

DJ knew the statement to be true. Joshua was a legal beast when it came to 4th Amendment search and seizure law. Based on everything he'd heard about him, he was a solid dude, not the lawyer who sold out poorer clients to get better deals for the richer ones. There were countless hustlers, gangbangers, and drug dealers who presently walked the streets because Joshua Delaney had picked apart the false testimony of some thirsty ass cop.

At the condominium's front door, Angel again told DJ how amazing it was to see him. Scheduled to leave the country in two days, she was adamant about negotiating the plaza deal, one on one, the next day. With no expectations on the type of arrangement, they agreed to meet at Carlos's restaurant and then take it from there. DJ chose the restaurant because he wanted to do what he failed to do seven years ago—introduce her to his brother.

"Okay, mister," Angel said, giving him one last hug. "Your brother's restaurant, noon sharp."

"Noon! Thought you said three in the afternoon." His tone was playful.

"I did not. Would you like a wake-up call?"

He handed her a slick grin. "Turn my phone off."

"You can sleep here if you'd like. I have two spare rooms. We can get breakfast."

"Nigga stay here, he try'na eat sumpt'n... and it ain't no breakfast."

"Oh, really?"

"Really."

She punched his arm. "Big picture, Jack. The plaza can be an amazing opportunity for both of us. But I'll only do it if you're on board."

"Calm down, woman," he said, rubbing his arm in mock pain. "I'll be there."

*****

DJ reignited the blunt and took another long pull, wondering if the plaza was a chance to bring the darkest parts of his life to a formal end. Maybe even pick up where they left off before Jason's death.

The beep of an arriving text snapped him back to the present. **This is not a wrong number, Jack.**

Angel.

DJ felt stupid for not having considered the obvious. Then again, she hadn't had his number before tonight. Hadn't called to say hi, or to ask what he was doing, or whether he'd be interested in running a plaza together. He typed a response, hit send, and closed his eyes.

*****

Angel read: **Oh, guess I should'a spent the night.**

Her stomach tightened. She typed: **You would've gotten a wonderful night's sleep.** She added a winking emoji and hit send.

She lay the phone on the satin sheet, and again surveyed the engagement ring. Not the half million-dollar nugget Joshua had given her, but the much smaller one, seven to ten thousand, less than the cost of her sky-blue Louis Vuitton bag—the ring DJ gave her the night he and his brothers murdered nine people. The ring forever tied to her soul.

He looked amazing. Sounded amazing. But he wants nothing to do with you. Not like before. He'll be friends, is open to sex—what man wasn't—but nothing more.

Still, she wasn't disappointed. Like he said when eyeing Joshua's ring, "Here ain't there."

And he was right. Here wasn't there. A lot had changed since they last saw each other. For starters, she was no longer the innocent girl he once knew. Fully grown, fully herself, Angel was a boss who took no prisoners in getting what she wanted. And though she had lied to DJ then, telling him she'd only been with three other men, that was certainly no longer the case.

DJ was right about another thing. Had he stayed the night, sex was a given. *Inappropriate?* Perhaps. But watching from the balcony as he drove away, she'd fought the temptation to call the airport and prepare the jet. To put a *Do Not Disturb* sign on her life as she celebrated their reunion with a month-long trip around the world, eating, drinking, laughing, and fucking like newlyweds.

Angel settled on the midnight text instead. His failure to respond without delay caused her to consider a plethora of scenarios. Was he asleep? Was he out doing the dreadful things that caused their separation—and her sorrow—seven years ago? Or was he with another woman? She knew she had no right to be jealous. Psychologically, only a weak-minded person entertained such thoughts.

The jingle startled her. **Like the sleep you're getting right now?**

She wrote: **Meanie. Who can blame me?** Another emoji, this one a sad face. Hitting send, she considered Joshua.

Most people would think she was a horrible person for not feeling guilty. But guilt was for those who lacked perspective. This was bigger than her relationship with Joshua. Seven years ago, an evil person had gruesomely taken Jason's life, setting in place the unexpected turn of events that separated Angel from her true soulmate.

She read Joshua's earlier text: **Dad loved your idea. Administration is drafting the bill as I write. He thinks you'd make a skilled politician. He wasn't joking. See you soon. Love me**

She thought it sweet, but emotionally inconvenient. Since their first night of sex, Joshua couldn't get enough of her. And though they had sex at his home—a dozen times in all—hers was off-limits.

Angel cherished her privacy. Loved the freedom it gave her. To initiate sex whenever, wherever, and with whomever she pleased. Sex that never took place inside her home. As with her stipulations on marriage, Joshua could take it or leave it.

An adequate lover, he lacked the size and stamina to satisfy. Fortunately, he could do so orally, a lost art in itself. He had sensed her growing displeasure with his lackluster performances, and had since discovered what she required of him, licking every inch of her body until she was completely spent.

In contrast, Enrique was well endowed and knew how to use it. Some men didn't. Two years ago, a mutual friend—the wife of a prominent shipping mogul who loved art as much as Angel did—invited her to one of his shows. She introduced them and later explained his sexual prowess and ability to remain discreet.

After several business-like dates—in which they discussed his artistic aspirations—Angel decided he'd do. She asked to see sketches of his recent work and suggested they meet at a hotel suite the following night. Upon his arrival, she placed the portfolio on the living room table and escorted him to the bedroom, where he performed as advertised.

Two months into the sex-only relationship, the two had become friends. Wanting to avoid hotel suites, Angel presented him with a business proposal. He could work rent-free from the loft in her building. And when she was in town, they'd fuck once a week; to which she'd pay him $500 a session. Anything more and he'd have to sell his work. Fortunately for him, he was an incredible artist and regularly sold. Occasionally, however, his demure stature—he was five-seven, a hundred and fifty-seven pounds—and propensity to act like a diva diminished the experience. Even so, he was worth every penny.

On the other hand, her relationship with Joshua had everything to do with the prominent transition of life he and his family represented. In time, Angel wanted to get married, to start a family (with a surrogate), and solidify her children's destinies in a way that ensured greatness. There seemed no better choice than the John F. Kennedy Jr. of Las Vegas; who also was a nice guy.

Regardless, what took place last night threatened to change everything. Her first love had returned, completely seizing her mind, body, and soul. The perfect man, DJ was powerful, gorgeous, fearless, and far more endowed than even Enrique. While in his presence, Angel saw no one else. Wanted no one else.

She suddenly recalled that terrible night. How DJ had taken a knee and proposed to her like a knight in shining armor, fucked her like he never wanted to lose her; and then, when life could get no better, disconnected their souls in a fit of rage. And not your typical rage, nostrils flared, cursing, physical exaggeration. No, he had merely hung up the phone, turned to her, and said, "I gotta go. Jason's dead."

The news had brought her to tears, and before she knew what happened, he was gone. The next morning, she and the rest of Vegas found out what happened.

*****

The phone jingled again. Angel read: **Trust me, I'm still trying to figure it out. Either way, I'm glad you know the truth.**

She wrote: **So am I. Guess I'll try to get some sleep. Otherwise, I'll look horrible in the morning. Sweet dreams**. She hit send.

Angel had always wanted an explanation for the breaking of her heart. And last night, he gave it to her. To protect her from being kidnapped... raped... murdered.

Duh!

The explanation's sufficiency had far outweighed the suffering she endured. And DJ had suffered too. She found comfort in that. Not in his actual pain, but the reality she had not been alone in hers.

Despite that pain, and perhaps because of it, Angel had put her nose to the grindstone. *Eyes on the prize*, she told herself daily. She graduated with honors and wasted no time submitting the documentation to Mr. Clark. Within minutes, he slid the bank statement across his desk. "For completion of your MBA," he said, "the board deposited this into your account."

She read the amount: $2,000,000.

He slid the second document. "For making the honor roll."

$3,000,000. Tío Javy loved excellence.

She opened Serenity Corporation five days later and presented Mr. Clark with the documentation. Another $2 million... for operating costs. After that, it was a slot machine that always paid. Serenity Marketing: $2 million. Serenity Financial: $2 million. Investments Group... Real Estate...

To date, the trustees had yet to refuse compensation for any endeavor, though by now, she didn't need it. Last year alone, Serenity Corporation netted $212 million, thanks to the investment arm of her empire.

She read: **See you in the morning, baby girl. Noon. P.S. You could never look horrible. Love me.**

She wrote: **I will**, and hit send.

He wasted no time responding with a smiling emoji.

Chapter 14

"What Now?"

"And you took him to your condo?" Priscilla asked, seated at a patio table with Angel. "After he ran out on you?"

Though it sounded like an overreaction, Angel knew it wasn't. Priscilla was her best friend and confidante. The one person she trusted enough from which to gauge genuine feedback. Sometimes. This wasn't one of those times. The reason being, she had told Priscilla forty percent of the truth in relation to DJ. And ninety percent of that was heavily distorted.

"I thought he did," Angel said. "Before I forget, can you get me a bottle of green tea for the road?"

"Nice try. So, you're saying he didn't run out on you?"

"He did... but it's complicated."

"Tell you what's not complicated." Priscilla sipped the mocha latte, the newest selection from her café's growing menu. "Took you forever to get over him. If it weren't for Cat, I'm not sure you would have."

"But I did, so thank you very much." Angel stared at the passing cars, caught between her friend's justified concern, and the struggle to grasp the impact DJ's return to her life would soon have. If they agreed on a business structure, the impact would increase tenfold.

"So, how'd he look?" Priscilla asked.

Angel smiled, grateful for Priscilla's decision not to push further. "He's more muscular. But whoa."

"And he just stopped by the restaurant?"

"Not exactly."

Priscilla folded arms across her chest. "Are we playing twenty questions? What do you mean, *not exactly*?"

"The plaza I purchased. His brother owns one of the businesses."

"I'm confused."

"I plan to renovate… start fresh. I'm ending the leases on all ten businesses."

"So, he found out you're the one kicking his brother out?"

"Somehow. Again, it's complicated." Listening to herself explain the story, minus the relevant details, Angel was surprised at how ridiculous it sounded.

"Extremely complicated." Priscilla motioned to a young African American server as he passed the table. "Malik."

"Yes, Mrs. Hewlett?"

"Please get me a bottle of green tea?"

Greenish-blue eyes, his smile revealed two rows of perfect teeth. "Coming right up."

When he was out of range, she asked Angel, "What do you think?"

"Gorgeous. Where'd you find him?"

"He's studying communications at UNLV. And get this, he models. Nothing big. Local ads… online stuff."

"Certainly has the looks."

"Perhaps I'll keep my own black guy."

"If you're referring to Jack," Angel said, "he's not someone you keep."

"Did he tell you why he left?"

"I love you, Pree, but it's better you don't know. Let's just say, when we first met, he'd been to prison for beating up a guy."

"Geez! What are you going to do now?"

That was the million-dollar question, wasn't it? To which she still didn't have an obvious answer. "I'm not sure. I'd like his brother's help with the revitalization campaign. He has several other businesses and is a community figurehead."

"And by community, you mean ghetto."

"The plaza's not in the ghetto. It sits perfectly between the Strip and the Northside and has the potential to become an urban epicenter."

Priscilla bent a suspicious brow. "Does he know about Joshua?"

Angel held up the ring. "Hard not to."

"I didn't ask if he knew you were engaged. I asked if he knew about Joshua."

"I told him. And he was quite happy for me. Jack's always been a good-hearted person."

When he wasn't killing innocent people.

"Oh, I'm so sure he hasn't changed a bit in seven years. If I remember correctly—" Priscilla held her fingers eight inches apart, "he had the biggest heart you'd ever seen."

Angel held her fingers ten inches apart. "Bigger."

The two giggled like teenagers.

Malik walked up, green tea in hand. "Here you go, Mrs. Hewlett."

"Thank you." Keeping her eyes locked on Angel. "Malik, would you be interested in a side job? I'm thinking of rearranging my office."

"Whatever you want me to do, Mrs. Hewlett. I'm at your disposal." His tone was as smooth as his smile.

"Wonderful. I'll let you know."

He walked away.

"Be careful," Angel said. "Let's not forget the prenup." She referred to the part where Priscilla lost everything if he caught her cheating.

"Tell that to Raymond."

"Has he strayed again?"

"Hired another secretary."

"That's number four."

"Six."

"Asshole." Angel hated the double standard. "I keep telling you, we could—"

"Let's do it."

Angel's face brightened. "Are you sure?"

"I've had enough."

"I'll have my lawyer draw up the papers immediately."

*****

The valet closed a fist on the twenty-dollar bill and shut the door. Angel hung up the phone and drove off. Her lawyer had assured her the contract would be ready within seventy-two hours. Once Priscilla signed, Angel would own the *Priscilla's Cafe and Dessert* name (and franchises); purchased for the bargain price of $10,000.

From the beginning, Priscilla knew she should have opened the café with a loan from Angel, or her sister, Cat, but she was determined to go it alone. Partly because she wanted to prove she could be successful on her own, and partly because she believed in her marriage. The latter was the primary reason she signed that God-awful prenup.

After the first affair, which Raymond did little to hide, Angel encouraged Priscilla to divorce him. She decided instead to get even by fucking a bartender she'd met while accompanying Angel on a trip to London.

Following affair number two, Angel paid $7,000 to get a copy of the prenup, which, upon its signing, had been sealed through court order. She then had one of her lawyers review the document for loopholes. It was chock full. The simplest—nothing prohibited Priscilla from selling the franchise; or required her to inform Raymond if she planned to do so.

Once Angel took ownership, Priscilla could fuck her entire staff, and he'd only be entitled to the $10,000 *if* she still had it. She wouldn't. Meanwhile, Priscilla could get the divorce and buy back her business.

As Angel turned onto the freeway, she smiled inside. Raymond was going to be pissed. *Screw him*, she thought. If he tried to make trouble, Priscilla would show the pictures of him exiting a Delano suite with secretary number three. She'd then quote the part of the prenup that stated, should *she* catch him having an extramarital affair, she was to keep sole ownership of her businesses and receive ten million annually for life.

With that kind of compensation on the line, Raymond would have little to say.

The GPS alerted Angel to turn left at the next intersection. Typically, she traveled in the Phantom, allowing one of her drivers to handle such details as she tended to her phone. But she didn't want anyone waiting around while she dealt with the present situation, so she'd driven herself, taken the Bentley Continental GT because it was small and easy to maneuver.

Thankful for the morning spent with Priscilla, the playful banter allowed her the respite necessary to readjust her mental footing before meeting Carlos for the first time.

Last night, following what she thought was DJ's last text, he'd sent another. Said he had called his brother, told him about the reunion—she didn't know exactly what he told him—and the noon meeting at the restaurant. He said Carlos looked forward to meeting her and would reserve a parking space out front.

On her way to Priscilla's, Angel called the restaurant, asked for Carlos, and introduced herself. She then asked if he wouldn't mind sitting down an hour before DJ's arrival. She wanted to discuss business-related things. He happily agreed and told her to call ten minutes before she arrived. That way someone could meet her outside.

She had.

Nearing the restaurant, a wave of nerves washed over her. The inclement terrain of urban living had replaced the glitz and glamour of the Strip. Fast-food restaurants, weather-beaten buildings, and lower-class enterprises lined both sides of the street; and unlike the rapt gaze found on most visitors along the Strip, its pedestrians appeared morose and nomadic.

She took a deep breath, turned into the parking lot, and pulled in front of the restaurant. A tall, husky Mexican teen in a white tank top stood curbside. Upon seeing her car, he removed an orange traffic cone from the lone empty slot and motioned for her to pull inside.

Is that even legal?

Under any other circumstance, she wouldn't dare park, let alone get out.

Angel shut off the engine, lowered her Safilo sunglasses, and thanked him with a gentle wave. He nodded, and then entered the next-door business, a liquor store. Two doors down in the opposite direction, a group of teens gathered in front of a check-cashing place. Angel suddenly realized her social ineptitude. $400,000 vehicle... $500,000 Tiffany engagement ring... $17,000 Sidney Garber diamond earrings... $23,500 BVLGARI diamond necklace... $9,000 Piaget watch...

You've made yourself one hell of a target.

Just then, an extremely fit older man stepped through the restaurant door. Dark-skinned, medium height, he wore khaki slacks, a white dress shirt, and presented the biggest smile. A protective smile.

Carlos.

Angel exited, set her bag and attaché case across her left shoulder, and locked the door. The social ineptitude extended to her clothes. The light blue Kate Spade skirt and blouse, matching nylons, and Tom Ford pumps were better suited for brunch at Bardot Brasserie, not a place where they could be ruined by a carelessly placed packet of salsa.

Carlos approached with open arms. "Damn," he said. "DJ said you were fine, but he never said you were this fine."

"Thank you, Mr. Albizu."

"Carlos, mamí. Mr. Albizu was my pop."

"It's nice to finally meet you." Back then, she often wondered if he would have liked her, considered her a suitable match for his brother. Angel stepped into his embrace as though he were family. Solidly built, he felt like a man who worked out regularly. "And thank you for seeing me this early."

"No problem. I still can't believe you two went to school together—my landlord." He chuckled, opened the front door. "Set'chu up a booth."

Inside, a hoard of shabbily dressed diners mingled about the fifteen tables and booths, eating, chatting, staring into phones. At the counter, two female cashiers took orders, while a third dealt with customer pickup.

Angel made a quick study of the above menu. Numbered pictures of combination platters provided a mixture of cuisine: Mexican, Cuban, Caribbean, and other Latin dishes. "Super busy," she said. "And you deliver."

"Gotta lot of regulars."

"The bloodline of any good business. Do you have an app?"

He shook his head no. "We're small potatoes. That's for the heavy hitters."

"There's nothing small about *your* customer base," she said. "An app is simply an opportunity to grow that base by introducing your business to people who might not otherwise have the chance to see it. DoorDash, Grubhub, and Uber Eats offer potential revenue opportunities. If you have a menu on file, my team can develop one for you. See if it's something you'd be interested in."

With a bent lip, he considered her words. "Whatever you wanna do. DJ said you were super smart."

"Well, I appreciate the compliment."

Angel got the feeling DJ hadn't discussed a lot with his brother as it pertained to her. As she followed Carlos to the back, several diners eyed her curiously. When she and Carlos stopped at the booth, Angel gestured to the table's surface. "Mind if I place my tablet here?"

"Nah, go ahead. And I printed what you asked for."

Carlos motioned for a young girl in a red shirt and black apron. The girl reached below the counter, retrieved a binder, and marched it over. Her cute face glowed with excitement. She looked too young to work there, so Angel thought her someone's relative.

"Are you famous?" the girl asked in Spanish.

"Thank you," Angel said, "but no, I'm not famous."

"She's a very successful businesswoman," Carlos interjected.

"What's your name?" Angel asked.

"Nina."

"Nice to meet you, Nina. I'm Angel."

"You're like the most beautiful lady I've ever seen. How many Instagram followers do you have?"

"I'm not on social media. I'm sorta busy."

"I'd follow you."

Her last statement held a strange conviction. Found in most teens these days, Angel wasn't sure if it was a positive thing or something that could later manifest itself as an inferiority complex.

"I like your Gucci bag," Nina said. "Bella Hadid has a red one just like it."

"Thank you." Angel didn't know what else to say.

"Okay, míja," Carlos told Nina. "Me and Angel got stuff to talk about."

"It was awesome meeting you," Nina said.

"Pleasure was all mine."

The girl returned to work.

"She has big dreams," Carlos said. "Wants to be a fashion designer. Reads all the big magazines."

"How are her grades?"

"Pretty good, I think."

"My company has a young entrepreneur program. You're more than welcome to sign her up."

"I'll ask her mom." He nodded to a middle-aged woman. She looked tired as she wiped down a table. "But to be honest, I let Nina work part time, just to help her with school clothes."

"We offer scholarships. But if you think she'll take it seriously, I'll sponsor her myself."

"Ain't never seen her that excited. Got no doubt she'd take anything you offer serious." He checked his watch. "So what'chu wanna talk about?"

*****

Sunglasses atop her head, Angel ran a finger down the binder page, typed into the tablet.

"Hey, chica, those are some fat ass diamonds," the male voice said. "Are they real?"

Angel looked up. The man and his three friends sat at the table across from her. All were Latino and covered in tattoos. Their soulless glares looked ready to pounce. A blush of anxiety filled her face as she considered whether her worst nightmare had come to life. Although she wasn't on social media, she used it to keep up with news relevant to her business decisions. She'd read about the shootings, the fistfights, and yes, the people killed in the most dangerous part of town.

She surveyed the kitchen area. Following her talk with Carlos, he had entered through the swinging doors, checking on her periodically. "Uh, yes," she finally answered.

"I ain't never seen you." The man stood up. "Where you from?"

"Back up, ese," the male voice to the side of her barked.

Angel turned to see DJ moving across the room with two Mexicans. The first was Jason's brother, Raul. Older, he was heavier than when she last saw him. The other was younger, medium height, thin, with a skull tattooed over his face. *His entire face!* She had never seen a scarier person.

Angel shuffled to her feet and greeted DJ with a hug. He corralled her beneath his arm, turned to Raul and the tattooed-faced man. "Raul and Malo," he said.

"I could never forget, Raul," she told DJ, extending a hand to Raul. "How's momma Cecilia?"

Raul moved past her hand and hugged her. "Kick'n back with the grandbabies. She said to stop by as soon as you can. 'Bout went loco when this vato—" he motioned to DJ, "told 'er you was back. Use'ta ask about you all the time."

"Gave me hell after you left," DJ added.

"Is you try'na get killed!?" Malo asked the man in Spanish.

Upon seeing DJ, Raul, and Malo, the man had sat back down, obviously wanting no part of them.

"Come here, homz," Malo demanded.

The man hesitated, then stood and walked over. Face to face with Malo, the height differential was significant, with the man a foot taller. The fear in his eyes, however, made for a striking contrast.

"Fuck you talk'n to her for?" Malo asked.

DJ rubbed Angel's lower back, his touch sending a wave of calm shooting through her body.

"Ain't never seen her before," the man said. "I was just—"

"You try'na die, homz?"

He bowed his head. "No."

"Then say sorry 'for I smoke your ass." Malo pressed his fingers against the man's forehead as if his hand were a gun.

The man turned to Angel and said in Spanish, "I'm sorry."

She nodded, handed him a look of contempt.

Take that, asshole.

Malo told the others in Spanish, "You see her 'round here, you don't say shit to her."

They nodded in unison; the man rejoining them.

"Whoa—" Angel said in a whisper.

"It's all good, chicá," Malo said.

"Name's Angel, fool," Raul said.

"Simón." Malo gave her a respectful nod. "Angel."

"Gonna head back to the pad," Raul told DJ. "Make them calls."

"Oralé." DJ bumped fists with both. "I'll holla tonight."

"Is that your Bentley?" Malo asked, a giant child-like smile on his face.

"Uh, yes."

"Sweet. Can we cruise one of these days?"

"Calm down, fool," Raul said. He turned to Angel. "He's a big-time car head. Be going to all the shows."

"Oh," she said. Seeing DJ's amusement, peace filled her heart. *There's nothing to be afraid of, silly, they're on your side.* She took a deep breath. "Tell you what, if you have a driver's license, you can take the three of us for a ride along the Strip."

The tattoo bent into a wide smile. "Serious?"

"Absolutely."

Raul tapped Malo's chest. "Now you got a reason to get your license."

"Oralé." Malo was suddenly a kid at Christmas. He told DJ, "She's badass, homz."

As they left the restaurant, DJ released Angel and pulled up a chair.

Carlos stood tableside. She hadn't seen him emerge from the kitchen. He asked DJ, "You good?"

"Yeah."

Angel caught the inflection. *Good* had nothing to do with what had just happened.

DJ touched the open tablet. "Been here a minute?"

"About an hour," she said.

"Thought you said noon?"

"I did. However, I needed to discuss some things with Carlos."

"Things?"

"You and I will get to that later."

DJ grinned, asked Carlos, "She tell you how she use'ta bully me in class?"

"No," he said, strongly. "But she told me everything else."

Silence.

Angel stood and hugged Carlos. "It was a pleasure to meet you."

He kissed her cheek. "It was my honor, mamí."

When he returned to the kitchen area, DJ asked, "You didn't really tell him everything?"

"I did."

Chapter 15

"Club Xstasy"

Outside the restaurant, Angel opened the Bentley doors and told DJ to, "Get in." She had planned to ride and talk, but learned his house was nearby; that he had moved from the one he lived in the night he saved her.

"Rent or own?" she asked.

"Own."

"Do we live alone?"

"We do."

"May I see it?"

A half hour later, the two sat on his living room couch, drinking glasses of ice water. Angel had picked up from her previous night's inquiry, further delving into his friendship with Jason. "Were you friends for a long time?"

"Within the first six months after I got here."

"From New York?"

He nodded. "School I went to… the Mexicans weren't used to niggas like me. They talked a lot of shit."

"Because you weren't fully Hispanic?"

"That and my dark skin. Some of 'em would call me a mayaté.'"

"Mayaté?"

"Some racial shit. Closer to the word *cracker* than nigger. Called me that too."

"How terrible."

"For them. Carlos had me boxing at three. Kick boxing at six. By the time they got to talking shit, I was real nice with my hands. Knocked a few of 'em out. But eses ain't taking too many losses. Started plotting to smoke me."

"Kill you!?" Angel balled her fist unconsciously.

"Yeah. But Jay stepped in—put an end to that shit. He was all about Latinos being united."

"Thank god they listened to him."

"Had to. He was an Abregon."

"At his mother's birthday party, I had no clue who they were." She raised an eyebrow. "I've certainly learned a great deal since."

"Media put them on the map. All the *allegedly* stuff after that night. Most people think anybody with the last name is part of their family. Raul and Malo were his brothers. There's two more, and four sisters."

"The guys from the restaurant were scared shitless."

"Look at the potty mouth on you."

"I'm no longer the little girl you once knew."

"You never were."

"Really—then what was I?"

"A gangster. Only you didn't know it."

"Oh, I'm no gangster. I nearly peed myself at the restaurant."

"Gangsters ain't always on some criminal shit. Sometimes they're just people who are badass at what they do. Like you with the business."

Angel leaned back, pretended to hold a cigarette. She took an imaginary puff and exhaled. "Angel Dominguez—gangster."

"Oralé. And their nana loves the shit outta you. Trust me, somebody fuck with you and she's sending a hit squad."

The two laughed like old friends. "She was adorable. I certainly look forward to seeing her."

"Heads up, she'll be salty we ain't together."

"I'll keep that in mind. Do you have anything else to drink?"

DJ got up, took a step toward the kitchen. "I got orange juice, mineral water—"

"Something a little stronger." She rocked her calve. "Unless you have someplace to be?"

*****

Upon her request for something stronger, DJ offered the only two choices he had—Patron and Wild Turkey. Angel chose the Wild Turkey because she had tried it before and enjoyed the smooth taste. He chose the same because, well, he was following her lead.

"I really loved Jason," she said. "He was playful, but in a super serious way. Broke my heart when he died."

"Jay thought you were the perfect woman. Finest thing walking the planet, plus crazy smart. Said if I didn't get out the game because of you, I was the dumbest person on the planet."

Angel smirked, as if seconding the opinion. "Bet you miss him something fierce."

"Every day. Wanna hear something crazy?"

"Sure."

"He's the one who picked out the ring."

She reached below her neckline, took hold of the thin chain. Pulling it above her blouse, she said, "You mean this ring?"

DJ stared in amazement. "You kept it... after all these years."

"Close to my heart."

He set forearms on his knees. "I fucked up that night. But the way they did him—" his voice cracked. "It was the only thing that could've made me react that way."

Her eyes welled up. She reached into her bag, removed a Kleenex, and dabbed the corners of her eyes. "I kept waiting for you to call."

"I wanted to... but, like I said—"

"I get it. I do. And I love you for choosing to protect me."

"My life would've been over had something happened to you. Swear to God, I would've killed a hundred people."

A long silence.

"Thank you for allowing me to meet your brother."

"Should'a done it back in the day."

"I've been thinking about that. Actually, it's the reason I couldn't sleep last night." She placed her free hand into his. "We can't change the past, Jack."

"I know."

"If it wasn't for what happened to Jason, we'd be—" She took a healthy drink. "I don't want it looming over our heads."

"Hard not to. It's the worst decision I ever made. Not doing what I did, but the bailing part."

She scooted closer, moved her hand to his thigh. "I want to start fresh."

"How you figga we do that?"

"I'm not a hundred percent sure, but I want to begin with the business you and I talked about that night." She placed the glass onto the coffee table. "In fact, I've already established it under Serenity's corporate umbrella. Want to know the name?"

He scrunched his nose. "What?"

"Urban United International. Urban United for short."

"Sounds global as fuck."

"In due time. For now, we'll keep it simple, investing in communities of color. Particularly, black and brown businesses; though, I plan to work heavily with the Asian community since I have significant dealings across seas. My lawyers have appraised Carlos's businesses at three-hundred-sixty thousand. I have a lender ready to sign off on a three-hundred-thousand-dollar loan. Carlos will use it to purchase a forty-nine percent stake in your name."

"Fuck." He pondered the swift movement of her actions. She was setting him up to win, asap. "Wait. It sounds badass, but ain't no way you got that nigga to risk his businesses for me."

"He has already agreed in principle."

"You're serious?"

"Very. Remember the safe deposit box?" she asked, referring to the process she presented seven years ago.

"What was that formula—cost, plus ten percent?"

"Fifteen. But I'll place four-hundred thousand in the box. He'll get the key once we sign the papers. Only question is, can you make the plaza safe for white people?"

DJ chuckles. "Huh?"

"They're the reason I bought the plaza. It's twenty minutes from the Strip. I think this could be an incredible opportunity—if you can protect white people."

DJ heard everything she said, but Angel's intimate nature was getting the best of him. Her scent, her lips, the sight of her legs. He could feel his flesh inching down his thigh. If she kept her fingers there, it would eventually crawl beneath her palm. "You're in Napoleona mode, so you gotta walk me through this."

Angel crossed her legs. "I paid one point two million for the plaza. Fifteen years ago, it sold for eight million. I believe it's worth twelve... maybe more." Angel recrossed her legs, the skirt's hem riding her thighs. DJ did not hide his approval. "Do you know why it lost seven million in value?"

"Neighborhood's fucked up."

"Correct. In the last nine years, countless businesses have failed. And three months ago, a man was killed outside the club. Murdered. Media said it was gang related."

"It wasn't."

"Insurance alone was reason enough to balk."

"Then why buy it?"

"Because I'm privy to other information."

"What other information?"

"Nobody messes with anything related to Carlos's businesses. That includes his customers. For a month after he bought the laundry-mat, there were zero car thefts in the plaza. In fact, there was zero crime. No break-ins, robberies, nothing. That's because criminals needed to gauge his level of influence."

"Tried to steal your guy's car."

"Only car they knew for sure wasn't connected to your brother. But I can assure you, had they become partners, Ronan could have left the key in the ignition, and nothing would've happened. At any rate, the thefts resumed. As did the break-ins and robberies. Of course, no one dared to touch anyone, or anything associated with the laundry-mat, which told me criminals had discovered out what belonged to Carlos."

"We let them know."

"I figured as much. Anyway, that's when I implemented my plan."

"Plan?"

"As my lawyers negotiated the plaza, Ronan began eating at the restaurant. Once the deal on the plaza was final, I set the rumors in place."

"What rumors?"

"That the family of the murdered man was preparing to sue Derek Winslow; and the police would soon shut down his club. After that, it was easy for Ronan to step in and assume the lease. Cost me thirty thousand." She extended her hands like a magician. "And here we are."

A goddamn genius. Seven years ago, DJ had watched her annihilate classmates, listened to her talk about business strategies, but it was nothing compared to actually seeing the results. She had handled Derek like a straight up bitch.

"But why the club?"

"Because it was the easiest way for me to unite Ronan and Carlos. Eventually, he would have suggested they go in on the entire plaza, offering Carlos a piece of that as well."

"Think I know where you're going with this."

"I'm sure. The previous owner died five years ago. While liquidating his assets, the family put the property on the market, asking eight million—the exact price he paid, but there were no takers. Asking price had dropped six million before we made an offer."

"If we can get rid of the crime, the value returns?"

"Correct. More than that, we can turn it into something beautiful: an urban epicenter. All new businesses, owned and operated by minorities. What do you think?"

"You ain't gotta cut us in, mamí. We'll still ride with you."

"That's not an answer to my question."

"The idea is dope as hell. But I gotta ask—who's Ronan to you?"

"My tío's inheritance came with a list of men and women at my disposal. Specialists. Ronan's an expert in corporate espionage."

"Is your man part of this?"

"Joshua's not a part of anything I do. And he never will be. Nothing's changed, Jack. I'm still a very private person. My company's financial dealings are no one's business."

DJ corralled her body, set a hand on her thigh, and curved his long fingers so that the tips rested between her lower knees. "A'ight woman, what exactly do you want?"

Angel turned her body toward him, recrossed her legs, deliberately trapping his fingertips. "As I said, I want to turn the entire plaza into an urban epicenter. Nine thriving minority-owned businesses, with the club as its anchor."

"Ain't that kinda sleazy?"

"Not if we turn it into the classiest urban gentleman's club ever. The public has embraced the Palomino Club, Little Darlings, Sapphire, and Sophia's. They're advertised in tourist guides alongside the Bellagio and MGM Grand. I'm going to knock down the wall connecting the carpet store and remodel the entire club—adding several V.I.P. suites."

"You can do that?"

"Of course, it's my property. The entire plaza was a supply warehouse in the fifties, owned by the city's biggest contractor. That's why the club's ceilings are two stories high, just like the carpet store. You know the empty lot on the property's eastern side?"

"Fenced off section?"

"Correct."

"It's a junkyard. Grass, bunch of weeds, all kinds of trash."

"Semis made deliveries there." Excited, her body moved with each declaration, gently massaging his fingers. "My city ordinance person said the property line extends another three acres."

"You've thought this shit through."

"Absolutely. I already have a name for the club."

"Napoleona?"

"No, silly." Angel smiled, extended her arms, and presented an imaginary picture frame with her fingers. "Club... Ecstasy. Only we'll have a big pink neon X, followed by the smaller letters, s-t-a-s-y." She dropped her hands. "A high-end gentleman's club for corporate bosses. Or as you guys say in the streets—ballers. A place for urban entrepreneurs to commingle with corporate businesspeople. Not gang members, drug dealers, or anything like that; but local musicians, athletes, people looking to meet others not of their race or social background."

Angel eyed him, eager for a response.

DJ stood, moved into the open space in front of them. Angel was right. He could name a dozen white boys who visited Freaky T's. Even though they had above average courage—at least in being around real street niggas—they didn't always look comfortable with their surroundings. Angel was saying, if the King's welcomed them with open arms, treated them like bosses, protected them (which they could easily do), word would spread, and other white boys would show up. It'd be a fucking gold mine. "I love it. I fucking love it. We can get them all. Businessmen... lawyers... doctors... pro athletes."

Angel bolted from the couch, pointed at him. "Right. We'll do a media blitz. Late night commercials... radio ads... billboards... social media." She did a voiceover, "*Club Xstasy—where the bosses come to play.* It'll be the hottest club in Nevada."

DJ stepped closer. "Nevada?"

She jabbed at his chest. "We have to think bigger than big. We have to think franchise." She turned away, playfully shook her plump ass, and dropped the imaginary mic.

That was all it took. DJ turned her around and kissed her passionately. She did not resist.

Seconds later, she pulled away. "Do you have a passport?"

PART TWO

"Illuminati"

Chapter 16

"Isha Ra"

CAIRO, EGYPT, PRESENT DAY

"Hello, Princess Isha," the voice said in Spanish.

Isha turned and saw Corina leaning through the balcony doorway. She took a moment to consider the task at hand—saving Corina's mother from the sex traffickers who held her in a Mexican brothel. Prior to the kidnapping, the men had decapitated Corina's father, and brutally raped her mother. Fortunately, Corina had been staying at her grandmother's. Isha motioned for her to enter. "I told you to call me Isha."

Corina stepped onto the balcony in a summer dress and flats. Taller than Isha, she arched her shoulders, taking a subservient posture. "Grandmother said to always call you, Princess Isha."

Isha hated the title of Princess. Historically, they were ostentatious, often fragile, and always held in the highest regard, whether or not they had earned such esteem.

"We're friends." Isha handed her a disarming smile. "And friends don't require such…" she switched to English, "formality."

"What is—" Corina attempted the same English transition, only hers broken, "For-mal-tee?"

"It means we don't have to be so serious," Isha replied in Spanish, placing a hand on her shoulder. "I found your mother."

Without warning, Corina hugged her. But as quickly as the joy surfaced, so did the terror. "Please forgive me. Grandmother said never to touch you without permission."

Isha knew her grandmother had told her a great deal more. Like the fact Mother treated Isha like Israel's Ark of the Covenant; any person placing a hand on Isha without Godly permission, often lost that hand, if not their lives.

Although younger, Isha wiped Corina's tears like a big sister and took hold of her trembling hand. "It's okay, it's okay. Don't worry, I won't say anything."

Her words calmed Corina. "You will save my mother?"

"The Queen returns in a few days. I'm going to ask her then."

"And she will save my mother?"

Isha looked off into the distance. "I'm pretty sure."

Corina dropped to her knees and bowed before Isha. "Thank you, Princess Isha. I give my life to you."

Corina's humbled state saddened Isha. Such reverence came from Corina's belief that Isha was more powerful than her, and therefore worthy of willful submission.

Isha suddenly grew angry. *This is everything I want to change about the world.* Now fifteen years old, Isha pondered her next move. She had waited years for this opportunity—a reason to instigate the so-called *Baptism of Blood.* Believing she had covered every angle, Isha knew what she wanted to do, but the wanting was the simple part. The courage to demand it from the most powerful woman on earth was another thing altogether.

A tempest feared by everyone but the Dragon, Isha could not manipulate Mother; nor could she sway her to mercy through rational, moral conversation. No, if she would ever have the chance to save the world, Isha realized long ago that she needed to force Mother's hand. And the only way to do that was to fulfill prophecy.

"Have you eaten dinner?" Isha asked.

Corina shook her head no. "I help grandmother."

"Have Sonja make you whatever you want."

Corina beamed. "Even pizza?"

"Even pizza."

*****

PRINCESS OF DEATH

Olivia Rothschild, sat on the metal folding chair. Her tanned legs crossed; she examined the room once more. The table, other folding chair, open laptop. Everything was ready. Everything but her purpose for being there. "Where is this cretin?"

Vincent La Fontaine glimpsed his Blancpain. "In route, Your Highness."

"In route is not here."

The chiseled behemoth moved to a position behind her. "Forgive me, Your Highness, it appears I was not explicit enough. It shall not happen again."

"It had better not. And I don't wish to meander."

"Yes, Your Highness. We will be airborne ten minutes after you've secured the target."

She adjusted the 40.22-carat diamond necklace. The fifteen-million-dollar gift from a Russian oligarch occasionally shifted about her neck. "Have you updated my itinerary?"

"Yes, Your Highness. However, the North American Crown has provided a contact at the behest of the Supreme One."

"Clarify."

"A senior agent by the name of Woodard. He's been monitoring an associate of Mr. Esperanza."

"Clarify."

"A local man named William McNeil. There are some anomalies."

"Mr. Marquez is the only anomaly." She huffed, tapped a painted fingernail against her knee. Why would father involve local agency? She wondered. "It doesn't matter. Our stay will be brief. Augustine is meeting me in Paris."

Olivia closed her eyes and began to meditate. Her third trip to America in the last year, the current venture resulted from her nemesis' sustained interest in an ordinary street thug. To the naked eye, it seemed as though Joaquin "Monsta" Marquez were reaching out in boredom, something he did from time to time. Born and raised in New York, he kept a strong finger on the pulse of American street life: music, film, fashion, politics.

A decade of vigilance had taught Olivia that, bored or not, Monsta did nothing without motive, a reality not lost on the Illuminati (or Illuminati). Known today as the Twelve Crowns of the Bavarian Illuminati, her father, Supreme Crown (Supreme One) Malcolm Rothschild, governed the secret society with an iron fist.

To the Illuminati, Monsta was the biggest threat to the second covenant of peace with Queen of Suma'at, Sekhmet "Mother" Ra. She had presented the second covenant as a world-ending ultimatum.

The first covenant was agreed upon in 1990, shortly after Mother revealed herself to the Twelve Crowns via phone call. She had claimed to be the daughter of the former Crown of Africa, King Sargon X. He had fled in 1935, after learning of the plot by the Supreme One—then, Clarence Sickert—to kill the seven non-European crowns. A plot carried out months later, killing the other six.

Upon Mother's revelation, the Illuminati welcomed her back into the fold, long enough to attempt an assassination. Expecting such treachery, she positioned her decoy in a Madagascar village. The woman was blown to pieces by a ballistic missile.

Two weeks later, a video arrived on the doorsteps of an Illuminati clergy. The video showed a man, dressed in a black mask, standing beside eight subordinates, one tier removed from the Twelve Crowns. Four men, four women. The eight were strapped to altars. As the masked man read Mother's newly formed constitution—and the rules of engagement—the head of each were cut from their bodies.

The masked man warned that another attempt against the Queen of Suma'at and their family members would suffer the same fate. To ensure they understood, Mother sent them dossiers of every man, woman, and child.

Illuminati had no choice but to agree to her terms and enter the covenant of peace. At least until they could devise a planned that succeeded. However, they never got the chance because the covenant was broken four years later, following the brutal murders of Sir George Wellington (Crown of the United Kingdom of Great Britain), Thomas Stowe (Crown of Italy), their two wives, and ten dinner guests. All fourteen had been decapitated, their bodies hung from crystal chandeliers inside Wellington's London castle. Thirty people died that night. They spared only a servant to inform the Supreme Crown of the man responsible—Monsta.

Without delay, Malcolm Rothschild called for an emergency round table in a small cottage just outside La Chaux-de-Fonds, Switzerland. There, he and the remaining Crowns learned that Mother had given Monsta control of her army, known as Mexica (meh-Shee-ka). The then eighteen-year-old Monsta had used them to execute vengeance upon Wellington for ordering the murder of his closest friend, a New York music producer by the name of Pedro Campos, and Campos's girlfriend, Désira Davis, a ballet dancer from Congo, Africa.

At the round table's conclusion, Rothschild decided that, although Mother should not have allowed her army to be used in such a vulgar way, Monsta's death was the only act of attrition necessary to restore peace. He knew Mother was responsible but decided against war. For she was a woman smarter and more vicious than Illuminati had ever encountered.

Rothschild called Mother personally and demanded Monsta be handed over at once. He cited an edict from the first covenant, whereby such an act—the killing of a Crown—was punishable by Roman crucifixion.

Instead of debating the issue, Mother simply told Rothschild to direct one or all Illuminati satellites to a location five hundred miles off the west coast of New Zealand. A task that took his engineers minutes to accomplish. She then suggested he record the event for posterity.

He did, knowing her well.

Mother informed Rothschild of his exact location before giving the order to detonate a bomb one hundred fathoms beneath the ocean's surface. Illuminati generals quickly confirmed its atomic nature.

"Mr. Rothschild, I warned you once before," Mother said, her voice calm. "All that you love is in my sights. And though I too shall perish, if you harm my son, I will destroy you... even if all life on earth suffers in like manner. As a gesture of human mercy, I warn you one last time, do not test my resolve."

What concerned Rothschild most was not her warning or the fact she had achieved nuclear capability, but her identifying Monsta as her son. She often referred to occupants inside her kingdom as her children but had never given one the power of her right hand. Later, Rothschild discovered Monsta was not her actual son, but a person simply chosen to ascend above the rest.

Mother informed Rothschild that Wellington should not have killed her son's friends. Campos had uncovered an Illuminati plot to seize control of a particular genre of music, presently known as Rap music. Illuminati had spent millions studying the psychoacoustics and determined the music capable of inciting revolution.

To alter and market the music in a more sociably docile way, Illuminati had bought several American record companies; one of which had sent a handler to gain Campos as an asset. The maneuver backfired, with Campos beating the handler within an inch of his life. As a result, Wellington had the handler, Campos, and Davis murdered.

Mother told Rothschild she understood Illuminati could not have known Monsta was her son, since she had failed to disclose his name. Even so, she determined his vengeance justified and reiterated her nuclear intent if they ever attempted, in word or deed, the murder of her or her son.

Mother then presented Rothschild an olive branch in the form of a new covenant of peace; one that included the names of all her children. Thus, speculation was no more. Of course, Rothschild needed to do the same.

Under the new covenant, unless found in grave violation (like the killing of a crown), all named children—those with direct knowledge of the Illuminati, or the Suma'at Illuminati—were deemed off-limits. Associates and underlings—those without direct knowledge (pawns)—were fair game. If found in common breach, associates and underlings could be killed without repercussion. Common breach was a term loosely defined as, "An egregious attempt to deceive the spirit of the covenant."

Rothschild had no choice but to agree to her terms since Mother appeared suicidal in her desire to protect her son.

They enacted the second covenant on January 18, 1994.

In the years that followed, Monsta continually found Illuminati associates and underlings in common breach, extinguishing their lives at every turn, and in the most macabre ways. And Illuminati could do nothing but accept his actions, or search and kill Suma'at Illuminati associates and underlings found in similar breach. Which they did. Yet Monsta was not deterred in the least.

Not until 2005, when Rothschild assigned his then fifteen-year-old daughter to deal directly with Monsta, did his brutality subside.

Olivia Rothschild was raised to be a killer of the likes the world had never known. Her tutelage began at the Rite of Purification, a ceremony that ended with the then-six-year-old cutting the throat of a Scottish virgin upon the Alter of Illumination.

Afterward, Malcolm Rothschild gave his daughter the title of Curator of Death. Each crown had a Curator, also known as a Royal Skull, but only the Supreme Crown had the Curator of Death. And because women were the curators of life—for it was through their womb that humans entered the world—no woman had ever held the position of Curator of Death. Rothschild subsequently had his daughter's reproductive system removed.

As Curator of Death, Olivia possessed the power of cessation upon all living creatures; except, of course, Mother's named children within the second covenant of peace. She could order the death of her father and Illuminati soldiers would obey it without hesitation. Rather, she chose her only siblings, Lucas and Solomon. The message to her father was clear, If I cannot create life, neither shall your sons.

Aside from the power to execute death, Olivia's chief duty was the governance of population control, i.e., the rationing of natural resources.

Through the most intricate substrata ever created—war, disease, famine, and constructed viruses like Covid-19—each day, they systematically killed tens of thousands under the watchful eyes of her servants. As Illuminati law decreed, "Where there is death, so lies the power to rule."

In the first year of her reign, Olivia successfully oversaw eleven million deaths. With the help of a Wall Street-like structure, and a child-like desire to succeed, her second year saw significant increases. Such had been the case every year since. This one was no different. The Science Schemata, with the help of pharmaceutical substrata, were creating fresh forms of death daily.

Since her emergence more than a decade ago, Olivia had grown into a beautiful woman. Tall and statuesque, she loved one thing most in life: absolute power. All else of value was a mere byproduct. Wealth and men included. The latter she handled without emotion; for they were nothing more than a thing to be enjoyed physically and then discarded like the scraps of a satisfying meal.

Years ago, Mother had taken a liking to Olivia, giving her the nickname La Princesa de la Muerte: The Princess of Death. And despite his hatred for the Illuminati, Monsta held a deep affection for the lovely tyrant. She was by far mentally stronger than any man he knew.

Today, Olivia was Monsta's equal in every way. So much so, he referred to her as the 'Baddest bitch on the planet.'

It was a title she relished.

Chapter 17

"Wealthy Bloodlines"

Democratic congressional candidate, Paul Hope, stood atop the stage and gripped the podium's edge. The vast mixture of human diversity had clung to the hour-long speech as though Christ himself had spoken. His writer, crafting the last five minutes of the speech like a fantastic symphony, had linked its crescendo to the name and campaign slogan: Hope for a Better Tomorrow.

"Tell you something else most Americans don't know," Paul Hope said. "In the mid-nineteenth, early twentieth century, many of our ancestors in the west stood together in this hope. Hope in a place to call home, and a family to love and cherish. Hope in the chance to work for a fair wage. Hope in the opportunity to raise their children in a truly civilized nation. And that's the hope of today. The crux of the American dream. Whether you're white... black... Hispanic... Asian... Native American... it doesn't matter."

Paul Hope scanned the crowd of over five thousand constituents and paused for greater effect. He noticed the tears of an elderly woman and took a mental victory lap, certain that of the countless rallies this had been his most successful. With two months left before election day, the momentum was certainly on his side.

"What unified them in this hope was poverty. Yes, poverty. That's because poverty induces a psychological pain unlike any a human can face. Where will I live? What will I eat? How will I take care of my family? Poverty is relentless... heartless. And all we need to do is look at the rest of the world to see that it does not discriminate.

"In the end, that unified hope of our ancestors was infiltrated, compromised, and replaced with the manufactured wedge of racism. A racism implemented by the special interest groups of their time. Yes, they were around back then. Sadly enough, it was poor whites who were the executors of this wedge of racism. Why? Because much like they are today, poor whites were the majority. Therefore, they were promised better jobs, better wages, and a better life—if only the other people were put in their places.

"History tells us what happened next. Poor whites turned on their nonwhite brothers and sisters. Not all, but enough to cause the violence and death that ensued. A simple plan to divide and conquer, instigated by the real men in power—wealthy descendants of secret bloodlines which have played mankind like a game of chess for hundreds of years. And do you know who the favorite pawn of these bloodlines is?"

"The political sock puppet," a woman yelled.

The crowd roared. It was a phrase coined at the Buffalo New York rally, coming at the conclusion of his spirited ninety-minute speech. Candidate Paul Hope had told supporters that most politicians were nothing more than sock puppets, bought and sold to the highest bidder. Told them he was no sock puppet, but a devout

Christian humanitarian committed to a revolution of love. A man who accepted you for who you were, regardless of political affiliation, race, color, creed, gender, or sexual preference.

Writers called his words fresh, authentic, and long overdue. After the Buffalo rally, *#nopoliticalsockpuppet* trended for more than a week. It had since become a separate campaign slogan, plastered onto T-shirts, buttons, posters, and bumper stickers.

"Yes, yes, the political sock puppet," Paul Hope said. "And today, the descendants of these wealthy bloodlines want us to believe our country has entered the darkest era of its nearly three-hundred-year history. But like the Wizard of Oz, they don't tell us themselves. No, of course not." He shrugged like a comedian delivering a punchline. "I mean, where would they hold the press conference? On the upper deck of their hundred-million-dollar yacht?"

He let the wave of laughter subside.

"No. They use the fired-up rhetoric of the sock puppet. Give to him or her the bullhorn of media: Fox News... CNN... MSNBC... Twitter. They're all the same. Outlets controlled by the wealthy bloodlines. They pump divisive rhetoric into our stream of consciousness, day in and day out, until it's all we think about. Don't you see? It's designed to separate us. To keep us pointing fingers at one another and saying, 'you're the reason for my pain. For my struggle.' To keep us from once again unifying in hope. That ends today!"

Paul Hope slammed a fist onto the podium. Finally, a politician who was not fucking around.

"Understand, there are no evil empires... only evil men. For a country is not its dictator, supreme leader, or even its president. A country is and will always be, its people. Join me in returning to that great and unifying hope. Elect me and we will give these wealthy bloodlines a history lesson they will never forget."

The crowd exploded into cheers as the HOPE FOR CONGRESS signs bounced like an advancing army.

It wasn't long before Paul Hope's wife, Diana, and two teenage daughters, Joy and Tabitha, joined him on stage. The perfect family. The perfect image of a better tomorrow.

A short time later, the family descended into the crowd, shaking hands and thanking people for their support.

Democratic chairman, Ted Carpenter, stepped between Paul Hope and Diana. "We have a problem. I need for you to come with me right away."

Paul Hope smiled and pretended as if Carpenter had congratulated him. "Can't you see I'm in the middle of a fucking campaign."

"Presidential orders."

*****

Hope stood quietly next to Carpenter as the service elevator headed toward the basement. Behind them, two armed agents stood, hands crossed at the wrists.

Carpenter had not spoken since conveying the presidential order, other than to say he didn't know what it regarded. The lack of details frustrated Hope. They had forced him to leave his event, his time to shine in front of the same people who might one day elect him Commander-in-Chief. What frustrated him further was the fact that the same man he'd been trashing for months had ordered him to do so. But if the President had taught him anything, it was that you never stopped playing to your base.

Hope tweeted daily for five months, picking apart every presidential lie, contradiction, and racially charged comment. He then associated it with his opponent, whom the President campaigned for on three occasions. The strategy worked to perfection. Recent polls had him seventeen points ahead of congressional relic, Republican Thomas Summerset.

The elevator doors opened, and the four men stepped into the corridor. Hope scrunched a brow, noticing right away the row of heavily armed men lining the walls. The majority wore sunglasses, which made them look more like bodyguards than Secret Service. Some had beards, some long hair wrapped in ponytails, and some facial tattoos.

A tall, barrel-chested man approached, his face void of courtesy. He stepped toward the long corridor. "Follow me," he said in a heavy French accent.

Hope paused, turned to Carpenter. "The Presi—"

In one fluid motion, the Frenchman turned and pressed a massive hand along Hope's esophagus, pinning him against the nearest wall. He squeezed just enough to introduce the possibility of death. "Follow or die."

The Frenchman released him.

Hope fell to his knees and coughed violently. He regained his composure and glanced up at the two agents. They stared straight ahead, robotic-like, as if a mere extension of the Frenchman.

Hope proceeded down the corridor, staying close to Carpenter as he tried to reconcile what had just happened. But he couldn't, and merely grew angrier with each wobbled step.

How dare they let a man, a foreigner, handle me like some common hooligan? There's no way the President ordered this. And if he did, it was the end of his goddamn presidency. Once Hope reported the incident, the Democratic Party would rally around him. There'd be bipartisan investigations, hearings, impeachment.

They stopped at the last door on the right. Slightly ajar, another armed man stood out front.

The man nodded at the door. "Go."

Hope entered cautiously, feeling a twinge of nausea.

Inside the dimly lit room, two men stood like giant sentinels on opposite sides of the doorway, their faces dark and menacing. A small desk sat in the center of the room, an open laptop upon its surface. The screen pointed in Hope's direction. There were two chairs. One faced the laptop, the other held a strikingly beautiful woman with long legs crossed beneath a short skirt. Behind the woman, a bald man in dark shades stood like a giant gargoyle. A gargoyle that looked as if he could tear him apart with his bare hands.

*****

Olivia considered the man they had sent her to deal with. She had captured many like him. Bottom feeders. Men who swore they knew everything about human behavior yet knew nothing of their own.

She gestured to the empty folding chair. "Sit and say nothing."

"Who are—," Hope tried to speak, but the punch to the back of his head dropped him like a stumbling drunk.

The two guards dragged him across the room, wrestled him into the chair.

"I'm not a patient individual, Mr. Hope," Olivia said. "Therefore, I truly need you to remain quiet, lest you anger me."

Hunched over, Hope looked up, fear in his eyes. She knew his ears were ringing.

"Good," she said. "Now focus." Olivia took position behind him, leaned across his quivering shoulder. She swiped his left cheek with her breast and tapped the laptop's entry key.

The throaty grunts at once filled the room.

She watched as he carefully studied the video. It took several seconds for the recollection to set in, but when it did, his countenance fell to the floor like a dead man.

United States congressional candidate Paul Michael Hope was at the home of friend, billionaire media mogul, Barren Moffet. The room that Moffet said was private, had not been private after all. They never were.

Hope's eyes held a wave of disgust... then panic. It was obvious he had never positioned himself on the outside looking in, like a deviant viewing, over and over, the hidden video of a recent conquest. His thoughts were now an open book to her and came complete with visions of the breaking headlines and ghastly images blasted on every media outlet known to man.

As if trying to escape a living nightmare, Hope wrenched his eyes shut. "I don't know what to say."

"I think we can both agree, it speaks for itself."

"Please... I made a mistake. We were drinking."

Olivia shook her head. It never failed. A man's first instinct when caught was to make excuses. As though it somehow changed what he was. "I have a file with your name on it. Inside is every mistake you've made in the last six years. Malaysia... Singapore... Mexico... your recent trip to the Philippines."

His eyes danced wildly, searching for a way out. "I'll be ruined."

"That is certain. But let me ask you—have you ever heard of a snuff film?"

The odd question was like a bucket of water dropped on his head. Hope bent his neck, confused. "Huh?"

"A snuff film. Do you know what it is?"

"It's a movie... where... where someone is killed."

"Yes. Typically, a woman, raped beforehand."

"What do you want?"

"To ask what I want implies you have a choice, which you do not. I represent the bloodlines you love to blame for the plight of the world. And as you can see, they had nothing to do with your actions. They merely provided you with the opportunity. You will continue to indulge, Mr. Hope. Only now, I will grant you access to an incredibly special catalog. I'm confident your deviant appetites will find other indulgences far more enticing than sodomy of a fifteen-year-old runaway." She rubbed his back like a gentle lover. "You will serve me," she said. "Please Mr. Hope, say it for me."

Hope swallowed hard. "I will serve you."

She wrenched a handful of his hair, snapped his head backward. "Say it like you fucking mean it!"

"I will serve you." He sobbed. "I'll do whatever you want."

"Excellent." Olivia released him, took a step back. "Fret not, Mr. Hope, I have many servants… politicians, businesspeople… coroners. And like them, should you deviate from your servitude—like choosing to report our little talk here—you and your family will die in a tragic accident. The kind without a trace of forensic evidence; like an airliner that vanishes over the Atlantic.

Of course, none of you will die. No, your wife and lovely daughters will be added to that special catalog. And Mr. Hope, you will watch them star in their very own snuff films. After which, you will be flown to a restricted island and hunted like the animal you are." She paused. "Please tell me you understand."

"I understand." His tone was strikingly sober.

"And never forget, Mr. Hope, the eyes of those bloodlines will be upon you until the day you die."

Hope shifted his body, turned to Olivia. "It will be my honor to serve you."

Chapter 18

"Queen"

Mother seldom traveled for leisure, but when she did, it was quite the spectacle. Twelve black and gold armored plated SUVs—two rows of six—thundered along Djoser road. Above them, five Russian-made Ka-52 helicopters chopped through the warm air like steel dragons.

Years ago, such precautions were necessary to ensure her safety. That was no longer the case. Since the second covenant of peace, Monsta had built Mexica—which included every type of soldier on earth and was now equal in size to the Illuminati's United Nations Security Confederation—into a killing machine two million strong. The difference between the two was that eastern governments of color treated Mexica like brethren, while Illuminati soldiers were seen as nothing more than an extension of the *Elite White Supremacists* who governed them in secret.

It wasn't the sheer number of warriors that kept the Illuminati at bay, but the man who led them. Not only did Monsta have the capability of ending life on earth at the slightest provocation, at times he seemed eager to do so.

When the motorcade reached the Step pyramid, the first four vehicles continued along its base, as the trailing eight turned outward, and formed a wide half-circle around them.

The four vehicles parked at the pyramid's center, side by side, ten feet from one another. The first in the line of eight stopped twenty feet from the pyramid's farthest corner. At the other corner, the last vehicle did the same.

Two helicopters broke ranks and positioned themselves fifty yards in front of the motorcade, guns pointed outward. The remaining helicopters moved farther out, circled the pyramid at measured intervals.

Mexica General, Vladimir Markelov, spoke into the shoulder mic, "Move in."

Warriors exited the eight vehicles and took tactical positions as servants from two of the center vehicles began setting up accommodations.

Doors opened on the other two center vehicles, and Vladimir exited first. Dressed in black beret, brown and black fatigues, and wearing mirrored sunglasses, he scanned the location before reaching inside and taking hold of Mother's hand.

Adorned in a multicolored robe, headdress, and sandals, Mother stepped out of the vehicle. She tapped Vladimir's arm. "Thank you, my son," she said in Russian.

Isha exited the other vehicle. Dressed exactly like Vladimir—shades and all—she watched as the servants neared the end of the task.

*****

Mother and Isha sat upon portable chairs beneath the large canopy. After more than an hour of debate, Isha was convinced her last point had finally won over Mother's internal reasoning.

"Very well," Mother said in Arabic, sipping the iced water. "I shall grant the girl a luxurious life."

Isha dropped her shoulders, having become well acquainted with Mother's condescending tone. "That's not at all what I'm asking."

"No, you want me to resurrect the dead. To save a woman who decided her fate long ago when she chose to embrace the lifestyle her husband provided. Provided with the drugs he first helped to distribute, and then steal. At any point, she could have chosen a better life for the sake of her child. Open your eyes—she is the reason they were all forced to pay."

Isha handed Mother a confused look.

"Yes," Mother said. "The men who took her mother also raped Corina and her grandmother. You want me to save *that* woman!?" Mother waved a dismissive hand. "May she pay another thousand years."

"As I said earlier, this is not an exercise in morality."

"You're supposed to be studying the glory of Egypt. Why do you insist on corrupting academia with such trivial endeavors?"

"Because it's the godly thing to do."

"You know nothing of godly matters. If you did, you would understand that helping her means establishing your throne. It means the shedding of blood."

"The blood of evil men?"

Mother nodded. "For you are the judgment of Ra upon evil men."

Isha knew the prophetic allegation well. A prophecy that was revealed to her on her sixth birthday. "You shall speak verdict, my child," Mother had said, "and Ra will make it so."

Mother also said Isha was not the first person to have this ability. That other people had had it. Some evil like Hitler and Mussolini; and others good like Martin Luther King Jr., and Gandhi. But no human had, or would ever have it, on a greater scale than the child born with the mark of Ophiuchus—the thirteenth sign of Mazzaroth.

"Please, Mother," Isha begged. "Rescue her for me. Just this once."

"That would be like dropping a bomb on an anthill."

"With all honor due, that's an extreme parallel." Isha sighed and leaned forward. "Dragón would have no problem accomplishing such a menial task."

"If my parallel falls short, it is only in the magnitude of death." Mother pointed an aged finger at her. "And no task you set to accomplish shall ever be menial."

"I find your decision cruel. You and I both know governments intervene in these kinds of matters all the time."

"Governments execute Illuminati schemata, nothing more."

"I want her freed," Isha demanded.

Mother calmly sipped the water. "This you have thoroughly articulated."

"Then tell me what I must do to establish my throne."

"You know exactly what you must do."

"Very well, I consent to the shedding of blood."

Mother shifted her body, raised a hand for Isha to be silent. It was a gesture heavy enough to weaken the knees of most humans. She motioned to the soldiers... the helicopters... the totality of the moment. "You speak as though you understand this."

"I want my throne."

Mother dropped her eyes for a moment. "Then it is not I that you must convince, but Dragón."

"Unnecessary." Isha felt the wind at her back. "We shall proceed to the ceremony. Whatever it may be."

Vladimir looked down at her. "Does a mere child command the Queen!?"

Isha immediately realized her error in judgment. She jumped out of the chair and knelt before Mother. "No human commands the Queen of Suma'at. Please forgive my arrogance."

Vladimir stepped in and pushed Isha away, causing her to fall on her rear end. He extended a hand to Mother and helped her to stand. As they began walking toward her vehicle, Mother told Isha, "You leave at once."

Isha knew to remain silent. She went to get up, but a female Mexica lieutenant told her to, "Wait."

Not wanting to anger anyone else, Isha remained seated, placing her forearms on her knees, hand over wrists.

Certainly not what I had in mind, she thought.

The lieutenant spoke into the shoulder mic. One of the three helicopters broke away and landed twenty yards in front of the half-circle.

She stepped up to Isha and pointed toward the helicopter.

*****

REYNOSA, MEXICO

Lujuria was not a strip club. Not like in America, where a woman teased, a man paid, and at night's end all returned to the beaten path of life. Lujuria was a slaughterhouse.

Throughout the impoverished region, parents begged their young adults to stay away from the club, because once inside, they were at the mercy of corrupt government officials, police, and cartel members. Men who drank hard, plotted evil, and feasted upon weakened souls like gas station jerky.

On any given night, one might see a drug mule taken out back and shot in the head, his body dragged to a darkened section of heavy foliage where it would remain until henchmen got around to disposal. Or a boyfriend sitting quietly at a table glimpsing his watch, wondering why his lovely date was taking so long to pee; not knowing she was in the storage room next to the bathroom, being raped by the men who'd noticed her beauty the moment she entered.

Such crimes always went unpunished.

Seated alone at a back table, Macho leaned over the face of his iPhone and snorted a line of coke the size of a child's pinky. The *Federale* downed a shot of Cuervo and headed toward the front door. An enforcer for eastern Mexico's most feared drug lord, Octavio Ruiz, Macho supervised two dozen officers working both sides of the Mexico, U.S. border, from Nuevo Laredo to Matamoros. He routinely met with corrupt American Border Patrol agents to ensure each shipment crossed without incident.

Occasionally, Macho and his men ventured about late at night, stalking the women who walked to and from the countless factories; many of which were owned by American companies.

When they found one they wanted, they placed her in the backseat and drove to a secluded area. They then showed her the bag of drugs they planned to frame her with if she resisted.

Once done, they dropped her on the nearest road, handed her a fistful of pesos, and warned her not to tell anyone. They knew the warning pointless since no one ever went against Ruiz.

On the battered sidewalk outside the club, Macho snorted a chunk of cool air and let the coke-filled snot trickle down his throat. The ensuing rush filled his body with rage. He loved the feeling. How it invoked memories of his wife, who left him three years ago, escaped to Texas with the mechanic she'd been fucking behind his back.

Macho stepped into the street and surveyed the unpaved road. As the line of cars and trucks rumbled along, music from the club pressed against his neck like heat from the midday sun. He crossed the street, stopped at the wall of chest-high weeds, and walked parallel to the road until he came upon the makeshift doorway.

Stepping onto the hillside, he moved down the jagged path. Thirty yards in, he heard the erratic breaths, the full moon reflecting off the waddling silhouette. As the two crossed paths, the fat man greeted Macho with a labored nod. The sweat along the man's nose had extinguished the cigarette protruding from his bloated face.

Another fifty yards in, Macho came upon Lujuria's pressure valve: *Motel Apetito*, a business he and a handful of others safeguarded for Ruiz. Years ago, the single-story inn had been converted into the region's busiest whorehouse.

Outside the front office, a group of men stood on the cement walkway, talking, drinking, and smoking cigarettes. Upon seeing Macho, one man rushed to greet him. After a few words, the man pointed to room 1. Macho spoke sternly to the man, patted him on the back, and headed toward the room.

What made Motel Apetito extremely lucrative was that, while it reserved most of the rooms for traditional prostitution, it set the first four rooms up as movie locations. Sex took place in rooms 1 and 4, while men and women—seated in rooms 2 and 3—recorded the acts from multiple cameras mounted throughout.

Scenes were edited, faces blurred—depending on the type of site—and the finished product posted on several internet websites. Room 4 was part of a *Cheating Spouses* website. Complete with dialogue outlining the affair, they pretended to have snuck away before the actual sex, with some scenes recorded elsewhere for added realism.

Room 1 belonged to Apetito's most lucrative enterprise, an internet *Fantasy Rape* site. With fourteen thousand global subscribers, the site raked in more than $400,000 a month. Yet, there was nothing fantastic about room 1. They were not paid actresses engaged in mock scenes of sexual violence, but woman indebted to Ruiz's organization.

Macho stepped into room 2 and eyed the room 1 monitor. Three men wrestled a dark-haired woman onto the bed as part of a *Maid Rape* scene. She had arrived a brief time ago, believing she was there to work off her husband's theft from a local winery owned by Ruiz. Given a maid's uniform, she was told to change and begin in room 1.

Other scenarios like *Waitress Rape*, *Housekeeper Rape*, and *Babysitter Rape*, were filmed throughout Ruiz's vast territory. Most times, the woman entered the task believing she was there to work off a debt.

Macho exited the room and continued down the walkway. Beyond room 4, he eyed the row of plastic chairs in front of rooms 5 through 14. Reserved for regular prostitutes, throughout the day, men shuffled along the parking lot inspecting women like cuts of beef hanging from a butcher's window. Dressed in one of the various costumes at their disposal, the women spoke seductively and did their best to entice the men inside.

All but one chair was empty, a man in a cowboy hat blocked Macho from seeing who was left. As he passed each room, heavy moans echoed the backdrop like the chopped wailings of a wounded animal. Hearing the footsteps behind him, the cowboy hat turned. It was then Macho saw the eleven-year-old, dressed in what looked to be a princess costume.

"Good evening, sir," cowboy hat said.

Macho nodded, stepped beyond them, heard the door open and close.

*****

Dressed in a nurse's costume, the woman wrenched her fingers. The man known as Macho had emerged from around the corner, a look of demented fury on his brown pockmarked face. Because her room sat in the motel's rear, she could only see the headlights of vehicles coming from the road. If she wanted a better view of potential customers, she needed to step around the corner, which she only did when conversing with Adriana. But Adriana had been picked up earlier and taken to the birthday party of a local judge.

Still, the woman thought, she should have worn her glasses. That way she'd be hiding inside the room like she was sure many of the women were doing. Macho loved to abuse the girls, but preferred the light skinned ones, like Helena, who he strangled to death six months earlier. Rumor had it they buried her on the hillside.

Darker than most, the woman considered herself lucky, Macho had never chosen her. She greeted him with a salacious smile and set a relaxed mood. "Hello, daddy," she said in Spanish.

Macho reeled back and slapped her face. The force of the blow dropped her to the ground, dislodging one of her heels. He opened the door, grabbed a handful of her hair, and pulled her inside. Kicking the door shut, he dragged her to the bed, bent her torso across the edge, and pressed her face into the mattress. "Don't fucking move, bitch."

*****

Inside the front office, the nine-year-old girl sat atop the desk, her feet dangling from the edge like a car seated infant. She looked at El Heffe with terror in her eyes. Her father had tearfully dropped her off an hour ago, payment for the costly medication El Heffe provided to her youngest sister.

With the help of an older prostitute, the child's tattered appearance—a deliberate move by her father to make her less appealing—was refined with a bath, garish makeup, and a red dress borrowed from the motel's smallest prostitute.

"I help your family, yes?" El Heffe asked.

The child nodded.

He stepped closer.

Without warning, the office door burst open.

One by one, a dozen soldiers shuffled inside and quickly surrounded the two.

Silence.

Outside the door, the sound of metal scraped the walkway floor like fingernails along a classroom chalkboard. Octavio Ruiz entered but said nothing as the scraping drew closer.

Seconds later, a man entered the office. The hood of his sleeveless black sweat jacket set beyond his forehead, encasing his face in darkness. A 21st century Grim Reaper, he was muscular, covered in tattoos, and held a gun in his right hand. He dragged a three-foot machete in his left hand as if walking a sharped tooth hellhound. Though El Heffe had never met him, he knew it was the man known as El Dragón.

"Sir," El Heffe said, nervously to Octavio Ruiz. "I was not told you were coming."

Octavio Ruiz said nothing.

El Dragón motioned to the child. "Come here, little one," he said in Spanish.

She scooted off the desk, walked over, and stood warily in front of him. El Dragón gently placed the gun-hand atop her head. "Cover your ears."

She gingerly set fingers into her ears and winced her eyes shut.

"Very good, little one." El Dragón smiled, winked at El Heffe, and shot Octavio Ruiz in the head.

Suddenly, the roar of gunfire erupted outside the office.

Chapter 19

"Time To Get Out"

Inside the yacht's master suite, DJ lay atop the bed, Angel nestled between his legs. Glasses of scotch in hand, the two were naked, save a pair of black and gold Gucci boxers and her white thigh-high Versace nylons.

Through the ceiling to floor window, they gazed at the brightly lit shoreline as it flickered in the distance like a stream of Christmas lights. DJ wasn't the type to use the word romantic, but the sight was romantic, the type of scenery that easily melted any woman's heart.

"Shit's strange," he said.

Angel looked up at him. "What's strange?"

"Being the only two people on a yacht this big. Feel like we're Jay-Z and Beyoncé."

"We're not the only two."

"Yeah, but we never see them until they're serving drinks or food."

"Well, that's the point of getting away. I've used this crew for the better part of five years," she said, focusing again on the majestic view. "They're family run and know how to stay in their designated areas."

"Shit ain't hard when you're in a floating hotel."

"Anyway," Angel said with a giggle, "I received the last appraisal. Would you like to take a guess?"

"You know numbers ain't my thing." He sipped the drink. "Three million."

"Six and climbing. We've made back our investment and then some."

A year after they agreed to give the partnership a chance, Serenity Plaza had become a reality. With two million in renovations, it carried the look and feel of a small city. Unrecognizable, especially at night, the twenty-foot pink neon digital signage—of the same name—beamed like a Broadway display.

At the plaza's other end, a fifteen-foot digital advertising screen ran mini-commercials for the nine attractive (minority owned) businesses, including Roxy (a high-end urban clothing outlet), T-Mobile, Archangel Productions (a music and film company), and Club Xstasy, North Vegas's hottest new gentleman's club. Her corporation—acting under the subsidiary, Urban United International—was the financier of all nine.

Masterfully orchestrated, like most new owners did when buying a sports franchise with a history of losing, Angel had changed the culture from within. With Club Xstasy she wanted white businessmen to feel the stark cultural contrast between her club and the blasé aura of other places; all of which were owned by white men.

She had attended enough social gatherings, been hit on by enough corporate professionals to know what they desired, what they secretly hungered for: fiery women of color capable of injecting their souls with the heat her club provided.

Much to her surprise, the club had become the plaza's anchor, a place where suit and ties mingled with urban entrepreneurs as if two sides of the same coin. Since its grand opening—which included an extensive marketing campaign featuring those fiery women on billboards, in TV commercials, newspapers, and social media, asked, *'Are you a boss?'*—the club's popularity had increased tenfold.

In the last two months alone, famed paparazzi—TMZ, Daily Mail, and Page Six—roamed the streets outside, a byproduct of the countless actors, sports figures, and rap stars who visited weekly. Knowing the publicity alone was worth its weight in gold, Angel had Carlos—the club's main figurehead—greet each celebrity with a hostess, complimentary bottle of Champagne, and security personnel capable of retrieving thousands in one-dollar bills.

Angel kept $150,000 in singles locked in an eight-foot safe inside *El Matador*, the classic Mexican restaurant next door. A restaurant she co-owned with matriarch, Cecilia Abregon.

Crime-wise, the Kings had quietly done their part in pushing the criminal element over two miles down the road. Such was their effectiveness, *Vegas Lifestyles* magazine recently published an article titled, *Serene Overtures*. In the piece, they credited Urban United International's willingness to work with the surrounding community—via scholarships, a young entrepreneurial program, and other community-centered endeavors—for the incredible socioeconomic transformation of the once impoverished area.

Angel had protected DJ and the Kings at all costs. Ironically, she did so by hiring off-duty cops for security. She handled them diplomatically. If they focused on protecting customers and avoided any job-related agendas, i.e., harassing her urban clientele, she offered them $20 an hour. Those who stuck to the script worked as many hours as they wanted. Those who didn't—Noss easily sniffed out any potential investigations—were not called back.

Law enforcement soon forgot any criminal association in the area. Meanwhile, King soldiers came to respect Angel. Guard her. And the Abregons not only adored Angel, but they were also highly protective of her.

When a local rapper got drunk and told Angel to get on stage and "shake that ass", she simply had him escorted out. As far as she was concerned, that was the end of it. Not for mama Cecilia, who, upon learning the rapper's name from a dancer, called relatives in Mexico.

Three days later, the rapper, his girlfriend, and her brother were found dead in a Northside apartment. Someone had bound and gagged all three, cut their throats ear to ear.

Closer than ever, DJ told Angel everything there was to know about Noss. After hiring him to investigate a plot of land south of Reno, she learned firsthand about his extraordinary ability to see the unseen. The crucial information he provided went above and beyond what was legal; boundaries that Ronan and others educated her on years earlier. She knew Noss routinely broke Federal law through a myriad of cryptographic deceptions.

"He's the hacker our government spends millions to protect themselves from," Ronan said one afternoon as they shared drinks enroute to Japan. "The fact he has several highly sensitive government contracts means his ability to hide in plain sight is downright Machiavellian."

Angel laughed at Ronan's facial intensity. But he was right. Noss's ability to hide in plain sight was downright Machiavellian. Therefore, she did what any smart leader would do. She hired Gen-Tech to screen all Serenity Corporation employees. And she didn't stop there.

During the next seven months—and with DJ's blessing—she and Noss became good friends, regularly attending lunch together to discuss her business ventures. And she always left the door open to his investment. To date, Serenity Corporation had netted $78 million in additional money because of the intelligence Noss provided. The two were in the preliminary stages of a joint venture, a software company, Omega Technologies.

For his thirtieth wedding anniversary, Angel gifted Noss and his wife with a month-long trip to Asia and Europe, all expenses paid. She provided them with an assistant and a Bombardier Global 6000, telling Noss, "The pilots will take you wherever you wish to go." They just had to choose a destination, and the assistant ensured the red carpet was ready upon their arrival.

To say Noss was a fan of Angel would be an understatement.

*****

"That candle's dope as fuck. What is it?" DJ asked, breaking the relaxed silence as they continued to gaze upon the radiant shoreline.

"At seven hundred a piece, it should be. It's from Trudon's Tuileries collection."

"Shit sounds exotic."

"Best candles ever. I give them as gifts to my clients all the time. They love them."

"Got this whole cabin smelling right."

"Take them with me wherever I go."

"Anyway, you did your thing with the plaza. Swear to God, ain't no white people ever stopped in for directions, let alone to shop."

"Everyone wants to enjoy a life free from harm's way."

"You made that happen. Shit's safer than the Strip."

"I'd like to think so. Financially, Club Xstasy's the game changer. Especially now that celebrities have found us."

"Never thought I'd own a strip club."

"Why not?"

"It's… what's the phrase you be using all the time?"

"A cliché."

"Right, a cliché. Every movie you see got niggas with paper owning a strip club."

"Truth is, they're extremely lucrative. The only cliché is the fact most are owned by… what's the phrase you like to use?"

"Cracker ass crackers."

Angel let out a high-pitched laugh, kissed his forearm. "Do you ever think of us, Jack? The way we were before. The way we were supposed to be?"

He kissed the top of her head. "Sometimes."

"Really?"

"Why wouldn't I? Look at us—we work. Even when you were with dude."

She interlocked the fingers of her left hand with his but said nothing. It had been four months since she and Joshua broke up. Three since she and DJ started sleeping together again.

After the trip to London a year ago (and the accompanying fuck-fest), both agreed it was best not to make it a part of their revived friendship. Simply put, Angel needed time to figure out her and Joshua's future.

"You never told me what happened," DJ said.

A long silence passed. "All he used to talk about was getting married and having kids."

"Kids?"

"Then suddenly his father resigns from the board. Cites scheduling difficulties. After that, Joshua started acting weird... distant."

"What'chu think went down?"

Angel shrugged. "Don't know... don't care."

"Can I ask a personal question?"

"Of course."

"Did you want to marry him?"

"Joshua's a great guy. Sweet. And he doesn't have a malicious bone in his body. I was moving toward settling down and having a family."

"And why not a Delaney?"

"Why not, given the choices?"

DJ wasn't going any further. Angel never played games with her future. Whatever plans she and Joshua put down a year ago were, as far as she was concerned, an afterthought. She lived life under her terms, which DJ figured had to have made for a bizarre arrangement between them. Especially since she was prone to flying off at a moment's notice. DJ wondered how many guys had been part of those business trips.

This time around, the sex was different. Angel's body was still tight, immaculate, but she didn't hold back, fucking him with a greater level of aggression than before. And she loved role-play. Loved to dress up and act the shit out like they were starring in a porno.

He extended the glass toward the shoreline. "Can't believe you put this together."

"What do you mean?"

"Private jet... two-hundred-foot yacht... five days off the coast of Morocco."

"Two hundred and *seven*-foot yacht."

He held up the glass, toasting. "To Serenity Plaza."

"Salute," she said. "Besides, I love spending time with you."

"Best part of my life."

Angel took a moment to digest his words. She grabbed the remote from the open space next to them and killed the lights, leaving only the blueish moonlight and its reflection off the still water. "Isn't it beautiful?"

He nodded. It was beautiful. A million miles away from the Northside of Vegas, beautiful. He suddenly understood the purpose of her first question. "Were you planning to get pregnant once you got married?"

"Through a surrogate."

"Ain't trying to fuck up that perfect body."

"God no. And what about you? Do you want kids?" She poked his ribs with her elbow. "You're not getting any younger, mister."

"One day. If I find the right chick."

"What am I, chopped liver?"

"You're too busy."

"Busy's got nothing to do with it. We can afford ten nannies."

"You try'na start an argument."

"Perhaps, if you don't answer my question. What's wrong with me?"

"Ain't a mother fucking thing wrong with you. Except, you're who you've always been—La Chica Napoleona. You do you and can't nobody say shit."

"You could."

"Bullshit."

"Fair enough. But if we planned something together, I'd see it through. This brings us back to my initial question."

"What question?"

"Thinking... about the way we were supposed to be."

"Are you asking if I wish we'd gotten married?"

"Maybe."

"I wish for a lot of things. Marrying you... kids... getting all my niggas out the game."

DJ inhaled her perfume and let the energy shift. He'd given her the answer she wanted, knew she'd dial back the Q & A and return to enjoying the moment.

"The last part is a wish no more," she said. "Who knows what will happen once you leave that life for good."

He scrunched a brow; having come upon a statement he hadn't expected. Was she asking him to leave the game? To marry her and become the way they were supposed to be?

"What? The only way you'll have a kid with me is if I'm out of the game?"

"A kid... marriage. I could never raise a child with someone who constantly risked his life."

"Well, this has nothing to do with our conversation, but I'm done."

"For good?"

The fact she didn't look up at him told DJ his words had caught her off guard. She didn't want him to read her expression.

"Gotta tie up some loose ends, but I promise you, I'm out for good."

A few minutes passed before she wiped tears from her cheek, kissed his forearm. Keeping her eyes on the shoreline, she said, "Jason would be proud of you."

The brief session wasn't about re-imagining the past, it was about defining the future. Plaza was done. Kings were set. Her vision eight years ago had come to fruition. It was now his turn to make the next move. To leave the game behind and finish what they started. It wasn't an ultimatum but a gentle nudge in the right direction.

Chapter 20

"Kasper"

Kasper gripped the Best Buy shopping bag and walked the grounds of the Serene hotel. Leo Scarza, the steroid-bloated son of Bonucci capo, Joe Scarza, shuffled in front of him like a dog with a bone. Leo hoped to one day have his name called, to become a *made man* like his father, a man who had worked under the rule of legendary mob boss, Salvatore Bonucci. The elder Don had been one of only two bosses ever allowed to retire, leaving control of the family business to his son, Salvatore Jr.

Kasper and Leo were headed to the penthouse suite of Don Jr.'s nephew, Frankie Gravano. The three men split money pinched from a drug deal between supplier Smokey Esperanza, and the Las Vegas Kings. Kasper had negotiated the deal more than a year ago. Twice a month, Smokey supplied the Kings with a hundred pounds of marijuana and thirty kilos of cocaine.

Before the deal, Kasper had never moved more than two kilos. The reason was no one trusted him. Not enough to front him enormous amounts of money or drugs. Kasper had a reputation as a drug-using lush with an overactive libido. If he found a girl attractive, he partied with her long enough to offer drugs or money for sex. Starting at $300, he increased the amount until she agreed, walked away, or reached his predetermined max. They rarely walked away, and the max changed from girl to girl—which varied from strippers to high schoolers—and sex act. He'd once paid $3,000 to a college freshman for a ten-minute blowjob, swearing she was the spitting image of Ariana Grande.

Kasper's drug dealing ambitions changed the day he met Leo. Equally the sexual deviant, Leo worked part time as a bouncer at the Palomino Club. As a side hustle, he provided select businessmen with drugs and prostitutes, often buying the drugs from the same prostitutes, who seemed to know every dealer in Vegas.

A particular night, Leo bought three eight balls from a prostitute named Strawberry; one of the eight balls was for his personal use. A half gram into it, Leo thought the quality so good, he asked her to introduce him to the dealer. The next night, Strawberry arrived at his suite with Kasper. The men hit it off, partying with Strawberry and five others until morning, during which Kasper added in a half-ounce free.

They partied again a week later. Within a month, Kasper had joined forces with Leo inside the Palomino Club, building a sizable clientele. For Kasper, his association with Leo Scarza not only gave him credibility, but it also allowed him to expand his other customer base, strippers who supplemented their income by catering to men with forbidden tastes: married men, judges, lawyers, and doctors who loved to get high and fuck free from scandal.

One of those strippers, Snowflake—all the white ones had similar names—danced at Club Xstasy. Not long after she began buying from Kasper, she asked him the price for half a kilo.

Cautious, Kasper responded, "Who wants to know?"

"My man. Told him your shit's hella good."

Her man turned out to be Money Milz, an alleged member of the Las Vegas Kings. Ever in search of bigger gains, Kasper quoted her $9,000.

A day later, he met Milz at Snowflake's Northside apartment.

"Nine thousand," Milz said, handing him a knot of cash.

"Hold up," Kasper said. "I thought this was a meet. I didn't bring anything."

"Just call my bitch when you got it."

Kasper shoved the cash into his pocket, shook his head. "I'm surprised you trust me with this kind of money."

"You'd be the dumbest nigga in the world to fuck us."

Kasper understood *us* meant the Las Vegas Kings, not Milz and Snowflake. Like most people in the Vegas underworld, Kasper was aware of the Kings, Abregons, and the alleged Easy Times Massacre.

"I'm straight up, bro," Kasper said.

He called Snowflake ninety minutes later.

Milz purchased two more halves before inquiring into something larger.

"What are we talking about?" Kasper asked as the two again met in her apartment.

"Coke and weed. Hundred keys, and two hundred pounds a month."

"Let me see what I can do."

It was all Kasper could say, since the diabolical wheel inside his head was spinning out of control. That kind of weight meant tens of thousands in profit. And since nobody knew Smokey was his connection, if Kasper could orchestrate a deal like that, he might be able to cut into the cocaine without Milz knowing. Tens of thousands would become hundreds of thousands.

The *knowing* part was critical because clientele, especially dangerous clientele, allowed you to put a middleman fee on the backend—$300 to $1,000 per kilo—but you couldn't tamper with the shipment. That was stealing, and stealing got you killed, regardless of your associations.

The following night, Smokey agreed to meet Kasper outside Mandalay Bay.

"That's a lot of weight. Who's it for?" Smokey asked.

Kasper paused. If he told Smokey, there was always the chance he'd cut him out of the deal by contacting Milz himself. "Why does it matter?"

Smokey shot back, "I got people. Wanna make sure you ain't stepping on their toes."

"Ever heard of a guy called, Money Milz."

Smokey nodded. "He's a King."

"Yeah."

"I'll talk to my people."

A week later, Smokey said his people will do a biweekly shipment of twenty-five kilos (at $17,000 apiece), and a hundred pounds of weed (at $300 apiece).

The deal came with two conditions. First, it was cash on delivery. No exceptions. Second, it was contractual, structured in three-month increments. Every ninety days, either party could cancel for any reason. But once agreed upon, Kasper, not Milz, handled six payments of $455,000 ($2,730,000). If at any point he failed to deliver, the shipment was canceled, and the contract voided. And for wasting their time, Kasper owed his people $500,000 in cash. Death was the consequence of failing to pay the $500,000.

Kasper told him he needed to talk with Milz. Smokey gave him a week. For Kasper, the payoff far outweighed the risk. As he saw it, the only real problem was the cash on delivery. To cut into the shipment, he'd need a sizable window before meeting up with Milz. Twenty-four hours. To get that window, he'd need to borrow $455,000. There was only one person with access to that kind of cash.

Kasper rented a suite at the Days Inn at Wild Wild West and invited Leo to a party with him and four strippers. The group raided the mini-bar and smoked an ounce of crack (Leo often preferred smoking to sniffing powder). As they took turns fucking the women, Kasper sprinkled in bits of the deal to Leo; specifically, Kasper's desire to cut into the kilos, the potential profit split, and the costs to make it happen.

After the girls stumbled out the door, he continued to discuss the details.

"How much we talk'n?" Leo asked.

"Four hundred sixty thousand in cash."

"No, how many keys?"

"Oh, twenty-five, every two weeks."

"If we cut one into five... with a good compressor... that's ten a month."

Cutting *one into five* meant they'd have to break open five kilos at a time, mix in a kilo of additive—a vitamin supplement—and then separate, compress, and repackage six weighed kilos.

"That's two-twenty with the fifty on top," Kasper said. "Hundred ten thousand apiece."

"You told Milz about the offer yet?"

"Wanted to talk to you first. Why?"

"Since he doesn't know, you can add them in."

"Didn't think of that," Kasper said, his eyes red and glossy.

After taking a long moment to consider the plan, Leo said, "It'll have to be a four-way split."

Kasper frowned. "Four-way split!?"

"My cousin Mickey'll cut them. He's done it before. And Frankie'll front the cash."

"That's fifty-five apiece. I make fifty without touching the shipment. I'm not going through a bunch of bullshit for an extra five grand. Tell you what, I'll pay them ten grand apiece, per shipment."

"He ain't risking half mill for ten grand. And without his money, you got nothing."

"Somebody'll lend it to me."

"Bullshit," Leo said, his tone unusually sober. "And even if they did for ten grand, you're not seeing the big picture."

Kasper chuckles. "Trust me, I've analyzed this shit from every angle."

"Ya think? Okay, then tell me—why did Smokey make it conditional?"

"He don't waste his time."

"No, he did it to keep you from cutting the shipment."

"You're reaching."

"You based the whole deal on Milz not meeting him. Right?"

"Yeah."

"Because if you put them together, who's to say the Kings don't cut you out?"

"They absolutely would."

"So let's say, by some fucking miracle, you find a jackass stupid enough to let you hold that kinda money every two weeks—'cause remember, you'll need it every two weeks—what happens if the Kings don't want the shipment?"

"Why wouldn't they want it?"

"Maybe Smokey does a bait and switch, sends you some weak shit. Maybe the Kings get spooked, think you're the feds. Who knows? Question is, what happens if they don't want the shipment?"

Kasper suddenly got his point. Without the $455,000 on hand every time, there was no deal. Because even if someone gave him the cash to make the deal, if the Kings backed out, Kasper was stuck holding twenty-five kilos and a hundred pounds.

Meanwhile, the same people—he had no such people—would want their money back, asap. And the only people he knew with that kind of money were not people who'd stand around waiting for you to sell a bunch of dope. They'd kill you and take the dope.

Leo was right. The front money didn't just buy him time to cut the shipment, it protected him. Bought him two weeks to get rid of an abandoned shipment. Something he'd have to do until he fulfilled the contract.

"I'd be fucked!" Kasper said, wide-eyed.

"You'd be dead. Mickey guarantees some dumbass doesn't fuck up the mix, and Frankie guarantees the Kings don't rob you." Two more angles Kasper had not considered. "His uncle's the goddamn boss. It's a win, win."

A win, win. At least until I learn Mickey's cutting process, save up my front money, and cut all three of you out.

When the first shipment arrived, Kasper watched as Mickey broke down five kilos, peppered in the additive, mixed the batch, weighed each new kilo, compressed, and repackaged. A process which was repeated four more times, taking fifteen hours.

The actual test came when Kasper delivered the shipment to Milz. Frankie attended the exchange as a symbolic warning. Kasper waited with a knot in his stomach while Milz cut open a kilo, scooped out a sample with a knife, and tested it. Milz paused, then shrugged as if to say 'good enough.' Not until the cash exchanged hands did Kasper relax.

DJ and Raul showed up with Milz on the second shipment.

"Why are you guys here?" Frankie asked.

"To let *you* know," DJ said, eyeing Kasper, "you'll be dealing with *me* from now on."

"What's the difference?" Frankie asked with a nonchalant shrug.

"Difference is, if you ever try anything stupid, it won't matter who your uncle is. We're coming for everything you love, including your women."

Frankie glared but stayed quiet. The gestured surprised Kasper. He believed Frankie had intended to look unimpressed, but he looked rattled, like the bully who got punched in the nose for the first time.

The two sides had conducted solid business ever since. The only issue to date was that, on three separate occasions, Smokey had asked Kasper to see if he could get the Kings to deal with a Vegas problem for him.

The first time he asked, Kasper told Smokey, "But the Kings don't know you're my supplier."

"And they still won't. Just ask 'em if they'll do it for *your connect*."

Kasper did.

DJ had considered the request for a moment. "Depends on the favor."

Kasper relayed DJ's answer to Smokey, who then handed him a sealed envelope. "Tell DJ we'll add two free kilos to the next shipment. And listen, homz, this ain't got nothing to do with you. Jus' give him the envelope. My people find out you opened it, you're dead."

It happened so fast, Kasper merely nodded and took the envelope. Fretting over its contents—*Phone number? Message to the Kings to call Smokey?*—he met with Leo before delivery.

"Smokey doesn't need no envelope to contact them," Leo said. "It's a contract. A hit."

"Get the fuck outta here!"

"Two keys are thirty-four grand. That ain't broken kneecap money. It's nigger hitman money."

When the next shipment went off without a hitch—and included two extra kilos, which, of course, Mickey cut—Kasper thought nothing of it. Down the road, he delivered two more envelopes.

However, three weeks ago, everything changed. Smokey presented Kasper with another Vegas situation. Only he didn't call it that. He called it what Leo called it—a contract; a hit: a man, his girlfriend, and their kid. Smokey would double the shipment as payment and drop the price per kilo by a thousand.

Before telling DJ, Kasper again discussed it with Leo.

"You gotta get 'em to do it," Leo said, responding to the news like a kid at Christmas.

"Are you crazy!? We're talking about a woman and her kid!"

"Stop being a pussy. If they double, we double."

Kasper presented the offer to DJ, who refused, said he and the Kings didn't kill children. Relieved, Kasper informed Smokey of his decision. Leo was disappointed.

Smokey called a week later. Meeting on the street outside the Aria, he told Kasper his people had agreed to only the man and woman. For that, they'd still double the shipment. Kasper presented the counteroffer to DJ, who seemed surprised there was a counteroffer at all. After conferring with several Kings, DJ said they'd do it... on one condition; he wanted to meet the supplier, face to face.

"Seriously doubt they'll agree to that," Kasper said.

"Makes no difference to me," DJ said. "But I'm heading out in a week, so if they're try'na move, you need to holla at me before then."

Kasper had lied and told DJ he'd forward the message to Smokey. Instead, he told Smokey the Kings had decided not to help.

*****

Kasper and Leo stepped into the luxurious suite, a comp from the regional manager into the Bonucci's for $300,000. The running debt allowed Frankie to live in the hotel for free. He could even change rooms every week.

Seated on the leather sectional, Frankie ate fried rice from a box of Chinese food and stared trance-like at one of the parlor's 60-inch TVs. Two ESPN announcers discussed the severity of a sports figure's injury. A Bud Light and black .357 snub-nose sat on the glass table in front of him.

At the couch's other end, a shapely, half-naked black woman in a blue wig and matching fishnets lay with her legs across the armrest. Cordless buds lodged in her ears; she bopped her head to music from the suite in-house streaming service.

Leo surveyed the woman. "Who's this?"

"One of Vinny's girls," Frankie said, eyes locked on the TV.

"Paid for?"

Frankie checked the clock above the TV. "You got twenty-one minutes."

"You take the front, and I take the back?" Leo asked Kasper.

"Sure."

"Hold up," Frankie told Kasper. "We gotta talk."

Leo shrugged, scooped a condom off the table, and nudged the woman. She looked up, took out an earbud. He motioned toward the bedroom. "Let's go."

She turned to Frankie. "I thought we done."

"Get your ass in there."

She slid off the couch and followed Leo into the bedroom.

"What's up?" Kasper asked.

"Fucking Kershaw," Frankie said. "Piece of shit lost me five grand last night." He placed the food on the table and guzzled the beer. "That my money?"

"Yeah."

"Drop it on the bar."

Kasper moved to the bar and set the shopping bag on the counter. He then stepped behind it, opened a bottle of whiskey, and poured a drink.

In the year since the deal began, Kasper learned Frankie was nothing more than a spoiled man-child. A heavy gambler, his lifestyle mirrored Kasper's and Leo's: money, drugs, and women.

Kasper downed the drink. "Where's Mickey?"

"Running errands," Frankie said, as the sound of grunts and feigned female moans emanated from the cracked bedroom door. He motioned for Kasper to come over and sit in the recliner across from him.

Kasper poured another drink and took a seat. "What's up?"

"Leo told me about the second visit." Frankie wiped his mouth with a napkin. "What'cha thinking?"

"I'm not doing it. Too many things can happen."

"Like what?"

"For starters, DJ doesn't know Smokey's my supplier. And even though Smokey could've contacted him already, he hasn't. Ain't no need to tempt fate. And then I was thinking, what if DJ started asking questions? Like the times and dates of the last few shipments. Smokey ain't got no reason to lie."

"Nigger would know you sat on his product. Smart." Frankie leaned forward. "There's been some changes."

"Changes?"

"Yeah, Leo and Mickey are out. Mickey'll still cut the dope, but their money comes here from now on."

"Leo ain't say nothing about this."

"That's 'cause he don't know yet."

"If they're out, my end's half."

"That's not happening."

"Why not?"

"Because it's not."

"Then I'm done when the ninety days are up."

Frankie smiled, not in humor, but in growing contempt. "You know, I've been risking my ass helping you? Dealing drugs is against my family's code."

"You're not the only one risking your ass. I'm a dead man if the King's find out what I've been doing. All I'm saying is, if Leo and Mickey are out, we need to split their end, fifty-fifty." Kasper straightened his posture. "Otherwise, I'm done."

"Figga'd you might say some shit like that." Frankie slid his hand beneath the couch and moved to his feet. As he walked over to Kasper, he pressed the silencer-tipped nine-millimeter against his side like a set of car keys. "Listen, you little spic, once I gave you the money to get your scam going, it became *my* deal."

"You got your money back the second I collected. And you've made over six hundred thousand since. I don't owe you anything."

Frankie pointed the barrel at his face. "Don't make me kill you and this whore."

Kasper straightened his posture, remained quiet.

"Okay, tough guy." Frankie cocked the hammer.

Kasper withered like a dying flower. "It's not fair, and you know it."

"Yeah, well, life's not fair, pal." Frankie returned the gun to his side.

Chapter 21

"Monsta"

From the control center inside Mother's palace, the middle-aged Egyptian spooled the transmission across multiple satellites. Convinced the finest hackers in the world could not untangle his work, he spoke into the earpiece. "Monsta?"

"Let's go," Monsta said from his Mexico mansion.

"Mother, you're connected," the Egyptian spoke into the intercom.

Seated inside the colossal living room, Mother gestured for the assistant, Hector Pinero's, to remain standing.

"Monsta," she said.

"How you feeling?" Monsta asked, his voice echoing from the overhead speaker like a godly encounter.

"I shall live another hundred years."

"If anybody could."

"You were right my son; we have reached the Baptism. I've sent her to you."

"A'ight. Got my end in place."

"You should know, justice has risen from her soul like a great wave."

"Yeah, but she gonna learn it ain't that simple."

"Remember, Monsta, the woman was merely the catalyst."

"Got no problem with where Isha's going. But she's self-righteous. I'm about to burn that shit out of her."

"I expect nothing less." Mother folded hands in her lap. "Charles Wallace killed his father and the Royal Skull."

"When?"

"Four hours ago."

"And the seat?"

"I suppose he'll plead his case to the Supreme One."

"Doesn't matter," Monsta said. "Olivia's their only chance at survival, and they know it."

"Illuminati's first female Crown. I must admit, she has always been quite ambitious."

"If by ambitious you mean crazy."

"Perhaps you two will finally become one flesh."

"Think of what we could accomplish if I put a baby in her."

"I believe the Bible calls it, Antichrist."

"Look at you." Monsta chuckles. It was as close to a sense of humor as anyone could expect from Mother.

"When will you know if she's the one?" Mother asked.

"Soon."

"My children, Monsta. Though their eyes are opened, they cannot see. And now a fool has been set in place."

"A pawn. He's there to distract the Blind from the true agenda."

"Class reconstruction?"

"They've done it socially. My guess is they'll look to implement some very intricate substrata. Maybe even something catastrophic." Monsta paused. "After I'm done with him, everything will speed up."

"Very well, my son. Keep me informed."

"I will."

The line went dead.

Mother stood and moved into the palace foyer as Hector followed close behind.

"I want to know the instant Charles Wallace is dead," she said.

"Will they not even hear him out?"

"Curator of Death has the last word."

"Olivia? With all due respect, my queen, you think they'll consider her?"

"As Monsta rightly noted, they have no other choice. Once Isha speaks, the world will transform. More than it already has. Olivia alone can adapt."

"Received word she has left New York."

"The candidate?"

"It appears she's put an end to his antics."

"Illuminati does not end such things, they assimilate them."

"Of course. Shall I inform the Supreme One on how best to resolve the issue?"

Mother chuckled. "You wish to instruct Malcolm Rothschild?"

"Forgive me, my queen. I meant at your behest."

"Do not assume to know what I desire. Malcolm Rothschild will assign the candidate to matters of neutrality. If not, the candidate will die." Mother stopped in front of an eight-foot onyx statue of a Sphinx. She turned to Hector, acknowledged his apprehension with a nod. "You have concerns?"

"Olivia is extremely dangerous. She does not fear Dragón."

"She fears losing his affection."

"Forgive me, my queen, but I do not understand."

Mother continued toward the elevator. "Like Dragón, Olivia lost her mother as a child. Their similar journeys and fierce appetites have forged a unique relationship. They govern their kingdoms like children playing together in the Paris catacombs."

"But not for Armageddon, she would certainly kill him."

"Olivia loves Monsta. And I suspect, in some strange way, he loves her. Yet her love comes from the belief that he *is* darkness." The elevator door opened, made so by the technician following her every move. She entered and gazed upon the camera above her head, motioning for the technician to wait for her command. Hector remained outside. "And as long as the dragon lives, she knows she will never be alone in the truth that she too... is darkness."

Mother rolled an aged finger, and the elevator doors closed.

*****

Hector stood there, a slave to weakness. The concern he had was instinctive, but completely unnecessary. No one hindered Monsta, because to do so would ignite the fullest extent of Mother's wrath. As with the case of Charles Wren.

A member of the Law Society (and one of England's most distinguished judges), Wren was a pompous man. Believing himself above reproach, he did not hesitate to grant MI6 consent to search the London cottage of thirty-two-year-old gallery owner, Allison Crawley. A senior official investigating Crawley for ties to organized crime had determined proof might be found on her home computer.

Not part of England's elite, Wren hadn't known Monsta, nor the fact Crawley was his most beloved European diamond (a term he used for his countless women). Consequently, days before Wren signed the warrant, an older female judge warned him to avoid the Crawley case at all costs. Wren stubbornly enquired as to the reason. She told him the answer lay far beyond her paygrade. He thought the explanation unsatisfactory for a man of his stature—coming from a woman, no less—and authorized the search.

MI6 found nothing.

A week later, the box arrived on the castle doorsteps of Sir Richard Dodd, the Illuminati Crown of the United Kingdom of Great Britain. Dodd's great-granddaughter had noticed the box while playing with cousins. She alerted the nearest chambermaid and continued with her afternoon.

Upon hearing the knock on the study door, Dodd granted his chief guard permission to enter. The man presented the box to Dodd and informed his master that the chambermaid inadvertently examined its contents. She had believed the box contained costly spices on order from India. She was presently being attended to by the in-house physician.

Dodd waved for the chief guard to leave. He then opened the box and removed the letter from the glass jar. He unfolded the associated piece of paper, read the two words: chaos, order. It referenced the Illuminati maxim, "Out of chaos, we maintain order."

Days earlier, the Supreme Crown had informed Dodd of the situation. Wren's lovely wife, Aurora, had torn her ACL during a tennis match with friends. They rushed her to the hospital, her surgery scheduled for the following morning. While under anesthesia, several armed assailants entered the operating room and killed the surgeon and his two assistants.

Dodd raised the jar eye level. With a glint of admiration, he examined the ocean blue eyes of Aurora Wren. Mother had once again made the point regarding her beloved war-child, Monsta. No one was safe from retribution.

The jar's delivery was not an act of war or even one of insolence. It was merely a gentle request for Dodd to do her the small courtesy of contending with the Blind inside *his* kingdom.

That night, Charles Wren put a shotgun to his head and pulled the trigger. But not before he used the butt of the rifle to break apart his wife's once beautiful face. The suicide letter stated he'd done so out of guilt for being the person responsible for her initial disfigurement—the jealous byproduct of an alleged affair.

*****

Monsta rested on the living room sofa, his bare feet atop the silk ottoman. "You're spoiled, and you think you know every goddamn thing."

Isha looked back at him from the sixty-inch Sony on the wall. "I don't understand why she's so angry. It was a simple request."

Monsta turned his attention to the balcony's glass doors. The storm continued to rage as another bolt of lightning cut across the dark like cracks in a windshield. The ensuing thunder knocked heavily upon the suite's walls. "Ain't nothing simple with you. Been at my hip since day one, and all I ever dropped on you was jewels. You were supposed to see this shit a million miles away."

"See what?"

"Her grandmother played you."

Isha raised a calming hand. "Don't get mad, but as you well know, it's difficult for me to follow your American slang. Are you implying she used Corina to do her bidding?"

"Everybody knows you're a fucking crusader. Grandmother ain't stupid. She prepped her. Got her to pull at your little heartstrings.

And just so you know, her pop's trafficked the same drugs got him killed. And her mother lived like a queen off that shit."

"Mother informed me of their past. Though I admit, I did not consider the grandmother's hand in this, it doesn't negate the fact her father's dead. And they forced her mother into slavery. A daughter needs her mother."

"A daughter needs her mother! That's your fucking answer? You ain't been paying attention. World is filled with mothers sold into slavery. Bitches taking dick all day long because some grimy ass nigga draped them off. To change that, you gotta judge the world."

"You're extremely grouchy this morning. And you said there would be a time when my words mattered."

"I also said they would come at a price."

"Which I'm ready to pay."

Monsta grinned. "Then answer this, you hardheaded little shit. Is sex trafficking evil?"

"Of course it is."

"I need you to say it."

"Very well. Sex trafficking is evil."

"Then let the games begin."

"You'll do it? You'll save Corina's mo—"

Monsta hit the remote. Jennifer Garner replaced Isha. The actress stood inside a library, whispering something about the benefits of owning a Capital One card. The commercial ended with her catchphrase, "What's in your wallet."

Monsta tossed the phone onto the cushion and gazed up at the skylight as another wave of lightning jetted across the sky. The trailing thunder had less of a punch this time. He got up, entered the bedroom, and stood at the foot of the bed, admiring his two sleeping diamonds. Every man's fantasy, he was determined to bed such women until the day he died.

Monsta provided the women within his global harem the absolute best that life offered: living quarters inside his mansions, expensive clothes, jewelry, access to any car they wanted, and a sizable allowance. Money that many of them used to care for destitute family members. All he required in return were their souls.

Stepping onto the balcony, he surveyed the massive storm. Before Isha's call, he'd been awake channel surfing. The meteorologist—who in this region of the world was almost always a dark-haired Latina in a tight blouse, short skirt, and stripper heels— showed the storm pushing west. She'd been right. Stretched out along the Pacific, the storm appeared bigger and far more menacing than described on the news. The endless void of darkness carried an air of pending doom.

Monsta took a deep breath and calmly reflected on the people he had killed in the last forty-eight hours, and on those he planned to kill in the next forty-eight. For the man known by many names, death was nothing more than a symphonic tragedy conducted by the greatest maestro of all—God. And He alone understood what Monsta was, for as the Bible stated without apology, "I form the light, and create darkness: I make peace, and create evil: I the Lord do all these things."

It also stated, "The Lord has made everything for its own purpose, Even the wicked for the day of evil." And Monsta's purpose was the Godly annihilation of evil souls. A purpose he took immense pleasure in. Yet the orchestration of such things was not as easy as most people thought. Certainly not with annihilation. When did the hyena ever seek out the lion? Present itself as atonement for the murder of a young gazelle? Never. Judgment came from the executioner alone—was part of his DNA. And within that DNA,

God had programmed the thirst for blood... the desire and instinct to hunt... chase, and finally, the frenzied euphoria that came from tearing through living flesh, even as the prey screamed in agony.

Monsta considered the distant storm. It also had a purpose, representing the wave of doom headed toward the Illuminati. And though he had crafted that doom through veiled circumstances, Monsta was disappointed Isha had failed to see the trap. Throughout her young life, he repeatedly instructed her on the urgency of reflection. On going back and routing the course a situation had taken before entering her life. He warned her it was the only way to uncover the strings of deception.

Until Corina, Isha had done well in heeding that advice. A servant for less than a year, palace gossip had allowed Corina's grandmother to learn of Mother's power, and the future importance of Princess Isha Ra. Seeing the opportunity to rescue her daughter, the fifty-six-year-old carefully positioned her granddaughter.

What she didn't know was that Monsta had positioned her.

Prior to arriving in Egypt, she had worked for Tiodoso Perez, a political advisor for Monsta on the El Paso, Juarez border. One day, while visiting Perez, Corina's beauty struck Monsta. Perez had given her the part-time job of cleaning the pool. Ever in search of diamonds, Monsta inquired as to her age and association. Learning her story, he offered the grandmother an opportunity to work as a live-in housekeeper at his Cabo San Lucas mansion. A year removed from her daughter's kidnapping, she and Corina lived alone in a weather-beaten adobe shack.

Monsta promised them spacious living quarters and access to an abundance of resources, including a tutor for homeschooling Corina. The grandmother happily accepted.

Two months later, Monsta arranged for Isha to visit. As hoped, once he made introductions, the friendship was immediate. While educating Corina on the world outside her small breath of reality, Isha told her about the many palaces she lived in: France, Germany, Italy, Russia, Scotland, and Africa (her favorite). Corina listened in awe, stating how amazing it would be to one day see such places.

Scheduled for only a week, Isha's visit lasted over two before Mother ordered her prompt return. Of course, being the princess with the heart of gold—and who got everything she wanted, even a pet lion named Zulu—Isha suggested that her new friend returned with her to Egypt.

Corina thanked her but said she could never leave her grandmother's side.

Not to worry, Isha would take them both, adding her grandmother to the palace staff.

Mother balked at the idea. They vigorously vetted her servants; many had come from families with a long history of servitude to the Queen of Suma'at. But like the request to save Corina's mother, Isha had insisted... and insisted... and...

It took five months for the grandmother to understand her good fortune, and the boundaries from which to operate. The grandmother's later manipulation of Corina was but another step toward Baptism for Mother, an event that prophecy said the child had to request.

And Isha had just done that.

However, unbeknownst to Isha, her judgment—and any judgment made thereafter—was not of individuals, but of *the imbalance their specific evil caused* throughout mankind. Therefore, in her quest to save *one* soul, Isha had unknowingly sealed the fate of *all* sex traffickers on earth.

Like the course of experimental medicine, the extreme side effects of *her judgments* within human reasoning, i.e., once the bodies started piling up, was anyone's guess. Monsta was certain of one thing, though. Her *judgments* would eventually lead to war—not between countries, but social classes. The rich versus everyone else.

When the Illuminati created the substratum known as MK13 (social media), its architects realized that for the substratum to be truly effective, the Blind needed unrestricted global interaction. Despite the concerns of some—men and women who wished for further analysis; especially as it related to the sharing of economic, political, and religious belief—the potential benefits of MK13 were too great to halt.

Two years after its implementation, those concerns proved justified when the Blind, having achieved a universal voice, threatened to bring forth the Illuminati's greatest fear—a global revolution. In the years that followed, the Illuminati countered with a substratum (AAI9, or algorithmic artificial intelligence) that allowed them to categorize, monitor, and easily control the power behind MK13.

Today, the Illuminati believed themselves more powerful than ever.

Mother believed them more vulnerable.

The Baptism of Blood would determine who was right.

Chapter 22

"The Thumb-Drive"

Noss inserted the thumb-drive, waited. Seconds later, the file appeared on the screensaver of his grandson, Evan. The three-year-old kicked a soccer ball through a miniature goal. The picture was Noss's favorite, taken last year during a trip to Blue Diamond.

Noss checked the Mickey Mouse clock in the monitor's upper right corner. 9:33 p.m. Reminiscent of the wristwatch his mother bought him as a kid, he downloaded the clock from a website specializing in throwback imagery. He thought the clock befitting Evan's love of everything Disney.

"Can't believe this shit," DJ said, tapping a bottled water against his knee. "Ain't nobody even supposed to know about you."

"The fact they do is quite alarming," Noss said.

The package had arrived yesterday morning, hand-delivered to Alissa by a young Mexican minutes after opening. Addressed to Noss personally, it held no return address. Alissa brought it to him as he sat in the office reviewing code.

"A kid?" Noss had asked.

"Yes," Alissa said. "Looked ten or eleven."

"And he didn't say what it was for?"

"No. Just to make sure I gave it to you right away."

"Okay."

When she left, Noss cut open the package and removed the ball of bubble wrap. He peeled away the layers, discovered the Bic lighter, and examined the tiny sticker running down the lighter's side. *Password: Jack Johnson.*

Noss flicked the lighter, briefly igniting the one-inch flame. He let go of the button and held it eye level. Locating the slit, he pulled the lighter apart, tearing the sticker in the middle and revealing the thumb-drive. He scanned the files, hoping to learn who sent it. As DJ said, only the Abregon's and King leadership knew about Noss's *special* relationship with them.

The shock of what he discovered, folder after folder, led to a day of meticulous examination.

An afternoon of deep reflection, and, knowing DJ had returned from his vacation with Angel, he called and ask him to come by after closing.

Upon DJ's arrival, Noss directed him to the most secure room in the building, a smaller office inside the server room. He then spent the last half hour explaining the circumstances of the thumb-drive's delivery, while summarizing its contents.

"It has to be the shit with Kasper," DJ said.

DJ referred to their drug middleman. A year ago, Kasper had brokered a biweekly shipment between the Kings and an unknown associate of Kasper, who DJ called *the connect.* Since then, with Kasper acting as the go-between, the Kings had handled several Vegas *problems* for the connect; specifically, three contract killings.

Two men, one woman. Snitches. Alleged snitches. Noss had overseen all three.

"What makes you say that?"

DJ explains Kasper had stopped at Club Xstasy three weeks back and presented another *Vegas problem* on behalf of the connection. Only they wanted an entire family killed, which included a kid. DJ had declined the offer, letting Kasper know outright the Kings did not kill children. Kasper said he understood and left the club.

"Makes sense now," Noss said. "But an entire family?"

"After I told him no, I figga'd that was the end. But he showed up again right before me and Angel left for Morocco. Said they were cool with only the guy and his wife. Told him we'd do it if I met the connect, one on one. Ain't heard from him since."

"I thought part of the deal with Kasper was you never got to meet his supplier?"

"Right." DJ gulped the water. "Angel got us right. It's time to live."

"You were betting he wouldn't relay the message?" Noss seemed genuinely surprised. Walking away from the monthly deal meant DJ was serious about going legit. A thing he had been alluding to for weeks.

"Yeah."

"Getting out is the right move." Noss turned to the monitor. "Unfortunately, that might not be possible right now."

Noss dimmed the office light with a remote and clicked on the projector. The screensaver of Evan filled a fifty-five-inch section of the wall. The two men eyed the thumb-drive's folder: NEVADA. For Noss, the word itself implied bigness, as though the file belonged to a family of fifty states.

"Unlike the other three *problems*," Noss said, "this is far more than a simple hit."

He tapped the folder, and a password box appeared. He typed in DJ's full name and three new folders materialized.

ROBERTSON

ASSOCIATED

MISCELLANEOUS

"My biggest concern at the moment is the type of information," Noss said. "I've only seen this kind of detail in a government kill list."

"Kill list?"

"In two-thousand-six, I worked a yearlong contract overseeing government black-ops. Correspondence between U.S. military commanders and special forces stationed off the grid. Jason Bourne type soldiers. A month in, our daily transmissions included a list of names—hundreds of individuals scattered abroad. They linked each to a separate NSA database containing the same information as the thumb-drive: pictures, videos, and countless records: banking, real estate, and business.

"Some names I recognized from previous transmissions; known terrorists—individuals wanted for various crimes against the United States. But others were ordinary citizens, men and women involved in U.S. global interests. The names were listed in alphabetical order and had a correlating number beside it: one-eighteen. All except the first name, which had the number six-sixty-six. It was the only name *not* in alphabetical order, and it changed almost daily. And when it did, it disappeared from the list altogether.

"At first, I thought nothing of the ordinary citizens. Could be informants, planted moles, or just people under surveillance. Then one day I locked onto the first name—which had changed four times in six days. My curious nature got the better of me, so I went back to the first name and dug deeper."

"I thought they disappeared?"

"Photographic memory." Noss shifted in the seat. "I learned he was a German banker, murdered outside a Berlin nightclub the day *after* his name appeared. German news outlets reported it as a botched robbery. I did the second name. A Liberian businesswoman."

"Murdered?"

"Died of a massive heart attack a day after her name appeared. I quickly discovered—"

"Six-sixty-six was like a green light or something?"

"Not or something. It was a kill list. Targets in stasis. Number changes, and the assassination was made to look like an everyday occurrence."

Noss clicked the ROBERTSON folder. A group of files appeared. He opened the first, and a row of thumbnails ran down the screen. He clicked the first thumbnail. The picture of a black male filled the left side of the wall.

"This is the target Kasper's people want hit," Noss said. "Name's William Robertson. He's a former Arizona prison guard. Worked both sides of the fence for La eMe—the Mexican Mafia."

"This' Montoya's people? Thought the New Mexican Mafia ran Arizona."

"Sorry, it is the New eMe. A month ago, Robertson robbed two Aryans at gunpoint. Stole two-hundred-thirty-eight thousand in cash. By the time the New eMe got to his house, he had skipped town with the money, and the fourteen kilos they'd given him to make the deal. Resigned the next day over the phone. Left a White Hills, Arizona, P.O. Box as a forwarding address."

"Sloppy."

"Very." Noss clicked another thumbnail, replaced Robertson with the picture of a house. "Searchlight. Robertson lives there with his girlfriend and newborn son; under the alias, Gary Thompson."

"They wanted us to kill a baby?"

"Or to see how far you'd be willing to go. File has everything related to Robertson. The next file concerns me most. Deals with how we got here. Worthless information unless you're trying to send a message."

"Message?"

"These associates of Kasper are watching, even when a guy is doing good business."

"What about the *Miscellaneous* file?"

"I'll get to that in a moment." Noss replaced the house with a picture of a white male. "Bryan Carson. Long story short, he was also a prison guard. Worked six years for the New eMe. Made about two million, which he laundered through a Zales jewelry store in his wife's name. Quit a year ago. Handed the entire operation to Robertson. He'd been grooming him to take over."

Noss replaced Carson's picture with the picture of a woman in a silver cocktail dress. Attractive, she posed outside a storefront. "Natalie Carson," he said. "The picture's from their grand opening eight months ago."

He returned to the initial series of files and opened a new one. A row of video thumbnails emerged. He clicked the first. Four video screens opened simultaneously. He advanced the first video, the other three moving in unison, and clicked play.

On screen one, the sound of heavy machinery churned as a completely naked woman lay spread eagle, face down on a soiled mattress. Her wrists and ankles were tied to rope sewn through the mattress edging. She screamed as a white male, pants down to his ankles, thrust violently into her.

The code reader in the lower left-hand corner displayed the time and date: 09/01/2021, 07:52:23... 24... 25... 26....

"The wife?" DJ asked.

"And the Aryans. He's number eight or nine. Video's six hours long. As you can see, it's roughly about the time Kasper returned to the club with the counteroffer. Which makes this a very powerful message."

"What'chu mean?"

"They're saying, 'our organization, our business, has many arms that never cease movement. Even as you decide whether to help us.'"

Screen two showed a wider shot of the warehouse. A Mexican and a dozen tattooed Aryans stood beside the mattress as the man continued his assault.

Screen three held a black van, POLICÍA embossed in white letters on its side.

Screen four held a fifty-gallon drum with an industrial mixer fastened to its lid. A pile of opened boxes lay feet away, empty white jugs stacked beside them like bowling pins. Another drum and a pile of unopened boxes sat to the right.

Noss picked up a red laser, pointed to the drum. "Bryan Carson."

"Pozole," DJ said. "Like the Mexican soup. It's how they dispose of bodies in Mexico. Liquifies them in a couple days. Everything but the teeth."

"They've been reported missing, but there's a ton of confusion."

Noss tapped an audio file. A female voice said, "I could have closed on the second location an hour ago, but he never showed up with the paperwork."

"Did you call him?" A different female asked.

"Of course, I did. His stupid phone keeps going to voicemail."

"He's probably out drinking. You need to leave him for good this time."

"Not until I'm done. Anyway, I'm home."

"There was marital strife," Noss said turning off the audio file. "It will lead investigators down a rabbit hole. Phone records place the call at six-fifteen p.m., the day before."

He clicked another thumbnail. Two videos ran simultaneously. It was the inside of Bryan Carson's bedroom. The first showed Carson in a chair next to the bed, bound and gagged. The second was from the ceiling; it showed a different man raping his wife atop the bed.

"Bryan Carson couldn't answer his wife because this guy had sedated him." Noss pointed to the man raping Carson's wife. He was white, medium height, with grey hair. "Used a paralyzing agent on both. Caused them to remain fully cognizant. Surprised her coming in from the garage." Noss shook his head. "He's a real sick bastard. Talks to them the entire time. Moves like former military, so I'm guessing he's a mercenary. Once he's done, he turns her head toward Carson. Makes her watch as he suffocates him. They're then taken from the house and a second group comes in. They strip the bed sheets, wipe everything clean. Remove the cameras last."

"If all they want is for us to hit him, why send this shit?"

"Because they know I'll understand everything they're trying to say." Noss placed hands on the desk, interlocked fingers. "Carson and his wife are dead because he chose Robertson as his replacement. Which says a great deal about how these people do business. The additional information is there to show…"

"They got a file on us," DJ said. "That's why Kasper never got back to me. Why they came straight to you."

"Yes. And whoever *they* are, they're incredibly powerful."

"Don't make no sense. You did the research. Kasper's a trick. Other than fucking with the Bonucci's, he's nobody. Wait—you think this is from them?"

"Digital fingerprint says they're bigger than La Cosa Nostra. Much bigger."

"Digital fingerprint?"

"There's aerial footage from outside the house. At first, I thought it was a highly sophisticated drone. But then it showed certain capabilities. Particularly with magnification. I assumed it a government drone, but something told me to check the digital fingerprint just in case." Noss turned to DJ. "There's only a handful of people in the world who'd know where to look, and they all work for governments: Russia, China, here." Noss took the deepest breath yet. "Turns out I was wrong."

"About?"

"It being a government drone. It's satellites. Multiple satellites. Some are government, but most are from global corporations: Verizon, SpaceX. That led me to recheck all the in-house videos. I assumed cameras had been secretly placed while the Carson's were out. I was right about all but two. They came from their televisions."

"TVs?"

Noss nodded. "The reason we're in this room is that it has every technological safeguard known to man."

"You say'n this is some... what's that white-boy's name?"

"Edward Snowden. And yes, it is."

All at once, the severity hit DJ like an overhand right. "What the fuck do I do?"

"Handle the contract and then sever all ties with Kasper."

"I can't refuse it?"

"No. And there's a message at the end of the video. You're not to do the hit until I'm contacted."

"By who?"

"I have no clue."

"A'ight, let me know." DJ checked his watch.

"One last thing." Noss tapped open the MISCELLANEOUS file. It was a single Jpeg. "I have to warn you, it's quite personal." He clicked on the photo.

DJ studied the picture for a long moment. "Satellite?"

"Yes."

DJ remembered the moment well. It happened on the morning of their second day. Naked, he was seated on an outdoor sectional on the yacht's open deck as Angel rode him.

Chapter 23

"Psychopaths"

DJ drove steadily down I-95 South, oblivious to the growing traffic.

"One more thing." Noss's voice boomed from the truck's speakers. "Don't assume he knows everything."

"What'chu mean?"

"Remember the other situation, the second group were professional cleaners. My guess is everyone's on a different page."

"What's my move?"

"Let him do all the talking."

"A'ight."

DJ hung up the phone and checked the dashboard clock. 7:41 a.m. Noss had received the call at 7:12 a.m. Kasper's people wanted DJ to meet their guy outside Club Xstasy at 8:00 a.m. Sharp.

Although rushed out of bed, DJ had been mentally ready since last night. After leaving Gen-Tech, he had a feeling the shit would go down without a heads up, which was okay by him. The sooner he killed Robertson, the sooner he could let Kasper and his people know the Kings were done.

Problem was that the person who called Noss said the guy DJ was supposed to meet was the same scumbag who raped Carson's wife before killing him. Noss said they'd actually described him that way—the scumbag. Helping a piece of shit like that was the last thing DJ wanted to do, but satellites, wiretaps, and cameras inside televisions were the craziest shit he'd ever heard.

More than that, the picture on the yacht proved they had used the same surveillance on him, meaning their reservoir of knowledge was unimaginable. If DJ pulled a Tony Montana and killed the guy he was supposed to help, Kasper's people might retaliate against Angel, Carlos, or whoever.

*****

Monsta emerged from the platoon of warriors; the sheathed machete set against his shoulder like a baseball bat. Sleeveless black hoody, he watched as Isha exited the military helicopter. The weapons stocked vessel differed from those of Mother's fleet—Monsta preferred the Lockheed Martin Sikorsky UH-60 Black Hawk—and had greeted Isha's royal jet upon its arrival.

"You ready?" he asked.

Clothed in fatigues, Isha considered the line of armored SUVs and Mexica warriors. "Absolutely."

Monsta extended the machete. "Hang onto this for me."

Isha knew she needed to make things right. She had disrespected the Queen of Suma'at, ordered her around like a common servant. Anyone else would have died where they stood. Reconciliation begins in obedience. She grabbed the machete. It was surprisingly lightweight.

Monsta nodded at a female warrior. She opened the center vehicle's rear door. Isha stepped inside and took a seat. Monsta sat across from her. When he pulled out a phone, Isha got the message loud and clear—there was nothing left to talk about.

As the motorcade drove off, Isha reviewed her line of attack. Behavioral Science class taught her the bizarre condition of a psychopath was his or her inability to feel for others. The cerebral substance (conscience) needed for empathy was missing, and the primary reason they could harm people without remorse. Its lesser manifestation of sociopath quantified that although the substance was present, it was weak, and so they still committed the harm.

She knew Mother and Monsta were psychopaths.

Based on the many commentaries regarding the subjects, Isha determined that countless world leaders, seen and unseen, were one of the two. How else could a ruler sleep at night, knowing their people suffered at the hands of evil men? She also determined the mental condition had, more often than not, played a key role in their rise to power.

Isha believed the mental defect a cerebrally transmitted disease; a virus that infected the mind the way COVID-19 infected the lungs. Analogous to the Sin Nature, it drastically altered a person's ability to love anything or anyone outside their perceived reality. It was in that stream of consciousness whereby Isha concluded world leaders were not the only sociopaths. Illuminati schemata had injected the virus into the minds of millions by successfully joining the substratum MK 13 (social media) to well-established film, television, and gaming substrata, forming the most powerful brainwashing mechanism ever known.

Instagram, Snapchat, Twitter, Facebook, Reality TV, and every other medium announced in one sociopathic voice, "Look at me... love me... worship me." They ignored suffering in the world unless it provided a photo opportunity. Then it was, "Look at me march in protest; listen to me talk about injustice; watch me raise money for the solution."

Where was true selflessness? Rightly did Yeshua speak. "Let not the right hand know what the left does." And "When you do a good thing, do not tell the world, for then you shall receive your reward."

Presently, you had psychopaths and sociopaths (world leaders) governing and farming psychopaths and sociopaths (Blind).

Despite this, Isha also believed MK 13 could inject the cure, i.e., the truth of God. And she was determined to one day do that on a global level. For now, she needed to focus on the task at hand—getting Monsta to acknowledge Corina as a person. Or at the very least, get him to understand she saw her as a person; therefore, he should allow her the opportunity to rescue Corina's mother.

*****

DJ bolted from the truck and headed toward the club.

"Jack!" the male voice said in Spanish.

DJ turned.

The man stood in front of a Ford Explorer.

"Who's asking?" DJ replied in English. Though he hadn't seen his face in the video, he could tell it was the scumbag.

"I'm supposed to be meeting a big Spanish speaking black guy named Jack," he said in English. "You're a big black guy who understands Spanish, so I'll take it you're him. Name's Butch. Hop in."

DJ slid into the Explorer's front seat next to Butch. "Where're we going?"

"To pick up the merchandise." He eyed DJ curiously. "You know about the merchandise?"

"Not the terminology I'd use."

He shrugged. "Right. We usually work alone. Don't even know why I'm picking you up, but orders are orders."

Not to mention, they come from bosses, DJ thought. *The question is, who's yours?*

Butch stared hazily through the windshield as he exited the parking lot. He rested a wide palm against the steering wheel, the other against his red wrinkled face, elbow flat upon the windowsill. Thin grey eyebrows clung to a weathered mug that, on closer inspection, had spent far too many years in the sun.

Butch's calm demeanor reminded DJ how easily it was for crazy to hide among the population. Noss had once told him, statistically, five hundred active serial killers were wandering the country at any given time. They looked normal, acted normal, all as they hid in plain sight, sharing a smile, nod, or passing glance with potential victims. Even in prison, the guy's DJ knew with multiple kills, bodies buried, mutilated, acted like regular people. They watched soaps, gambled on sports, and even read the Bible.

Butch sparked a Camel, pulled onto I-15. "Done a lot of these?"

"I don't know what these are."

"Kidnap... murder. It's my specialty. Though I'm not as gruesome as you guys."

"You guys?"

"Yeah, the whole cutting off their heads thing."

Does he think I'm part of a cartel? DJ quickly reassessed the situation. Noss was right—the guy's either clueless as to who I am, or he's trying to rock me to sleep.

"Government called them Personnel Extractions," Butch continued. "Guess they thought it sounded more civilized. Got a hundred fifty under my belt. Iraq, Pakistan, Ukraine. Even gave me a few medals." He laughed scratchily. "Pay was slightly above average... but the extras—" he made a thrusting motion with his right arm and waist, "more than made up for it, if you know what I mean."

Know exactly what'chu mean, you maggot mother fucker.

*****

From her window, Isha watched as the caravan moved alongside a line of black SUVs, parked in what looked to be five rows of eight to ten. Twenty yards beyond the last SUV, they came upon a massive circle of armed Mexica warriors.

The caravan stopped outside the circle. Monsta opened the door and placed a foot on the ground. "Don't forget the blade."

Machete in hand, Isha got out and took position behind him. Monsta stepped between two warriors and entered the circle. He calmly walked to the center as Isha followed close behind. They came upon two Border Patrol vans, parked side by side, engines running. Six warriors stood at measured intervals around the vehicles. From that position, Isha thought the circle resembled an artificial arena.

A warrior opened the rear door of the first van. Isha saw a woman sitting on a wooden bench. With the warrior's help, she climbed out the van. Filthy, her matted hair twisted in every direction. She wore a nurse's uniform. No, a nurse's costume, the sexualized kind, meant to arouse. She had been crying, her mascara smeared face giving her the appearance of a raccoon.

Corina's mother?

Isha chastised herself for not expecting this. The warrior opened the rear door of the second van. At once, Isha felt sick. Piled atop one another like throw rugs, five men lay with their mouths duct-taped, ankles hogtied to wrists with interlocking cuffs. The chain on each cuff was fixed separately to a center ring, like a spider web.

Warriors took hold of the chains and pulled the men out of the van. The men groaned as the cuffs cut into their ankles and wrists. The warriors dragged the men across the desert floor and set them at Isha's feet. All five showed signs of abuse.

The torrid heat blurred the landscape as a slight wind blew dust into Isha's eyes. The knot in her stomach tightened like a noose, threatening to spew the orange juice and banana nut muffin she'd eaten for breakfast.

"Stay there," Monsta said, walking toward the woman.

Isha reminded herself of the promise made to Corina. On mental paper, the promise appeared simple, even if she had to endure the warped machinations of Mother and Monsta; derived, of course, from their distorted belief that evil men must die. Men like Pharaoh, Goliath, Sennacherib.

Isha took a controlled breath and considered how Suma'atan prophecy had delivered her to this moment in time—determined her the judgment upon the world of evil men. Before she could ponder further, a Mexica lieutenant handed Monsta a double-barrel shotgun.

Monsta placed the shotgun to the woman's head, causing her bladder to release.

Isha fought to stabilize her mental footing. A warrior removed the machete from her hand. He unsheathed the blade and handed it back.

"To save her," Monsta said, "you gotta know blood."

The lunatic glow in his eyes told her exactly what was happening.

Isha softened her posture. "I can't do this."

"Kept telling you—this ain't no superhero movie. Ain't no Avengers gonna fly down and save this bitch. And you wanna know why? Because they don't exist. Yet every time I turn around, a fucking superhero is saving the world." Monsta held the shotgun outward, pontificating. "Saving the world, not from real evil, like rogue cops who kill blacks; or from pedophiles, rapists, and bankers who jack old ladies out of their homes. Nah, it's always a fucking caricature of evil. Thanos, Bane, the fucking Joker." He gripped the shotgun with both hands, held it at the waist. "But this is the actual world. And in this world, we judge real evil. The first maggot in front of you..." The man squirmed. "When we got to his room, he was with a ten-year-old girl. And when I say with a ten-year-old girl, I mean—"

"Please," Isha said. "Just save her for me this one time. I won't ever ask again."

"Oh no. No, no, no, no, no. People don't pay billions to watch Iron Man turn bitch 'cause he can't handle the cost of war. People want to see... need to see the villain get fucked up."

"Please."

Frustrated by her failure to get beyond the pending horror, Monsta took a step toward the woman and returned the shotgun to her head. "Ten... nine...."

Fighting to keep her right leg from shaking, Isha locked eyes with her victim. For the first time in her young life, she saw it. What Monsta called the death-stare. A terrible daze that filled a man's eyes like a broken blood vessel when he realized his life was coming to a tragic end.

Isha raised the machete above her head. The man begged through the duct-tape. Suddenly, it all made sense to her. That is why he asked me if sex trafficking was evil! He painted me into a corner, the prophetic process no longer ambiguous. Amen Ra had sent the priestess to teach the child about evil. However, when the time came for the child to judge that evil, it was the Dragon, not the child, who executed that judgment.

"Four..."

Tears fell from her eyes. "Please, I promise!"

"Three..."

Like the superhero movies, Monsta had made himself a ticking time-bomb. And the only way to stop it... stop him... was to kill the man.

"Two..."

Isha dropped the machete to the ground and fell to her knees. She covered her eyes. "I'm begging you, please!"

But begging was not killing.

"One."

The bomb exploded.

Isha looked up. Her face contorted into a silent scream as the headless woman lay on the ground, a red mist hovering above her body like a swarm of gnats. Isha had never seen a ghastlier sight. Had never felt more sickened to her soul.

Monsta walked over to her, his eyes dark and distant. "She's dead. Ain't no amount of tears gonna change that." He motioned to the iPhone a warrior aimed at her. Isha hadn't noticed it before. "You just showed Mother you don't know shit about blood."

Isha looked into the camera. "I have failed you, Mother. Please, stop him."

"Only thing you did wrong was puff out that flat chest of yours," Monsta said. "Never do it again. You are the judgment. I am the mother fucking wrath. And so you never forget the difference—"

Monsta handed the shotgun to a nearby soldier and picked up the machete. He walked over to the first man, knelt beside him, and snatched off the duct tape.

"Please help me, Jesus! Forgive me for my sins," he cried in Spanish.

Isha's mind shifted at once. Hearing the name of Jesus, she realized it wasn't about saving the men but restoring balance to an evil world.

"Are you fucking serious?" Monsta turned to Isha. "He's calling your homey, Jesus. The nigga who said it was better to be tossed in the ocean with a millstone around your neck, than to rape a child."

"Why do you even care!?"

"I don't." He pointed the machete at the five men. "Aside from running a whorehouse that included children as young as nine, they operated a fantasy rape site. Only it wasn't no fantasy. I mean, who's gonna check, anyway? No, Princess Isha, these were real rapes. Women whose husbands owed the local boss. But you ain't gotta worry about him. I already blew his fucking brains out. Anyway," Monsta pointed the machete at the second man, "the women reported to this piece of shit. Showed up ready to scrub toilets in order to save the lives of their sorry ass husbands. Men like your little friend's father."

"I was trying to help her." Isha huffed as she gained strength. "I know helping people is a concept unfamiliar to you."

"Unfamiliar? You stupid little shit, that's what the fuck I'm doing right now. Helping you understand what it's gonna take to sit on that throne." Monsta stepped up to the first man. "Ain't no millstone, but it'll do."

He brought the machete down across the man's forearm.

Thwack!

The man screamed, and, as if trying to run from the pain, rolled onto his side. The severed forearm, still attached to the cuff, dragged the ground behind. He rolled back onto his stomach and pressed the nub into the ground. Shock. The forearm dangled from the chain like a puppet.

Monsta stepped to the man's rear.

Thwack! He hacked off his foot just above the ankle.

The man screamed again, rolled sideways, and then back onto his stomach, his appearance that of a hideous, spider-like human.

The other men twisted and groaned. And why shouldn't they, Isha thought. They'd been captured by an actual monster. His name had never been more fitting. Nor his title as the Dragon.

In the hazy wind of insanity, she at last got the point. The Dragon's point. Avengers did not exist. Superheroes did not exist. She'd always known that. What she didn't know, what she was discovering now, face to face with genuine evil, was that their fictional existence was nothing more than a psychological red herring. An image designed to keep humans from fully digesting the truth that devils were real and living among us. They snatched children from parks, murdered the innocent, and even governed the lives we lived. Here, they had raped a mother... grandmother... Corina.

Monsta raised the machete.

Isha looked down, closed her eyes.

Thwack, Thwack, Thwack, Thwack, Thwack, Thwack, Thwack, Thwack....

The hacking stopped, replaced by the muffled cries of condemned men.

Isha sensed a weightier horror, though.

"Open your eyes," Monsta demanded.

She did.

He had lodged the machete in the man's upper body. The rest of him lay in scattered chunks. All except his head, which Monsta held in his right hand, inches from her face.

The vomit exploded, splashing the man's face.

Monsta raised the head eye level. "Sprayed you like an infant, nigga."

He tossed the head to the ground like a coconut, took a step back, and peeled off the hoody. Musclebound and covered in tattoos, he dropped the hoody to the ground and returned to the body. Dislodging the machete, he calmly walked up to the next man in line, pressed a boot against his shin, and tipped him sideways. Shifting the boot to the linkage connecting the ankle cuff to the metal ring, he raised both arms. "God, I thank you for being such a fucking gangster."

It was the worship of a madman. An absolute madman.

Monsta brought the machete down across the man's thigh, splitting it wide open. The man screamed into the duct-tape, the blood spurting like a punctured hose. Monsta moved to the side of the gaping wound, raised the machete above his head.

Isha again dropped her eyes to the ground.

Thwack, Thwack, Thwack, Thwack...

I need to look, she reasoned. To remember the day, if only for its infamy. She took a deep breath and lifted her eyes, quickly zoning in on the horror. A new gurgle of vomit splashed from her mouth. She didn't care. The man, scarcely coherent, flopped about frantically, instinctively. The bloody nub jerked back and forth, as if searching for the fat limb that dangled from the ankle cuff like a pig in a slaughterhouse.

"Fuck you doing?" Monsta asked him.

Isha squeezed her eyes shut. Baby steps.

The hacking resumed, and went on for what seemed like an eternity before Isha heard the machete hit the ground.

"Ain't got time for this shit," Monsta said.

Isha opened her eyes.

Monsta walked over to a warrior, grabbed her machine gun, and nodded at the two warriors next to Isha. They lifted her wilted body off the ground and carried her several feet away. The two then shielded her as Monsta stood over the remaining men.

"Millstones for everybody," he said, emptying the weapon into their faces.

Isha watched the entire event. Could do so by bending her neck just a bit. Three killed at one time. The act, although still terrible, was not as terrible as the hacking to pieces.

Another warrior traded machine guns with Monsta. The Dragon was not done. He aimed and repeated the process. Monsta tossed the machine gun back to the warrior, retrieved the hoody from the ground, and headed toward the SUV.

A warrior placed a gentle hand on Isha's shoulder. "Time to go."

Chapter 24

"Café Adrenochrome"

"When did you get here?" Angel rushed into Cat's arms.

Angel had received the text an hour ago, sprinkled between Michael's confirmation of her meeting with restauranteur Glenn Skinner, and a picture of DJ's surprise birthday gift, sent from her dealership—a black 2021 Dodge Charger SRT Hellcat.

"Yesterday morning," Cat said, squeezing gently.

The two stood in the cafe's foyer. Across the room, Priscilla, Amber, and Brittany waited. Angel hadn't spoken to Cat since she and her husband, tech giant, Theodore Radcliff, moved to Paris more than a year ago. Fearing what the other might say, but not wanting to discuss matters at length on the phone, they agreed to speak before sitting down with the rest of the girls.

"Why didn't you call?" Angel asked. "I would have stopped everything."

Cat kissed her cheek, placed a hand on the small of her back. "I wasn't sure where we stood."

Angel had wondered, too. But seeing Cat again quickly released the pent-up love. "I'm sorry. I never meant to hurt you."

"It wasn't your fault. You and I were together long before he entered the picture."

"I can't believe it's really you." Teary-eyed, Angel stepped back to survey the five-ten bombshell. A slender brunette with light green eyes and long legs, she referred to her as the dark-haired Giselle. Cat wore a grey Marciano top and skirt, matching nylons, and Céline shoes. She finished the breathtaking look with a diamond choker and the rock she called a wedding ring. A diamond so big the average person believed it costume jewelry. "How long will you be in town?"

"Purchased a penthouse at the Panorama Towers." Cat loved the Vegas strip. Called it her Emerald City. "My things are being shipped as we speak."

"That must've been a pretty penny."

"Fifteen million. The view outside my bedroom window is to die for."

"You haven't changed a bit—other than looking as beautiful as ever."

"Perhaps. But God, as my witness, you're still the most delicious morsel on the planet. Having spent the last year in Paris, I would know."

When the two arrived at the private patio table, Angel hung her bag on the back of the chair and made her rounds. "Sorry I'm late," she told Priscilla, hugging her first.

"Not to worry." Priscilla pushed a lidded tea into the space next to Cat. Within the group of friends, only Priscilla knew about the relationship between Angel and her sister. "If it's not hot enough, I'll get you another one."

"Why didn't you text me she was back?" Angel asked.

Priscilla smirked. "Uh, I did, but you never answered. Even drove by your place, but *someone* wasn't home."

"Slept at Jack's place. We barely got in."

Cat curved a brow. "Jack?"

"Yes," Angel said. "We went to Morocco."

An extraordinary social acumen allowed Angel to mingle in diverse circles: Hispanic, African American, Asian, and the current white click of millionaire (and billionaire) wives and girlfriends she met with twice a month for brunch.

They gathered every first and third Wednesday to laugh, gossip, and expound on the socialite world of Vegas's elite. This morning was cause to celebrate. Luxor CEO Clifford DuPont had finally proposed to Amber. Like the others, the former pageant contestant—all but Angel was—had landed her wealthy fiancé through a combination of rare beauty and cunning sensuality.

It was a fiery combination that made them the center of attention everywhere they went. Even now, as they chatted in the cafe's isolated section—Priscilla's version of a V.I.P. lounge—men and women stared incessantly.

Since its grand opening four years ago, Priscilla's Cafe and Dessert had found its Vegas niche. With the help of Serenity Marketing, all three locations were five-star hangouts—Starbucks for wealthy millennials. A place they could happily nibble on $20 muffins, drink exotic blends, and chat with great physical exaggeration.

Priscilla now owned her franchises outright. When the deal to purchase went through a year ago, she had expected Raymond to be livid. His prenuptial trap thwarted. But he wasn't. He had called Angel and told her he was relieved. He then asked to meet with her privately. Over lunch, he said he absolutely loved Priscilla but needed a great deal more sexually. His words were both confessional and an invitation to indulge.

Angel declined the latter. She told him she knew about the other secretaries and was only protecting her friend's monetary interests. Knowing Angel to be a cunning businesswoman, he conceded.

They signed the divorce papers three months later, changed the $10 million annually into a lump sum payment of $35 million. Priscilla was simply happy to be rid of him.

"So, what made you leave Paree?" Angel asked Cat.

"It had run its course."

Angel kissed Amber on the cheek, took hold of her hand, and examined the heart-shaped diamond. "It's beautiful."

"Love it," Amber gushes.

Angel moved to Brittany, admired her necklace. "Is this new?" She made sure to praise her girlfriends, who were extremely sensitive about their looks and social status.

"Russel got it for our anniversary," Brittany said.

"Gorgeous." Angel shuffled back to her place next to Cat. She reached below the table, set her left hand on Cat's knee. "Run its course?"

"It's a long story."

"Did you at least enjoy living there?"

"Loved it," Cat said, locking eyes with her.

"I want details."

"Stop by the new place. We can drink wine and catch up."

Cat's self-assuredness was beyond measure. As mentally strong as Angel, she had always been the alpha female. Never one to mince words, her crude sense of humor was something Angel sorely missed; life forever seemed a joke only they were in on. Sitting there, her energy let Angel know she had truly gotten over the issue that separated them a year ago.

"I'm sure you two are still settling in," Angel said.

"It's only me."

"Oh. You said your things were being shipped?"

"Wardrobe, paintings, antiques, things of that nature. Designers are starting from scratch."

"Why don't you stay with me for a few days. At least until your things arrive."

"I'd like that very much."

"I'm down the street from you."

"I know."

Angel sipped the tea, grinned.

"Tell me about this magnificent plaza of yours," Cat said.

"Purchased it a year ago. Nine businesses, including a gentleman's club on the west end. Renovated the entire structure. Truth is, I had no idea it was going to be so successful."

"It was on TMZ again," Brittany said, giddily. "Two days ago."

"The stars have taken notice," Amber said.

"Yes, but our main clientele are businessmen and pro-athletes."

"I think it's the name," Cat said. "After all, who doesn't enjoy a little ecstasy in their lives."

"My sentiment exactly."

Cat again leaned in. "Sounds like a place one might find an incredible orgasm."

"Multiple."

"Speaking of which, have you tried the caramel mocha. Pree said it's new."

"First week," Priscilla added, "and it's already my second-best seller."

"Too rich for my blood," Angel said.

"Nonsense." Cat flicked a fingernail at the nearest server. "Would you be so kind as to get this beautiful creature a caramel mocha?"

The man bowed slightly and headed for the kitchen.

Cat winked at Angel. "Just a taste."

"A taste. Nothing more."

"Oh, I'd do nothing to mar that perfect body of yours."

"I can't believe he proposed so quickly," Brittany said, referring to Amber's engagement ring. "I had to wait a year."

"And you got your millionaire," Cat said, assessing the ring. "Hundred fifty thousand."

"How rude." Priscilla sucked her teeth. "It's the thought that counts."

"Anything less than a hundred thousand constitutes an afterthought." Cat extended her ring. "Or in my case, one point seven."

"Cat's right," Brittany said. "You don't want him being a cheapskate."

"Your smartest conviction yet," Cat said, a sarcastic glint in her eye. "And look what else you stand to acquire. A million-dollar suite, and a semi-handsome frump."

"Money has nothing to do with it," Priscilla snapped.

"It has everything to do with it. Just ask any of the girls at the Bunny Ranch. They'll tell you the same thing—as soon as they removed the cock from their mouth."

Brittany chuckles loudly. She then looked at Priscilla, who glared from across the table. "What? It was funny."

Angel laughed. "It was."

After taking a moment to reconsider the joke, Priscilla cracked a smile. "It was."

*****

"Remember the Kardashian bitch?" Butch puffed the third Camel in the last fifteen minutes. "The guys had her duct-taped and ready to go. Fucking amateurs. I know people who would've paid a couple million for that mount."

DJ said little as Butch continues his *personal extraction* story. Earlier, he had explained how the capturing of his targets was the easiest part. He likened them to deer and sheep and other animals who wandered about their dull existence, oblivious to the horror lurking nearby. The current job had taken a week to set up, which he'd done from the comfort of his Texas ranch. He said that with the right team, and for the right price, they could snatch anyone, even a judge, politician, or entertainer.

As Butch rambled on, DJ envisioned the scene from Scarface. Tony Montana had been chauffeuring The Shadow through the streets of New York, waiting for the moment when he could detonate the bomb, killing the target, his wife, and two children. At present, Butch's chatter played like Tony's mental escalation prior to killing The Shadow.

Butch flicked the Camel out the window, turned into the winding driveway. DJ took a swift inventory of the wooded terrain. Vastly different from the countless subdivisions that had sprouted in the last two decades, the dense grove of trees and native foliage granted the fenced luxury home absolute privacy. Robertson had chosen a new name, a new place in the sticks, believing that it gave him the best chance to hide. But he'd only given his enemies the seclusion needed to carry out their plan.

"Most shitheads around here got a local stake," Butch said. "Insurance company, restaurant... fucking jewelry store."

The statement brought back the image of Natalie Carson standing outside her jewelry store. DJ wondered if her success had somehow fueled his brutality against her.

They pulled into the multi-acre property and Butch parked in front of a two-story home. A white Land Rover and a black BMW sat on opposite sides of the two-car garage. Visually, there wasn't another home in sight.

No less than seven hundred thousand, DJ thought.

He followed Butch through the front door and into the dining room area. He could see the kitchen and living room simultaneously, three armed men posted at various intervals.

"Sir, targets are secure," one man said to Butch.

Sir? Noss was right, they're mercenaries.

Butch nodded, turned to DJ. "Upstairs."

They climbed the carpeted staircase and another armed man standing outside a closed door greeted them.

"Sir," he said, opening the door for Butch.

Inside, man number five stood next to an oak bureau, arms folded behind his back.

"Give us a minute," Butch said.

The man exited.

It was the same setup as the Carson video. Collared shirt, jeans, Robertson sat tied to an office chair. Tears ran down his cheeks as the terror burned through his eyes like a blowtorch.

The girlfriend lay atop the bed, eyes opened. Paralyzed, she stared up at the ceiling, her mascara tears trickling the sides of her face like ink from an exploded fountain pen. Medium height, pretty, she was dressed in a blouse, skirt, heels, and a fortune in jewelry. She looked a mixture of black and Asian. Based on their appearance, DJ guessed the men had surprised the couple as they readied for work.

Butch sat on the bed, placed a hand atop the woman's bare thigh. "Now, now, love, it'll be over shortly." He eased the hand up her skirt, turned to DJ. "Torture causes the brain to release adrenochrome into the blood. Gives you amazing power... as long as you drink it within forty-eight hours."

DJ handed him a look of disdain, said nothing.

"You think I'm crazy," Butch said.

"I think your business is your business."

Butch ripped the lace panties from her body and inhaled her scent like a bouquet of roses. He turned his attention to Robertson. "Let me tell you what's going to happen. First, me and my men are going to fuck your girlfriend. And I mean, really... really... fuck her. Then I'm going to kill you while she watches. After that, you'll both be flown across the border. And while you're dissolving in a drum of hydrochloric acid, others will really... really... fuck her." He mounted her thighs and brought his face nose to nose with hers. "And when you're done being a cum receptacle—guess what? You'll get your very own drum."

He had described Carson's fate to a tee. His words, joined with the blood drinking comment, were as if Butch knew each syllable— like a temperature gauge—were slowly increasing the level of psychological torture. Adrenochrome.

"Where's the kid?" DJ asked, suddenly aware he hadn't seen him.

Butch grinned, savoring the agony in the woman's eyes. "On ice. Banged his little head against the downstairs coffee table. Plan to drain him first." He placed a hand on his belt buckle. "You want in?"

"I'll be outside," DJ said, exiting the room.

*****

Butch had driven to McCarran International Airport, gained entrance with a wave of his credentials, and parked inside a private hangar. DJ stood outside the vehicle and watched as Butch's men loaded Robertson and his girlfriend onto a private jet. She was unconscious. He was dead as a zapped mosquito. One man saluted Butch and assured they would deliver him the blood by noon tomorrow. The last part still had DJ's head spinning.

A half hour later, they had returned to the club.

"Why were you even there?" Butch asked.

"Following orders, just like you."

"What? To evaluate my team?"

"We're done."

DJ exited, closed the door, and walked away. As Butch swerved out the parking lot, DJ decided the guy knew little about anything other than his job. The so-called *personnel extractions* he boasted about, although incredibly detailed, were nothing unusual. If there was anything unusual, it was the brain sick idea that drinking the blood of tortured victims somehow gave him power.

DJ called Noss.

"You were right," DJ said. "He didn't know shit. Thought I was there to evaluate him."

"Excellent. Means he has no clue who he works for."

"What now?"

"Have Kasper meet you at the club. Tell him you're done... with everything."

Chapter 25

"War with Illuminati"

Settled in the heat of the jacuzzi, Isha heard two knocks on the suite door. It was Reina, her assistant while in Mexico. Three knocks meant it was a servant. Four knocks, Mexica. Monsta simply pounded a heavy fist before entering.

"Come in."

The latch clicked and Reina called, "Princess Isha?"

"I do not wish to be disturbed."

"Yes, of course. But I've been sent to inform you the Queen will call at any moment."

"Go."

The latch clicked. It had been many hours since she and Monsta arrived at his mansion. Quickly parting ways, she was quite content to never see him again. Ever. Reina had escorted Isha to her favorite suite—it was one of only three with a private terrace overlooking the Pacific—and asked if she needed anything. She hadn't. Alone, Isha changed into her bathing suit, got into the jacuzzi, and unpacked the events leading to the dreadful day.

She began with the people responsible. First was Corina's grandmother. For the better part of a year, she had disguised herself as an outwardly brittle, harmless woman. In the end, she was as calculatingly ruthless as the rest, deliberately setting the wheels in motion that led to this morning's deaths—her daughters included.

What disturbed Isha most about the grandmother was how, knowing the potentially murderous results, she had so easily followed through with her plan. If nothing else, Isha's eyes were opened to a new level of reality—that vengeance could transform even the love of a mother into psychopathy.

Isha pondered her own role in the event. Her desire to be a crusader, as Monsta put it, had caused their deaths. That led her to consider the true culprits in the matter, Mother and Monsta. Both had desired fulfillment of a prophecy whose explicitness was becoming more lucid every day. Its true expectation, however, still escaped her.

If humankind's imbalance resulted from King Sargon III's manipulation of Alexander the Great, was Isha supposed to counteract *all* evil that had taken place since? The Pax Romana? Crucifixion of the Godman Christ? Dark Ages? Theft of America? Slavery? The Holocaust? The idea seemed absurd. Was absurd. Absolutely absurd.

Yet Mother and Monsta were committed to the idea, a concept as strange as the prophecy itself. Monsta was the last person anyone should enlist for such a godly reckoning. The six murders proved that, if they proved anything.

But Isha also knew an overwhelming majority of the Blind would have considered the men evil, and worthy of death. Not her. It didn't matter how wicked they were, only the Master Architect had the right to judge. Had the right to destroy ITS creation as IT did with Sodom and Gomorrah, or spare them as IT did Manasseh, King of Judah, who killed more than a million people, including his own children.

Isha could still hear the faint groans of dying men, still see the mutilated bodies. She wondered if the sounds, the images, would forever haunt her dreams.

*****

"Are you alright?" Mother asked in Arabic.

Seated in the center of the long couch, Isha stared groggily at the camera above the TV, the bathrobe's hood atop her head. "I know why they call him Dragón," she replied, the earlier despair gone, replaced by a resolute scowl. "He is evil, Mother. Pure evil."

"He is the reason Illuminati abides by the covenant," Mother said. "But let me ask you—why Corina's mother?"

"Excuse me?"

"The brothel had thirty-two women and eight girls. Children. The youngest of which was nine. Do their lives not have value in your eyes?"

"I didn't know about the children."

"You didn't know because you had no desire to know. Your justice, like those who claim to dictate the earth's moral agenda, is self-serving." Mother paused, giving Isha the chance to digest her words. "Let me ask you another question, unjust princess. Do you suppose these children prayed to your God for rescue?"

"My god?"

"Yahweh."

Mother had discovered her affinity toward the Hebrew God, YHVH. From her religious professor, no doubt. Though she'd been taught most world religions, she favored the God of Abraham. Particularly the idea IT had visited earth in human form.

"Yes, I do believe they may have prayed for rescue."

"Then perhaps He answered *their* prayers, and not your feebleminded attempt at liberation. Don't you see, the Dragon reflected God's love for the children."

"With all respect due, Mother, I don't believe a man who murders six people is at all a reflection of God's love."

"Have you not read the Bible in its entirety?"

"Many times."

"He is a God of both life... and death. Oh, you foolish girl, the Dragon did not judge six, but seventy people according to *your* will. Fourteen were women."

"Women?"

"Who were as evil as the men they cast their lots with." Mother dismissed further analysis with a wave of her hand. "The prophecy has begun."

Isha dropped her shoulders. "War with Illuminati?"

Mother motioned to someone off camera and told Isha, "You shall remain with the Dragon until further notice."

The camera shifted to Corina. "Hello, Princess Isha."

A deer caught in the moral headlights; Isha felt her heart sink to the floor. "Corina? I, uh..."

Suddenly, an unfamiliar woman joined Corina on screen. "Princess Isha," she said, in Spanish. "Thank you for—"

The screen was cut off.

"Corina!" Isha called, her mouth open.

"Meet me upstairs," the voice said evenly.

Isha turned, eyeing Monsta's back as he walked away.

*****

DJ hung up the phone and motioned for Kasper to stay silent.

Milz scanned Kasper's body for cameras and wiretaps using Noss's modified MCD-22. "Nigga's clean."

Kasper took a seat across from DJ. "We have a serious problem."

"What?"

"Told them what you said. That you were done."

"And?"

"We've been called to Tucson."

"Who's been called?"

"Me and you. I don't understand why." Kasper wiped sweat from his brow. "I never told them you wanted a face to face. I mean, I told you I would tell them, but I never did."

"Then what the fuck did you tell them?"

"That you didn't want the job."

DJ paused. Something about Kasper's statement was wrong, but the seriousness of the moment kept him from trying to figure out what. "First off, ain't nobody calling me anywhere. Second—"

"It's Smokey Esperanza," Kasper blurted.

"Are you fucking serious?" DJ bolted from his seat, came around the desk. "You said the connect was out of state. That they had no ties to Vegas."

"He doesn't."

"Fuck you mean he doesn't? You know who his brother is?"

"No."

"Spider Esperanza!"

"Who's that?"

"He's the only mother fucker in Vegas connected to the Malverdé cartel," Milz said. "The same niggas killed Montoya's brother."

Kasper dropped his eyes. "Fuck!"

"Milz specifically asked you if the shipment had anything to do with Malverdé," DJ said. "If it had, we wouldn't have done the deal."

"What are we gonna do? We can't tell them no."

"You can't." DJ suddenly remembered what Butch said. *I'm not as gruesome as you guys... the whole cutting off their heads.* DJ thought, *I should'a fucking known.*

A knock came from the door.

Kasper bent forward. "I'm gonna throw up."

"You better not," DJ said.

Raul opened the door.

Angel entered with Lethal, her six-seven, two-hundred eighty-pound escort (when she was at the plaza). A King soldier and cage fighter, Lethal greeted the five with a respectful nod as Angel walked over to the desk. She held a thick legal envelope in her right hand.

A rose among thorns, she sensed the tension. "Am I interrupting?"

"You're good," DJ said.

She handed Kasper a look of disgust, turned to DJ. "We have things to discuss."

DJ told Kasper, "Get a lap dance."

"Wait," Angel said, pointing a manicured fingernail at Kasper. "Francine told me you were inappropriate."

He handed her a puzzled look. "Who's Francine?"

"Ginger," DJ said.

"It wasn't like that, Angel—"

"Don't you dare call me by my first name," she snapped. Lethal took a step toward Kasper, leaning over him like a three-hundred-pound anvil.

"It's Ms. Dominguez to you," Angel said. "And this is the last time I'm going to tell you—my girls are not for sale. Do I make myself clear?"

"Crystal," he said, apathetically.

"Good." She pointed to Malo and told Kasper, "The next time you solicit one of my girls, you'll have to deal with him."

The blood drained from Kasper's face.

"Your night is done," she finished. "Lethal, please escort him out."

DJ told Kasper, "I'll call you in a little while."

"What about Tucson?"

"A little while."

Lethal tapped Kasper's shoulder, motioned toward the door. Kasper got up and lumbered like an angry child.

When he exited, Angel said, "I don't like him. He's a creep."

"Want us to bury him?" DJ joked.

"I want you to make him respect the girls." She spun on a heel, addressing the group. "I get it, they're beautiful, and every guy coming through that door wants to sleep with them. But this is not a whorehouse. Look, they don't just work for me, they work for you. We're in this together."

"Oralé," Raul said.

"And please inform Kevin not to refer to my girls as female dogs."

"Already checked him," Gun said. "Gotta give the nigga some time, he just got out the pen."

"I understand, but he needs to adjust quickly." She gestured to the office's second door. It led to the parking lot. "Remember, starting Monday, you'll need to use that door."

DJ cracked a bottled water. "Explain that shit again."

"Monday through Friday, ten to three, we'll be the Renaissance Lounge, a restaurant for professionals."

"Restaurant? We ain't got no kitchen," DJ said.

"Which is why I had the connecting door built." She studied their confused grimaces. "Into El Matador?" Still nothing. "Geez, do you guys pay attention to anything?"

Silence.

"Mama Cecelia will oversee the food," she said. "It'll be a cigar lounge without the smoke. Suit and tie only. We'll have a live Jazz band and a different group of girls. Dressed classier, they'll provide company upon request. I've hired several men for the female professional."

"We're banned from the club?" Malo asked.

"From every room but this one. Doubt you guys will notice. None of you show up until five, anyway. If I'm right on this, I've already scouted a second location."

"I bet." DJ checked his Rolex. "Carlos said he ain't seen you all day."

"Pree's sister, Catherine, is back from Paris. Don't know if you remember her?"

"The model chic."

"Yes. Anyway, we had lunch. She'll be staying with me while her things are being shipped. If you have time, I'd like for you to stop by."

"Cool." He tapped the envelope. "What's the deal?"

"Tax forms, as per our discussion. Need signatures." She headed for the door. "Leave them with Carlos."

"A'ight," DJ said.

When she exited, Gun said, "Whatta we do about this Malverdé shit?"

DJ picked up his jacket, told Milz to, "Hold down the spot."

"Got it."

DJ gestured to the other three. "Let's take a ride."

Chapter 26

"Unseen Hand"

GENESIS TECHNOLOGIES

Noss had gotten the call minutes after closing for the night. Physically and emotionally spent, the urgent message—DJ had never requested an emergency meeting with all four leaders present—only added to the growing dread the thumb-drive created.

"You said Kasper never conveyed your request to meet?" Noss asked.

The four sat in chairs borrowed from the front office.

"Yeah," DJ said. "He jus' told them we didn't wanna do it. Why?"

"If that's true—"

"They knew he was lying," DJ said before Noss could make his point. He had known something was wrong with Kasper's statement.

"Right. Which means they found out about your request to meet some other way."

"I'll check the office video, but we keep the MCD on twenty-four-seven, like you said."

"Any cellphones there when you requested to meet his people?"

"Yeah, but we turn 'em off when talking business."

"That's my fault," Noss said. He stood, moved to the wall of servers. "They have not investigated you guys in so long, I got lax. There's technology that can listen even when they're turned off, but the government can't use it legally. Based on the thumb-drive, I'm sure these people would have access to it." He paused. "Though that may not be what happened here."

"How else could they know about us trying to meet them?" Gun asked.

"Kasper. You said he likes to talk. Gossip."

"Nigga brags... name drops," Gun said. "That's the word from the bitches he fucks with."

"I'll check the flypaper," Noss said. "Though he rarely talks business, I may be able to glean something from the follow-up calls."

Flypaper were wiretaps placed on King associates. At Noss's request, Angel had ordered all club personnel—and any visitor, before entering the office—to leave their phones in the car. If they wanted, they could leave them in the club's safe. Noss knew most people feared theft of their phones and would rather leave them secured in a safe. It took five seconds for Carlos to swipe the phone and upload Noss's program.

"Either way, ain't no more phones in the office when we're talking business," DJ said.

"I'll make you a special box to put them in," Noss said.

"Cool." DJ stood. He hadn't expected to have *the conversation*. "I got an announcement to make."

"Announcement?" Raul asked.

"Earlier today, I told Kasper I'm out the game."

"The game, game?" Gun asked.

"Yeah. And I'm hoping you're with me. All of you."

"You wanna end the Kings?" Raul asked.

"Never. We'll still call the shots, but no more monthly shipments, or handling the work. I'll put money in the streets every month so the soldiers can eat. But that's it. Whatever they make is theirs."

The silence played like a sigh of relief. In that instant, DJ knew he had underestimated his brothers desire to leave the game too. Clearly, if given the chance, they, like him, wanted to lead a life, not necessarily of peace, but one where the feds were out of the picture.

"When you start thinking about this?" Gun asked.

"Last year—after me and Angel reconnected. Back in the day, we had made a plan with Jason." The statement wasn't entirely true. DJ and Angel had made a plan he believed Jason would've supported had he not been killed. "She'd wash our money and make us legit. Then we'd put a chunk back into the streets to keep niggas fed. Apart from that, we'd stay out of it."

"Mí hermano wanted out?" Malo asked.

DJ nodded, sure of the answer. "He knew we couldn't stop soldiers from hustling, but we could watch over them. Protect them from the feds. Even create a lane for the ones who wanted out the game."

"What we gotta do?" Raul asked.

"Nothing. Earlier—the paperwork Angel dropped off. It's for a tax number so you can fall back and collect a fat ass payroll check. She even put together a business portfolio for each of you." He tilted his head. "If you agree to fall back."

"From everything?" Gun asked. "Even the small shit?"

"Anything that can put a black eye on her corporation. But don't get it twisted, if niggas try us, we go."

"How much we talk'n?" Malo asked.

"Eleven stacks a week, for now. About six hundred thousand a year."

Malo's faced brightened. "Legit!?"

DJ grinned. If the craziest nigga walked away from the game, Raul and Gun were a given. "Hundred percent."

"Six hundred a year," Gun said, equally excited, "and I ain't gotta rip and run no more. Where the fuck I sign?"

DJ eyed Raul, who smiled and said, "Oralé."

"Now all we gotta do is figure out why Malverdé wants to meet with me and Kasper."

"You're the only link to Robertson," Gun said.

"What? You think the vatos might try something?" Raul asked.

"That's not it," Noss said. "They know you guys move as a unit. If DJ saw the thumb-drive, you all saw it. Or at the very least, know about it." Noss rubbed his eyes. "This has to be read between the lines. A call to Tucson means that, although you guys are a unit, ultimately, they may see DJ as the leader."

"Ain't no leader," DJ said. "We designed it that way."

"I know, but if we're honest, you're the glue that holds it together." Everyone nodded in agreement. "And that's critical, because we have to consider the worst-case scenario."

"Worst case scenario?" Gun asked.

"Yes," Noss said, somberly. "That you might not be able to walk away from this life. Not until we know who and what we're dealing with."

*****

After meeting with the Kings, Noss called his wife, Emily, and told her he'd be home late. He lied, said he needed to deal with a data breach regarding one of his major clients. Emily forgave his tardiness when it pertained to something she was familiar with. And thanks to the media, she and the rest of the world understood security breaches, particularly the hacking of personal data.

Emily told him not to worry, to take as long as was necessary. He knew her acquiescence stemmed more from potential liability than anything else. The company's success had allotted her a substantial increase in lifestyle. Bigger home, cars, clothes, amenities. Thus, every Gen-Tech problem was a threat to that increase in lifestyle.

Having set her mind at ease, Noss hung up the phone and cracked open a bottle of whiskey. Slumped behind his desk, he continued to dissect the night's events. Along the way, he'd gotten drunk, which ironically had the opposite effect for Noss. It enabled him to feel the dilemma's true gravity and to plot accordingly. And the Malverdé situation was as grave a dilemma as he had ever encountered.

The new and mysterious cartel was separate from all the other organizations he'd managed to navigate through. When it came to the Abregons, Kings, Oscar Montoya, Bonucci crime family, and to some degree, the U.S. government, Noss had been able to name the key players. Leaders. But he knew nothing about the Malverdé cartel, except for the fact that although they maneuvered in Vegas, government intel was virtually silent on who and what they were. An oddity.

To date, Renulfo Abregon was the only person he knew that confirmed their existence. Renulfo never said how he knew, only that his family was to avoid anything having to do with the cartel. Said it with a tinge of fear. Another oddity.

At first, the worst-case scenario Noss presented to the Kings had not been well received.

"Noss, you're my nigga and all," DJ had replied. "But I don't give a fuck if Jesus Christ is in Tucson, we're done."

"That is not realistic, nor is it prudent," Noss had contested. "These people have access to our lives through mechanisms I can only fathom. We need to understand who they are, and what they want. If we treat them with anything less than our absolute respect, the results could be tragic."

His words were a bucket of ice water.

"You're right," DJ said after a long moment.

DJ then changed the subject, focusing on a plan to feed the street soldiers. Of the four current suppliers, they agreed to part ways with three, Kasper being one of them. They'd then purchase ten to fifteen kilos a month from the remaining supplier and disperse them to key lieutenants.

At that point, barring unforeseen circumstances, they were done. Gun suggested using Smokey for the monthly kilos. That way, Malverdé wouldn't feel left out. Not to mention they'd get to cut Kasper out of the deal for being a scandalous piece of shit.

"That's a good idea," DJ said. "I'll let them know."

"You're going to Tucson?" Noss asked.

"Yeah."

DJ had decided to let Smokey know, face to face, the Kings were done. He believed it was the honorable way to cut ties; or at the very least, come to a downsized alternative until—as Noss put it—they discovered who and with what they were dealing. But Noss saw it differently, though he kept it to himself. Going to Tucson meant the Kings were willfully stepping into whatever obscure plan Malverdé had in store.

Noss gulped the whiskey and stared hazily at the computer screen. Natalie Carson howled as the final Aryan, done with his rape, tore into her rectum with an empty tequila bottle. The low volume caused her screams to play like a warbled stream of jazz.

Noss set the whiskey bottle on his lap. "Animals."

Appalled that a couple—an American couple—could be wiped so easily from the face of the earth, he wanted nothing more than to send the video to the feds and see those responsible brought to justice. But if anything on the thumb-drive ever surfaced, more than likely, he was dead.

Why include me? he wondered. *Your genius ability to dissect and articulate intricate patterns. That's why.*

An ability the Abregon's, nor the Kings could ever fully appreciate. And how could they? How could anyone, unless they understood the way his mind worked?

Noss took another drink and reset the four video screens to the beginning. Blindfolded, gagged, Natalie Carson lay tied to the mattress as a forklift removed the pallet containing her husband's drum from the *Policía* van. The driver carefully placed it between the mixer's latches and then parked the forklift in the warehouse's corner.

He jumped off the forklift, removed a mask from a side compartment, and walked over to the mixer. He strapped it into place with a pulley, pried open the lid and filled the drum with gallons of acid taken from the stack of boxes. He resealed the lid and flipped the switch.

Nhug, nhug, nhug, nhug, nhug.

The man discarded the mask, untied Natalie Carson, and allowed her to use the bathroom. Despite her pleas for help, he again bound, gagged, and blindfolded her. The man moved to a small coffee table where a bowl of condoms, half a dozen shot glasses, and an unopened bottle of tequila sat. He removed a condom, returned to the mattress, and raped her.

During the next few hours, over two dozen men entered the warehouse to do the same. Only the Aryans had sodomized her, refusing to wear condoms as they did.

The Carson's murder differed vastly from that of Robertson. If Bryan Carson had worked for Malverdé, except for the choice of replacement, he'd done his job well. And so, if death was the remedy for the sole mistake, then Malverdé should have killed him. Killed his wife if they thought she was a threat. But gangrape and torture—Noss assumed the same fate for Robertson's girlfriend—was a fate far worse than she deserved. Certainly, far worse than what Robertson got, the person responsible. That meant the Malverdé cartel played by no rules.

Noss turned off the video, shifted his thoughts to the Carson family. Since the news of their disappearance, the marital strife had run detectives down a rabbit hole. Presently, the investigation was centered squarely on the idea Bryan Carson had probably killed and buried his cheating wife, and then disappeared. Maybe to Mexico. Because he and Robertson hadn't worked together in more than a year, once news of Robertson's disappearance surfaced, only a former coworker—or one hell of a detective—would see the connection. Complicating matters was the fact Robertson fled to Searchlight and taken up an alias.

Noss scratched the bottle's label. He struggled with the idea his daughters were under the same Malverdé surveillance. The thumb-drive more than guaranteed it the case for anyone associated with him and the Kings.

He spun the chair, eyeing the wall of servers. He desperately wanted to protect his family, to understand Malverdé's angle, and thought to review the thumb-drive once more but decided against it.

As his eyes grew weary, Noss considered the Tucson invitation. It appeared salutary. DJ and the Kings had solved a Malverdé problem and would be commended for a job well done. But having viewed the entire thumb-drive, Noss knew better. After the Aryans raped, tortured, and suffocated Natalie Carson, a man entered and hung her upside down by the ankles. He cut her jugular and drained her blood into a small drum.

Noss's gut told him DJ was about to come face to face, not with the Malverdé cartel, but something bigger. And far more powerful.

Chapter 27

"Malverdé"

TUCSON, ARIZONA

DJ followed the line of passengers as they marched across the hushed terminal. Two twenty-something white males continued to laugh it up. Based on the conversation he'd listened to during the forty-seven-minute flight, he knew they were locals returning with a weekend of Sin City memories. Kasper moved in step with them, trying his best to blend in.

DJ continued down the corridor, checking the signs above the access which directed passengers to the first-floor baggage claim.

Kasper finally looked back to find him. Locking eyes, DJ nodded. Kasper's face remained consistent with what DJ had observed throughout the flight. Kasper had stared aimlessly at the inflight pamphlet, made three trips to the bathroom, and awkwardly joked with the attendant about a fear of flying. DJ knew that fear was less about flying, and more a byproduct of the unknown journey.

The events of the last twenty-four hours had forced DJ to put Kasper under the strongest of microscopes. He had lied to the Kings. First about not knowing Spider. Everybody who was anybody knew of Spider Esperanza, especially if they dealt with his little brother. Smokey would have made sure of it. He then lied about telling Smokey the Kings would do the hit.

In both instances, his motivation for lying was the same: greed. DJ had seen it before. People said anything, promised anything, to get what they wanted. Most ended up in the trunk of a car. The trunk was still a strong possibility for Kasper.

An alleged member of the Malverdé Cartel, Spider was a respected killer. DJ had crossed paths with him many times over the years, and the respect was always mutual. Long before Milz approached Kasper, Renulfo Abregon had set the parameters in place. When getting any new supplier—the Kings had several, but nothing as big as they were intending to propose to Kasper—if the shipment was tied to Malverdé, it was a *no go.*

DJ had never seen Renulfo express fear of anyone, but he could tell he feared the Malverdé cartel. DJ believed it had to do with the cartel's alleged ability to kill at will. Since no one knew who they were—Noss had tried and come up empty—retaliation was impossible. *How do you fight what you can't see?*

Last night, after bringing the news to Renulfo, he reaffirmed Spider's association and told DJ to be very careful during the trip.

DJ knew he had nobody to blame but himself for having underestimated Kasper's reputation as a drug using trick. Truth was, after Frankie Gravano showed up to the first delivery, he assumed the Bonucci crime family was behind the shipments.

Midway down the escalator, DJ surveyed the area. Within seconds, he found the sign next to the newsstand, exactly where

Kasper was told it would be. Written in black magic marker, the name read: Michael Richards.

A dark-skinned Latina held the sign between French manicured fingernails. Model beautiful, she was five-six or seven, curvaceous, with a white blouse and a beige thigh-high skirt. Her shapely hips and bubble ass had every guy from the flight doing a double take. Sheen brown legs stood atop four-inch sandals whose straps circled her ankles before tying off. French pedicure and black-rimmed glasses—giving her the appearance of a sexy librarian—completed the jaw-dropping look.

Pure fire.

Under the circumstances, a potentially dangerous fire.

"I'm Kasper."

His voice sounded halfway together.

The woman smiled and bowed slightly. "I'm Veró," she said, the '*r*' rolling off her tongue like a cherry lifesaver. She pivoted to a nearby trashcan, tossed the sign, and licked her plump lips. "Do you have any luggage?"

Kasper patted the gym bag across his right shoulder. "Got everything I need right here."

Veró flicked the fingernails of her right hand at DJ. "And you?"

"Two suitcases."

She gestured three conveyors down. Most of the passengers from his flight had already corralled inside the baggage claim rails. "Your flight." She grabbed Kasper's hand. "We'll be in the limo across the street."

Before DJ could respond, Veró pulled Kasper's shit-eating grin toward the automatic doors.

DJ stepped into the baggage claim area and stood at the front of the conveyor. A squatty white woman in uniform entered through a side door, took position next to a waist-high gate.

As voices echoed from behind the flaps of the lifeless conveyor, DJ eyed the entryway's large windows. With a clear line of sight, he saw the limousine parked on the outermost row. Beside the front driver's side door, a stout Mexican man stood with hands folded at the waist. He couldn't see Kasper or his new friend.

Renulfo told him Malverdé might roll out the red carpet. Not to trust it if they did, they'd do the same for someone they planned to kill. DJ took a deep breath, reminded himself of the two rules when it came to the unknown. *Keep your eyes open at all times* and *Trust no one.*

The rules were one of the countless differences between DJ and Kasper. Another was the fact Kasper believed he didn't need to make a good impression; that a year of doing business with Smokey had already done so. Experience taught DJ impressions were not associated with formal introductions or prolonged business, but character tested over time. The thumb-drive demonstrated that.

The conveyor hummed to life. Within seconds, DJ's luggage slid through the rubber fingers and down onto the merry-go-round.

He stepped through the doors, took a moment to consider the distant mountains. The hue of the descending sun coated them like a cap of orange snow. Tucson was relaxed. It reminded him of the towns on the outskirts of Vegas, the ones whose social energy was purposely dialed down as a soothing alternative to the flashier Strip.

As he approached the driver, the man's posture softened. Up close, DJ thought he resembled more of a Native American.

"Welcome to Tucson," the man said, taking one of the suitcases from DJ.

DJ nodded. "Thanks."

He followed the driver to the limousine's rear, set the other suitcase on the ground. The driver opened the trunk and began situating the first suitcase. DJ moved to the rear driver's side door, opened it. Briefly stunned, he quickly shut the door, the sharp image burning his eyes like the beam from a police flashlight. Veró was on her knees in the middle of the carpeted floor. Kasper, his eyes tightly shut, held a hand on the back of her rapidly bobbing head. Though he knew both heard the door open, neither tried to acknowledge his presence.

DJ returns to the rear, told the driver, "I'm gonna ride up front with you."

"Okie Dokie"

Once seated, DJ took a deep breath, focused on the two rules. The Malverdé red carpet was in full effect, and it came with a dime piece capable of rocking Kasper to sleep in the time it took to grab a couple of high-priced suitcases.

The limousine exited the parking lot.

DJ pressed the armrest control and dropped the window midway. The desert air mixed with the flow of AC, the opposing temperatures relaxing his mind as he tried to block visions of the back seat. Except for the surrounding desert, Tucson was nothing like Vegas. He'd seen that much as the plane circled toward the runway. But few places were. Still, Tucson held peace that enabled him to keep the trip front and center.

The driver turned on the radio, and the bumpy cadence of a narcocorrido filled the space between them. Stopping at the first red light, a jolt of anger rushed up from inside DJ. Even with its shock absorbing frame, the limo rocked heavily as the male grunts emanated from the other side of the tinted divider.

This nigga can't be that simple. The Malverdé cartel awaited them, and Kasper was treating the shit like a game. It was the reason Angel couldn't stand him. The reason no one could. The nigga had zero self-control.

Not missing a beat, the driver calmly raised the volume.

DJ tightened the reigns of his mind. He had fucked up. Should have sat down with Kasper before leaving, explained to him how he and the Kings conducted business. How he expected Kasper to act during the trip. Angel did shit like that. Stuck a polished fingernail in a person's chest and told them exactly what she expected. It's what made her a better leader than any King, including himself.

Suddenly, a rush of fear entered his mind. *What if I never see her again?* He took another deep breath and spit out the fear like a swig of spoiled milk.

*****

Tejano music drifted above the backdrop like the faint whispers of a once vivid dream. Miles from the airport, the scene had changed drastically; fast-food restaurants, gas stations, and ordinary storefronts had replaced the travel related comforts of the airport region.

The limousine stopped at the intersection of 12th and Valencia. DJ took a swift inventory of the neighborhood. No black faces. No white faces. Only brown faces. They pumped gas, stood in front of a Western Union, and pushed carts along a supermarket parking lot.

The driver turned right onto 12th and went another quarter mile before swerving into a narrow lot, parking longways in front of a small Mexican restaurant. It reminded DJ of the eateries on the outskirts of Vegas. The ones with slot machines that whirred cracked melodies, coughed up grease-stained nickels, and prepped users for the true dream killers at Gotham's center.

DJ opened the door and joined Vero and Kasper on the sidewalk. He glimpsed the sign on the restaurant door. *Closed.*

"Follow me," Vero said.

Kasper handed DJ an idiot's grin and marched behind Vero like a lost puppy.

Inside, the place was nearly empty, immaculate, and carried the feel of a high-end restaurant. Banda music played softly on a speaker above the sole register next to the doorway. The wall clock read 7:29.

Atop the handful of tables and booths, the candlelight mixed with the blood red tablecloth to create a Santeria vibe. DJ thought it odd the restaurant was closed so early on a Friday night. He mentally laughed at himself, realizing the observation resulted from Angel's business influence on his life, i.e. *Why aren't they making money?*

DJ turned his attention to the four men seated at a back table. Smokey, Spider, and two unknowns. Seeing Veró, Smokey got up from the table and approached. When he reached them, he nodded at Veró and bumped fists with Kasper. "Hey, homz."

The gesture relaxed Kasper. It also caused his chest to puff up a little. "What's up, bro," Kasper said. He acknowledged Veró with a nod. "Wow."

DJ wanted to slap the shit out of him. The rules of the game were set in stone. One of the main decrees was you never paid tribute to sex because it offered your adversary an exploitive window into your state of mind.

Smokey grinned. "She's fine, eh?"

"Hell yeah."

Smokey told Veró, "I'll tell big homey you took care of the vato."

She smiled pridefully, like *big homey* was somebody she wanted to impress.

"We got rooms downtown, ese," Smokey told Kasper. "Ain't the big Vegas, but it's mí raza." He tilted his head toward Veró. "You still got business with la chicá?"

"Definitely," Kasper gushes.

DJ had enough of Kasper. He'd let Spider know—without coming across like a snake—that he and the Kings were there apart from him. In assessing whatever purpose Spider's people had for the meet, they didn't need to lump them in with this certified jackass.

"Take care of the vato," Smokey said, handing Veŕo a thick envelope.

She shoved the envelope into her purse and exited.

Smokey extended an arm toward Spider and the others. "Mí casa, su casa."

As they walked in the table's direction, DJ swept the floor with his eyes. During his life, he'd been in four wet-work rooms. Two were at businesses, one was inside an office trailer, and one a home. On all four occasions, the floors—and in one instance, the walls—were lined with reams of plastic. The host had informed everyone the place was under construction. All but the target knew they were standing on an oversized body bag.

With no plastic in sight, DJ made quick assessment of the men. Spider sat on the opposite side of the table. Although the two had crossed paths numerous times, they had only spoken once. The other times, they had simply exchanged respectful nods.

Coincidentally, the one time they spoke was about two months ago, when Spider dined at El Matador with a white woman DJ knew to be a criminal defense attorney. As she used the restroom, the two men, both wearing Oakland Raiders gear, shared excitement about the team's chances in the upcoming season. The brief conversation had been smooth.

Reaching the table, DJ focused his attention on the man standing to Spider's left. A sturdy giant, he guessed him six-six, three-eighty. The other man was seated to the giant's right. Short and lean, he wore a cowboy hat and a thick goatee.

When all three moved around the table to greet Kasper, DJ caught the giant's slight wobble, the unstable movement of most nonathletic big men. A solid kick to either knee would drop him instantly.

Smokey introduced Kasper and DJ as, "The vatos from Vegas." He pointed at the giant, told Kasper, "That's Oso." He continued down the line. "Mí hermano, Spider. Mí tío, Naco."

As the only black man ever permitted inside the Abregon family, DJ was well-versed in all things Mexican. Barrio royalty, the Abregons had taught him the difference between a Chicano mafioso (Abregons, La eMe), and the Ismael "El Mayo" Zambada, Joaquin "El Chapo" Guzman, and Arellano Felix cartel mafioso from Mexico. Both factions would smoke you where you stood. The only difference was the cartel mafioso didn't have to worry about federal repercussions, so they didn't give a fuck if you were standing next to a cop when they pulled the trigger.

Naco was cartel. *But Malverdé?* He wore an aqua blue rodeo shirt, aqua blue suede cowboy boots, and snug fitting Levi's with a diamond encrusted aqua blue belt buckle that, if real, was worth at least twenty thousand.

Kasper greeted all three with a flimsy handshake. "Hey, guys." He motioned to DJ. "This is DJ."

"Good to meet you," Naco said in Spanish.

Spider gave DJ a dap. "We need a quarterback, homz."

"And a new coach," DJ said. *Time to separate from this lame.* "I'm tired of fucking wit' Gruden."

"You two know each other?" Kasper asked.

Spider ignored the question. "We got some decent players."

"Tight end is a savage." DJ suddenly remembered the season tickets Angel said she'd reserved. Fifty-yard line. Said she was looking into the cost of a company box. That it was a great way to land new clients. Damn, he loved her. If she wanted to fuck with chicks, it was fine by him. "Appreciate the invite."

"Wasn't me, homz. Big homey put this together. He's on the way."

"Right on." DJ didn't know what else to say.

Naco called to a young girl who had emerged from what DJ guessed was the kitchen area. She carried a spray bottle and rag and had been wiping down the front counter. Her presence told DJ the restaurant had closed before their arrival; maybe even because of it.

She finished wiping down the counter, left the bottle and rag, and headed over to them. Late teens, nerdy in a cute way, she wore gold circular rimmed glasses and a long black and white dress that fell inches from her shoes. Her long brown hair was wrapped tightly in a bun, a red rose pinned to its center.

"Mí sobrina (niece), Selena," Naco said.

DJ and Kasper greeted her with a smile.

She returned the smile and added a timid wave. The gesture further put Kasper at ease. His body movement was that of a man who believed himself among friends. It was early in the game and DJ had yet to see any street sense from him. He wondered if he had any sense at all. For the moment, everything seemed legit, but that didn't mean the girl wasn't part of a bigger plan to get them to drop their guard.

Selena returned to the counter, picked up her supplies, and pushed beyond a set of swinging doors.

"She beddy smart," Naco said in broken English. He paused. "Mí gurlfriend burtday, I go begas. Es beddy bright."

DJ knew Naco was saying he'd taken his girlfriend to Vegas for her birthday.

"The Strip," Kasper chimed in. "We run that shit."

An awkward silence lingered before Naco, Smokey, and Oso laughed in unison. Though it sounded lighthearted and easygoing, the cadence held a slight glimmer of intent.

They're laughing at this nigga. Is it because of the obvious exaggeration, or the acknowledgment of a fool oblivious to the fate that awaited him?

Like Spider, DJ remained poker-faced.

Naco flexed a scrawny bicep, pointed at DJ's arms. "Big muscles," he said in Spanish.

"He's a badass fighter," Spider said in Spanish. He turned to DJ and switched to English. "Kickboxing, right?"

"Before I caught a case."

"I remember. Mí tío, Flaco, got a gym."

"Guerrero Boxing," DJ said. "Heard he added some MMA cages. That he got a couple of young eses cold with their hands."

"Simón." Spider nodded. "You should come through. Show the youngsters some stuff."

Coming through implied returning home. A positive statement, but not one DJ was ready to bet his life on. "Anytime. Jus' let me know."

"I go begas more time," Naco interjected, "Ju mí fend?"

He was asking DJ if he would watch over him the next time he went to Vegas. Although DJ had easily separated himself from Kasper, it was a chance to lay the softened mentality he'd later need; particularly after he told them he was out of the game. "Next time you there," he said in Spanish, "you'll have an army with you."

Naco made praying hands, kissing them as a sign of gratitude. The gesture surprised DJ.

"Yeah," Kasper said. "Whatever you want. Pussy. Coke."

The comment played like a broken piano key. Naco glared at him, asked Smokey in Spanish, "Is he slow?"

They were less than twenty minutes into the biggest meeting of their lives, and Kasper was done. DJ took a deep mental breath. The fact Naco asked in Spanish told DJ he knew Kasper didn't speak the language. Which reminded DJ that they probably had a file on Kasper. Not probably—definitely. Suddenly, the dots connected themselves. At the airport, the Vero chick had taken Kasper by the hand and walked him to the limo, playing him for the trick he was. Any file on DJ would have told them the opposite, which is why she didn't give him a second look.

From this point on, pay attention to how they treat you.

If DJ had any chance of getting out of the game, he'd have to walk the tightest of ropes between Kasper's idiocy and Malverdé's true intent.

Smokey laughed, waved off Naco's comment. "He just likes to party."

Naco slapped the table, let out a fit of laughter. "Den let's partee."

Kasper grinned as everyone joined in the laughter. Everyone except Spider and DJ.

Chapter 28

"Worst Case Scenario"

When the laughter subsided, Kasper lured Naco and Smokey into a brief Q & A regarding his access to model caliber prostitutes in Vegas. He named dropped, Frankie Gravano, no less than half a dozen times. Like DJ, Smokey and Spider would know Gravano was the nephew of Bonucci crime boss, Salvatore Bonucci Jr. Although Kasper's presentation was sloppy, he'd finally shown some street sense by letting everyone know his Vegas ties of influence did not stop at the Kings.

The Bonucci's were more powerful than the Kings. For all its lavishness, Vegas's underworld was straightforward, with La Cosa Nostra sitting atop the list. Malverdé was new and remained somewhat of a wildcard. Since the two organizations had yet to bump heads, no one could say for sure who was stronger.

Smokey was in the middle of asking a question when he and everyone elsc disengaged at once. DJ's eyes were off the front door, so he'd caught Naco's reaction first, the most drastic. His face had wilted, like the plug in his soul had suddenly been pulled.

DJ pressed a thigh against the closest chair. He shifted his body toward the entrance, turning just in time to see the man two tables away, three black teens trailing close behind. Mid to late forties, with the physique of an NFL linebacker, DJ guessed him five-ten, two-thirty. His face was stone, like that of a man who didn't fuck around in life. All the same, the immediate threat stood at the front door: six men, a mixture of black, white, and Hispanic. Arms crossed at the wrist, they carried the look of skilled violence, the type capable of ending life quickly.

The man reached their table, and the teens broke away, moving to adjacent tables. DJ made a swift assessment. The first two were male, late teens. Each had a crisply folded bandanna hanging from their back pocket: one red, one blue.

Bloods and Crips?

The third teen was a girl. Younger than the boys—fourteen or fifteen—she looked African, a mini-Lupita Nyongo.

DJ noticed she had made it a point to sit at a different table from the boys, in a spot where the candlelight was less intrusive. Placing both hands atop the table, she leaned forward, observant. Dressed in jeans and a white hoody, her dark baby face possessed a glint of determination. Her hair was lustrous and twisted in thick tight corn rolls, two of which fell down the front of her hoody.

As a byproduct of Club Xstasy's growing success, celebrities had showed up regularly. Because of the security Angel provided them— and in coordination with their bodyguards—ordinary people were forced to stare, whisper, and admire them from afar. It allowed DJ to see how the public reacted when they were around someone famous. The look was always the same—respect mixed with awe. That's what he saw in the faces of Spider, Smokey, Naco, and Oso.

Spider softened his posture. It was the biggest tell yet. Whoever the man was, he was *the fucking man*.

"Monsta," Spider said.

"Where's Vero?"

Spider motioned to Kasper. "Vato wasn't finished, so she headed out."

Monsta nodded, asked Kasper, "She there on time?"

"Ohhh yeeaah."

Are... you... fucking... serious?

No one can be that stupid. As fast as DJ thought it, Monsta gave Kasper a look that acknowledged he was, in fact, that fucking stupid.

Monsta turned to DJ. "DJ."

The file.

DJ extended a hand. "Good to meet you, O.G."

Monsta shook. "Call me Monster. Only I spell it like a New York nigga say it. S-T-A at the end."

Though he sounded relaxed, Monsta carried the heavy flow of a man who rarely said anything without substance.

"Caught the accent," DJ said. "Grew up in Brooklyn."

"I know." He motioned to the Crip. "I'm out the B-X."

The Crip pulled a pack of Newport's from his jacket and tossed them to Monsta. He removed a cigarette, tossed the pack back to the kid, lit it. Taking a long pull, he blew the smoke in Kasper's direction, told DJ, "Sorry about the Butch nigga."

DJ shrugged with his eyes. "Nigga got the job done."

"Ain't gotta bite your tongue wit' me—he's a bona fide piece of shit. And just so you know, he lied about their kid. Little nigga's a'ight. He's with good people with a whole lotta money." Monsta bent his neck. "Bet the computer homey tripped on the info. Probably schooled you on a ton of shit."

Monsta left no room for guessing. *They had a file on everyone.*

"Most thorough shit he'd ever seen," DJ said, shifting to the language of code. From that moment, he'd use words only Monsta understood. As a gesture of respect, he would leave it up to Monsta to add any details he wanted.

"What was?" Kasper asked, the piano key still broken.

Monsta ignored the question, motioned to the young girl. She got up and walked over. "This is Princess, Isha Ra," he said, directing his words to DJ. "If everything goes well, you and her gonna be working on a special project for me."

Isha nodded. "Nice to meet you."

Her flow carried an air of discipline. "Never met a real princess before," DJ said. "It's an honor."

"Please, call me Isha."

On second listen, she sounded like Angel—an intellectual.

Monsta asked Naco in Spanish, "Where's my lil one?"

Naco yells into the kitchen. Seconds later, a short woman in a sauce-spattered apron appeared, Selena in tow. She placed the apron on the nearest table and inspected the men at the door before walking over.

DJ thought, *I get it. It's a family owned mafioso spot, like El Matador.*

The woman stood before Isha, gave a slight bow. "Hello, Your Highness," she said in Spanish.

Isha waved, replied in Spanish, "Good to see you both."

A Spanish speaking African princess?

Another slight bow and the woman asked Monsta, "Mí Monsta, where have you been?"

"Working." Monsta hugged her, and told Selena, "I heard you handled your S-A-T's."

"Hey tío." She hugged him. "Should've done better."

"This one's gonna be a doctor," Monsta said to everyone as he motioned to the Blood. The kid pulled a gift-wrapped box from his jacket pocket, handed it to Selena.

"What's this?" she asked.

"Deals a deal," Monsta said.

She unwrapped the box and removed the newest iPhone. Beaming, she again hugged Monsta. "Thank you, tío, but the deal was if I got into Harvard."

Monsta waved a dismissive hand. "That was the easy part. Hard part was proving you belonged."

"Really?"

"Mother's proud of you. Got you a place off campus. You'll have a car and a weekly allowance."

"*Your* mother's proud of me?"

"Everybody's proud of you, míja," Isha said.

Selena cried. "Thank you so much. I won't let you down, I promise."

"Know you won't." Monsta kissed her forehead. "Now scram."

The woman gave Selena a congratulatory hug, and the two floated back to the kitchen.

A Latina strolled up, kissed Monsta on the cheek. "She loves you so much." She eyed Isha, gave her the same slight bow. "Your Highness."

Isha smiled. "Dolores."

Another dime piece, DJ had seen her walk up, take notice of the situation, and fall back until Selena was done. A taller, slightly curvier Gina Rodriguez, she was dressed in a tight red top, tighter Capri pants—which her lusciously round ass nearly swallowed up—and black pumps. No less than $25,000 in diamond laced charms sat atop her perfectly round breast.

DJ hoped she wasn't Monsta's woman because Kasper's salivating stare was outright disrespectful.

"Selena's one of the few reasons I still give a shit," Monsta said. He tilted his head at Isha. "She's the main reason."

Isha seemed unimpressed by the praise and responded in what sounded like Arabic.

Trilingual?

Dolores again kissed Monsta. "What can I get you?"

He removed strands of hair from her green eyes. "Patron En Lalique for everyone."

"Okay, baby."

As she walked toward the kitchen, Monsta locked onto Kasper, who couldn't take his eyes off her ass. "Tomorrow, we cross the border. Got big plans for you and DJ."

Kasper grinned ear to ear. "I'm all in."

"Good." Monsta turned to Spider. "Where we at?"

"They barely got here."

Monsta puffed the Newport. "I'm a Nuyorican," he told DJ. "Like Big Punisher."

"Got rest the nigga's soul."

"Best we ever had. Love my native soil, but back in the day, they taught me to think nobody knows the game like us. Learned different. When I cross paths with niggas from the east I can work with, I build them empires."

The last statement caused the Blood and Crip to smile, revealing a mouth full of platinum and diamonds. The sight added a bizarre twist, since the only other person DJ knew with a similar grill was a nigga named Dice. But his shit had cost fourteen thousand and wasn't even close to what the teens had, which, if DJ had to guess, was in the neighborhood of sixty thousand.

"I don't give a fuck about money over bitches, or money, power, and respect," Monsta said. "In this family, it's allegiance beyond riches. ABR."

The statement hung in the air like a puff of smoke.

Dolores returned with the gold-colored tequila and began setting down the shots. Starting with Isha—who pushed hers away—she served each person, including the teens. Clearly Monsta's order to serve everybody superseded the legal age. When Dolores was done, she took position next to Monsta. He placed an arm across her shoulder, kissed her lips. She then headed toward the kitchen without saying another word.

Monsta walked over to Isha's table and picked up her shot. He drank and set the glass on the table in front of her. She again pushed it away. The energy between them carried a father, rebellious daughter vibe. Monsta retrieved his shot of Patron and motioned for everyone else to do the same.

They did.

"To the future," Monsta said, downing the shot.

Everyone drank.

DJ placed the glass on the table.

Monsta extinguished the Newport on an empty plate and asked DJ, "What'chu think of baby girl brought us the drinks?"

"Pure fire."

"She got'chu tonight."

DJ grinned, appreciative. "No disrespect, brah, but I'm good. And truth be told, I'm just trying to understand why I'm here."

"Like I said, I got plans for you. We'll talk about it tomorrow when we cross the border. Jus' relax tonight—blow out her back."

"Again, no disrespect, but I'm good."

"It's cool," Kasper said. "He don't know it's the way you do business."

"I beg your pardon," Isha said. "What's the way he does business?"

Click! Kasper had finally stepped on a landmine.

Before DJ realized what happened, three of the men from the entrance were halfway to the tables. He shifted his body in time to watch them stop in their tracks. Confused, he turned to Isha as she lowered her hand, having halted their movement with a single gesture.

"You know... the girls," Kasper said, eyeing Monsta, as if he could help explained.

"Are you implying he treats women like accessories?" Isha asked.

Kasper thought long and hard. "No."

"You shall address her as Your highness," one man ordered in a weighty voice.

Kasper had one chance to clean that shit up.

"No, Your Highness. Just running my stupid mouth."

It was the smartest thing DJ had ever heard him say, borderline genius.

Monsta chuckled. "Gotta be more careful, brah. She's a feminist." He slapped Kasper's brittle shoulder. "Think you can handle a hub?"

As if awakening from a coma, Kasper asked, "Are you serious?"

"Ninety-nine percent of the time."

"Yeah, I can handle one."

"We gonna see," Monsta said, eyeing DJ. "But it sounds like you ain't trying to work with me."

"Not personally," DJ said.

"Why not?"

"Was on my way out the game—even before the deal with the Butch nigga. But I got people who'll help in whatever you're putting down."

"I only fuck with bosses."

"Appreciate the props, but we're a council. Ain't no bosses."

Monsta ruminated for a long moment. "Tell you what, let's do breakfast. See if I can change your mind."

DJ paused, nodded. "We can break bread."

"But you ain't try'na change your mind."

"I'd be lying if I said it was possible."

"Head back," Monsta told Isha.

Without saying a word, she got up and headed toward the front door, surrounded by the three men.

Monsta then told the others, "I want to talk to the brotha alone."

Monsta didn't sound angry, but he felt some way. Everyone but those in the kitchen did as he asked, even Kasper, who looked like he wanted an explanation.

When the place emptied, Monsta leaned against the table opposite DJ. "Is you retiring?"

"You sent the thumb-drive, O.G.—you know the legitimate shit I got going on."

"Club Xstasy?"

"And some other shit. Ain't trying to fuck that up."

"You think fucking with me, gonna fuck that up?"

"I think if a nigga's in the mix, there's always a chance shit'll go sideways."

"The chick, Angel. That your girl?"

"She's my heart," DJ said, defensively.

"You love her?"

"To death."

Monsta held his stare for a moment. "Nigga she was engaged to—"

"—Joshua Delaney."

"I know. He's the son of Senator James Delaney. What *you* don't know is that the senator has been secretly planning to make a run in the next election."

"What? President?"

"Yeah. And when any politician talks shit like that, they instantly come to the attention of some powerful people. Very powerful people. And the goal of these very powerful people is not to debate policy in hopes of making the world a better place. No. All they want, is to control it by any means necessary. In Delaney's case, it's through the political machine. They achieve this by capturing men like Delaney and making them pawns in a much bigger game."

"Blackmail?"

"Blackmail."

"Are you one of these people?"

"Wrong question… for now. The right question is, how does it affect your girl? In scraping Delaney's life for dirt, they discovered his son's fiancé, Angelica Athena Dominguez. Discovered the rich uncle who left her a fortune. A nigga that worked for the late great, Pablo Escobar."

"You're kidding?"

"One thing you'll learn quickly about me, I'm always serious— even when I'm not. Once they discovered that information, they placed her under the strongest microscope possible. Since then, they've uncovered a long list of back-alley deals. Mostly bribes. She's paid to play. Delaney's son even handled a few. Then there's her association with—"

"Me." DJ shook his head, feeling the weight of Monsta's revelation.

"The Kings… the Abregons."

"But my nigga, Noss—"

"Has always focused on you and your crew."

DJ paced the floor with his eyes. "She's a beast with the business shit. Ain't no way she let herself get caught slipping."

"I've done the research, and you're right, she's a beast. And real talk, the shit she's done, ain't no different from what the business cracker been doing since they stole this country. But you know how the shit works—they control the legal system. Which means they control the rules of the game." Monsta nodded. "They're coming for her."

"Who?"

"The Feds."

"That's why the nigga resigned from Angel's board," DJ said, reflectively. "Why his son got to acting funny with her."

"To be President, Delaney can't be associated with corruption. They've already used what they have on her as leverage against him. The shit he votes on. Legislation. Bills. If he's obedient enough, they might even choose for him to run, which gives them greater leverage."

"You said they're coming for her?"

"She'll be indicted on multiple counts, including money laundering."

DJ could no longer hold back, wrenching his face in his hands. "What happens then?"

"Feds'll question her. Get her to dig a twenty-year hole for perjury. Manipulate the media to create a narrative. After that, they'll use RICO to take everything she has: bank accounts... businesses... property." Monsta shrugged. "Will she turn on you?"

"Ain't nothing to turn on. I've always kept her out of the way... to protect her."

"What if I said you have the power to save her? But to do that, it might cost you your life."

DJ looked up. "Save her?"

"She keeps everything. Everybody keeps everything. But like I said, it might cost you your life."

DJ softened his posture. The idea of dying for Angel... his people... gave him hope. "Tell me what I gotta do."

"You can start by not retiring."

And just like that, they were back to square one. It was then DJ saw Angel for what Monsta intended her to be: leverage.

"Okay," DJ said. "But I gotta ask. How you gonna keep the feds off her?"

"Easy." Monsta's face twisted into a cruel smile. "Think of it as a chessboard. The Department of Justice is nothing but a chess piece, a fancier pawn. One of many such pawns controlled by the powers that be. The true powers that be. And me and those true powers have an understanding."

"What kind of understanding?"

"You really want to know?"

"If I'm gonna die for her, I need to make sure she'll be safe."

"Gotta tell you, my nigga, that's some gangster shit," Monsta said. "But the deal is simple. These powerful people understand that if they fuck with mine, I will kill everyone they love. And I will start by cutting off the heads of their women and children." Monsta laughed. "'Cause I'm fucked up like that."

To be continued...

THE STREET

ILLUMINATI 3

"CHILD OF WAR"

Chapter 1

"Proper protocol"

LAS VEGAS, NEVADA

Olivia Rothschild emerged from the Boeing 757, grasped the staircase rail. Vincent positioned himself at her right shoulder. She evaluated the scene before her. The red carpet ran a hundred feet along the private hanger. On one side sat her motorcade of armor plated 1-ton SUVs. On the other, twenty-five armed soldiers, shoulder to shoulder, in ranks of five. The Armani suited men were hybrid trained—French Foreign Legion and American Navy Seal—and descended from the bloodline of the Knights Templar.

Two men stood in front of them. The first was Illuminati General Christopher Knigge, Commander of the North American Division. Beside him was veteran NSA agent, Leonard Woodard. Woodard carried a leather briefcase.

Christopher marched forward and climbed the staircase. Taking a knee, he extended a right hand. "Your Highness."

Olivia acknowledged him with a nod, seized his hand, and navigated the steps. Vincent matched her stride for stride. When they reached the hanger floor, Christopher took position at her left shoulder.

Olivia examined the plane. "I want her cleaned."

"Yes, Your Highness," Vincent said.

Agent Woodard approached. "Welcome to America, Your Highness. I'm agent Leonard Woodard." He motioned toward the motorcade's center vehicle as a lone Knight held the rear door open. "Right this way, please."

"Director Chaney assigned you to me?" she asked.

"Secretary of Defense."

Olivia strolled to the vehicle and surveyed the enormous cabin. It held four luxury recliners. Christopher entered first, sitting in the rear passenger side seat, his back toward the front of the vehicle. He again took Olivia's hand and guided her to the seat across from him. Vincent entered the other side, took the seat to her left, Woodard across from him.

As the motorcade drove off, Olivia asked Woodard, "What do you have for me?"

He removed a file from the briefcase, handed it to her. She crossed her legs, thumbed it open, and studied the intel.

"His name is Roberto Esperanza," Woodard said. "He—"

"Amazing, that's the exact name beneath the photo."

Woodard grimaced, her comment playing like a backhand to the face. He let a moment pass. "Esperanza is some sort of henchman for Marquez."

Olivia looked up from the document. "Please refer to him as Mr. Marquez."

"I beg your pardon?"

"You heard me. Have his whereabouts been determined?"

"They have not." Woodard's voice held a hint of agitation. "M-I six refused to share much on the purpose for your visit."

"Why would they?"

"With all due respect, the United States government is not some sort of diplomatic caregiver."

Christopher and Vincent each turned their attention to Woodard as Olivia closed the file.

"Do you have any idea who you're talking to?" Vincent asked.

"I was not told your country of origin." Woodard directed his words to Olivia. "But again, with all due respect, that's beside the point. They have entrusted me to protect and assist you in any way possible. However, that task is hindered when I don't know who you are, and why you're here."

"I beg to differ, agent Woodard," Christopher said. "Who she is, is all that matters. You told me they instructed you on the proper decorum when addressing, Your Highness."

"I was."

"And what did the Secretary tell you?"

Woodard handed Christopher a look of disdain. "Answer questions she may have. And speak... only when spoken to."

"You have violated that protocol," Vincent added. "Therefore, I now command your silence."

"Excuse me?"

The motorcade turned onto Reno Avenue as Olivia stared out the window.

"Very well." Olivia retrieved her phone, pressed a number, waited. After a moment, she said, "It is I."

She listened.

"I am," she said, "but I'm ending his service."

Christopher slid a hand inside his jacket.

"Your apology is pointless," she said. "My assistant will notify you."

Olivia hung up the phone, set it on her lap.

Fwump!

Woodard's entire body shuttered. Mouth open, his eyes flickered in ghastly desperation. Christopher had plunged a massive ten-inch blade into his chest, down to the handle.

She sneered at Woodard. "I am Olivia Rothschild. My father is Supreme Crown, Malcolm Rothschild, the most powerful human the world has ever known. And well, you... you are no one." She turned to Vincent. "Have the autopsy reflect cardiac arrest."

"Yes, Your Highness."

Christopher removed the knife.

Eyes open, Woodard was gone.

"Pull over," Olivia ordered. "I want to change vehicles before this thing shits itself."

"Yes, Your Highness." Christopher reached for his shoulder mic.

Outside, the motorcade pulled over.

*****

"We good?" Monsta asked DJ as the two stood ready to leave the restaurant.

"We good," DJ said.

Following Monsta's statement that he'd cut off the heads of women and children, DJ's mind went numb. The declaration wasn't one of drive-by shootings, or even, in the Carson's case, a home invasion where individuals were kidnapped and murdered. No, this was some Al Qaeda shit. Barbaric. Still, Monsta was composed, as though he were beyond that type of brutality, unless, like he said, provoked.

"You'll be staying the night at one of my places," Monsta said. "Go put your things up. I'll holla in a minute."

DJ nodded and headed for the door.

"You and him ain't here for the same reason," Monsta added, his tone cryptic. "Tell 'em that when he asks."

"A'ight, O.G."

*****

In the parking lot, the limo was gone, replaced by a Lincoln Lexani SUV. DJ opened the rear right door, sat in a leather recliner, and made a quick assessment of the interior. Gleaming from top to bottom it looked like a miniature Vegas suite: a bar with crystal glasses, 65-inch TV, oak trimming.

He leaned against the armrest and eyed Kasper. It was a look that said *'don't say shit to me.'*

DJ needed to get his head straight and the last thing he wanted was for the clown to start asking questions about things that had nothing to do with him. But Kasper was lost in his own reflection. He stared straight ahead, half mesmerized by the vehicle's luxuriousness, half dazed by what just happened. The seriousness of the meeting—even his small part in it—weighed heavy upon his shoulders.

DJ had no clue what Kasper thought he was getting himself into prior to leaving Vegas, but like him, he now had to consider the roller coaster he was on: Malverdé, the African princess, young Bloods and Crips, deadly bodyguards, and the presence of death at every glance. Oddly enough, though they came to Tucson with different objectives—Kasper probably thought they were the same—each had to now reevaluate those objectives.

For DJ it was all about protecting Angel and the Kings. Kasper, if he was smart enough, which DJ doubted, it was about the opportunity to run a hub, along with the realization he might be in way over his head. And he was.

Although the young princess had brought the bitch out of him, she was wrong for doing so. Kasper's words were stupid, but they were the truth. By offering Dolores for the night, Monsta had treated her like an accessory. A fuck toy, like Vero.

DJ stared out the limo's window and checked his watch. 9:35 p.m. The people were still wandering about. A lively, permanent fixture in a land that had two faces. One, a hardworking gaze that searched with diligence for a small part of the American dream. The other, a dark and fearless scowl that declared *poverty is not an option!*

As his mind settled down, DJ's natural ability to process even the most hostile environment began to take over.

Yesterday, he was convinced he'd be able to persuade whoever he encountered that the Kings were done. But Monsta was a street vet and easily blindsided him with a twist. An all or none twist. Now, instead of having set the record straight, letting everybody know that he and the Kings were out the game, DJ was headed toward a world unknown, with a nigga who wreaked of power. Not just street power, but political power.

If he were believed, Monsta knew about Joshua's dad and the people who controlled him. People capable of treating senators like pawns on a global chessboard. The same people had discovered Angel's background, backdoor dealings, and her uncle's pass with Pablo Escobar, which even now DJ struggled to comprehend.

The idea of Angel losing everything, her businesses, homes, cars, way of life, was unconceivable. Ever since he'd known her, she'd always had money, lived in some form of luxury. A luxury provided by her uncle and built upon through her genius. DJ had no doubt she could survive losing her wealth—people like her always found a way to rise again—but prison was another thing. To go from Guy Savoy's artichoke and black truffle soup, toasted mushroom brioche, to twenty years of prison slop would be too drastic a change. Angel was not built for that kind of change. Not many people were.

So, in the end it was simple, DJ's life for her life. That decision was easy to make because DJ's instinct told him Angel was never in danger. Monsta knew he would change his mind to save the one person he genuinely loved.

When the SUV curled onto the interstate's ramp, DJ considered the rollercoaster's next curve. Prior to Monsta's statement that saving Angel *"might cost you your life,"* he had already said, *"This is Princess, Isha Ra. If everything goes well, you and her gonna be working on a special project for me."*

That was a vital clue for DJ because Monsta had also stated Isha was the reason he still gave a fuck.

Any smart person wouldn't dare put someone whose life might be in danger next to the same person you value most, DJ thought. And Monsta was a smart person

More to the point, bosses on Monsta's level, who needed bosses like DJ—on the lower level—weren't going to waste time putting them in harm's way. Obviously, DJ would have to take penitentiary risks, but those risks would come with massive rewards. Whatever the situation, only time would tell.

Kasper leaned forward and reached into the bar. He cracked a bottle of Glenlivet XXV and gulped heavily.

"They got glasses, nigga," DJ said.

Kasper removed the bottle from his lips and smiled, letting out an exaggerated sigh as he did. He gulped again, this time much longer. Afterward, he held the bottle in his lap and used the armrest control to turn up the radio volume. "Looks like he changed your mind."

"Stay out my business," DJ warned in a low growl.

"Thought our business was the same."

"It's not. I'll tell you what he told me, we're not here for the same reason. So just focus on what the nigga offered you."

"A hub," Kasper said firmly.

"Right, so you need to focus on not fucking it up."

"Ain't worried about that. Got people stronger than Malverdé who'll back me up."

DJ rested an arm on the window's edge. "The Bonucci's."

Kasper gulped once more. "Which means this Monsta guy knows nobody's gonna fuck with me. Tomorrow's major. He's talking about shipping lines. I can feel it. They open that shit up to me and I'll be a millionaire."

"What the fuck is shipping lines?" DJ asked though he already knew. He wanted to hear Kasper's definition.

"It's a different type of hub. Arizona, New Mexico, California, and Texas are all red flag states. Feds monitor Mid-west and East Coast movement linked to these states. Post Office, U-Haul, rental cars, them cocksuckers know all about that shit. But Vegas is international. They can't fuck with the businesses because they carry a higher level of civil repercussion."

The statement was confirmation of Bonucci influence. Knowing they'd get a piece of any deal offered to Kasper, they had prepped him. DJ wondered, since Monsta's surveillance was so thorough, he had to know about the Bonucci's. Which meant he knew the control they had over Kasper. And without a doubt, Monsta wasn't the kind of nigga to allow the Bonucci's any say in his business. Regarding Kasper, things just got interesting.

DJ stretched his legs, folded hands across his lap. "So what'chu think he wants from you?"

"To be a boss. To manage. Malverdé'll take care of everything. They'll drop and align their drivers, then tell 'em when to hit the road. I'll get anywhere from four to seven percent. Plus, I get to piggy-back."

"Piggy-back?"

"Monsta knows the Bonucci's can protect his network. In return, he'll let me control Vegas distribution. Let's say a shipment comes in. They'll bring an extra hundred kilos and give 'em to me at cost. Nine, ten thousand a key. I flip 'em in Vegas for eighteen. Like I said, I'll be a millionaire in a few months." Kasper ran fingers along the bottle and surveyed the SUV's interior. "Might get one of these. Have someone drive me around like your girl, Angel."

DJ lowered the radio's volume to zero and leaned forward. "Don't mention her name again or you'll be going to Mexico with a black eye."

Kasper smirked. "Okay, no more names."

This nigga ain't built to run a hub. A hub wasn't sixty kilos, two hundred pounds of weed a month shit. Like the clown said, it was millions. It was responsibility for other organizations. If he didn't give it the respect necessary, it was a hundred-person federal indictment moving through ten states. DJ was sure Malverdé had a file on Kasper. Knew his mother's name, cousins, aunts, uncles. When he fucked up, and he would, a whole lot of people were going to suffer the consequences. Butch nigga consequences.

"Deal like that comes with a code," DJ said. "A code built on loyalty capable of doing a life sentence."

Kasper frowned, gulped from the bottle one last time. "Don't need a teacher, DJ. Was hustling way before I met you."

Have it your way, clown.